About the Author

I started writing in 2017 when I started thinking about my mortality. A big part of who I am as a person is in my daydreams and imagination. We do not know what the future will bring, and I wanted to make sure I have a record of the stories I have been playing in my head. That was the start of the passion I now have for writing.

I am a new writer who has found his artistic self in his writing.

I am the father of four young adults and teenagers. I see my writing appealing to this age bracket or older.

My hobbies include writing, coaching AFL and Camping.

Writing is a hobby as I have a full-time job as a mining engineer and a family which keeps me occupied. I am grateful for the opportunity I have been given to publish this story.

THE WORCHESTER CHRONICLES BOOK 1:
A FRAGMENTED LAND UNITES

Dennis Hunt

THE WORCHESTER CHRONICLES BOOK 1:

A FRAGMENTED LAND UNITES

Vanguard Press

VANGUARD PAPERBACK

© Copyright 2023
Dennis Hunt

The right of Dennis Hunt to be identified as author of
this work has been asserted by him in accordance with the
Copyright, Designs and Patents Act 1988.

All Rights Reserved

No reproduction, copy or transmission of this publication
may be made without written permission.
No paragraph of this publication may be reproduced,
copied or transmitted save with the written permission of the publisher,
or in accordance with the provisions
of the Copyright Act 1956 (as amended).

Any person who commits any unauthorised act in relation to
this publication may be liable to criminal
prosecution and civil claims for damages.

A CIP catalogue record for this title is
available from the British Library.

ISBN 978-1-80016-457-4

*Vanguard Press is an imprint of
Pegasus Elliot Mackenzie Publishers Ltd.*
www.pegasuspublishers.com

First Published in 2023

**Vanguard Press
Sheraton House Castle Park
Cambridge England**

Printed & Bound in Great Britain

I dedicate this adventure to my children, and I hope they can use its completion as inspiration in their lives.

I also dedicate A Fragmented Land Unites to my late Mother who always encouraged reading and the love of books.

Acknowledgements

I acknowledge all those who have encouraged me with my writing. Included in this group is Dave Bardon who pestered me for a copy of the completed book. This persistence drove me to complete the trilogy, an adventure I loved writing.

Contents

Chapter 1 — The Attack	11
Chapter 2 — Building Blocks	20
Chapter 3 — Upheaval	32
Chapter 4 — The Boar	41
Chapter 5 — Raids	54
Chapter 6 — Betrayal	72
Chapter 7 — Expansion	85
Chapter 8 — Revenge and Power	107
Chapter 9 — The Picts	132
Chapter 10 — Building for War	151
Chapter 11 — Wessex	166
Chapter 12 — Aethelswith	184
Chapter 13 — Conquest, Treaties and Betrayals	193
Chapter 14 — Union	210
Chapter 15 — The Fight for Survival	224
Chapter 16 — Bad News for King Knut	240
Chapter 17 — War to the End	242
Chapter 18 — Reunion	246

Chapter 1 — The Attack

We knew our parents would be cross if they found out. However, it was Saturday and we wanted to see the markets. Although we had been there before, the lure of the smells and sounds had compelled us to return. Our parents would never have let us go to the markets on our own, and they hardly ever went themselves. Egbert and I had to sneak away from our homes to be a part of this experience.

The markets are on the last Saturday of every month. Market day is when farmers and villagers from around the valley bring their produce into town. On market day Worchester becomes a bustling centre with more than half of all the people in the valley attending. There are hundreds of men and women, girls and boys who come in from the surrounding district. Many bring animals for a day out while others bring their animals to sell. There is a cacophony of sound and smells, some good and some bad.

I am Godric and I am the son of the town blacksmith, Osgar Amity. Amity means friendship, or so I have been told since I can first remember. I see this as a good family name and an excuse for me to be out making friends. We live a mile outside of Worchester at the foot of the Malvern Hills. Father has a workshop in town but does most of his work out on our property where we also have a forge. Osgar inherited the blacksmith's role from his father, Wulfstan when Wulfstan was killed by the Vikings. This raid was before I can remember, and I know that this is the reason Father is so hard on me. He keeps telling me that these are dangerous times and directs me to stay away from town and trouble.

Godiva is my beloved, patient mother. I have one older sister called Hilda, two younger sisters, Wassa and Cyneburg, and a younger brother called Tata. Mother and Father keep us busy on the farm and as the eldest boy I help with the forge and have been trained to follow my father as a blacksmith. This is hard, and I find it hot and exhausting work. During winter it is bearable as during the day it is the only warm place around the farm. We all gather around the fireplace in the house at the end of each day, although it is usually only started when dinner is being prepared.

My best friend is Egbert. Egbert lives in town with his family. Because of the distance we must work hard convincing our parents we need each other. Egbert is the same age as I am and has an older brother, Leofric, and a younger sister, Sunngifu. Egbert's father is the town mayor and public notary. I don't know what a public notary is, however I know he is responsible for all the legal disputes and does a lot of paperwork. Leofric is six years older than Egbert so Egbert is not close to him. Egbert had two older sisters but they both died when they were young, and they are not spoken about.

In Worchester everyone knows everyone so Father and John, Egbert's father, know each other and catch up on the rare occasions Father goes to town. One such visit is how Egbert and I became friends.

That day's market day was perfect as the weather was mild with the air still holding a hint of warmth. It was the last Saturday in September, so the best weather was behind us as the season moved closer to winter. Egbert and I had just been chased away from a stall selling freshly baked buns. Egbert had managed to nab one of the buns before the straw broom came down on my head. We were off behind father's forge to share in our booty. We were growing boys and we were always hungry. Meals were a good size but it always seemed like forever between them. I expect the stall holders knew that they would have some of their produce pilfered before they got the chance to sell it as they never really looked unhappy, or so I thought. In other areas of the markets there were also games going on such as egg and spoon and sack races. We could even see bobbing apples which is always messy but popular.

On the back wall of father's stone forge building, Egbert and I had found footholds in the stone which enabled us to scale the wall and get up onto the roof. We had found this route up on our last visit into town. This had not been market day but rather one of the days Father worked from town. Father usually worked from town on the Friday of each week. Up on the roof we had the best vantage point to view the whole town and especially the markets. We knew that we had to be very careful to make sure no one saw us, or we would be in for it again. Discipline was harsh and neither Egbert nor I wanted it. For me it was usually an iron rod across the backside. Father would pull down my breeches and give me five hard whacks across the backside. I never cried out as I had been taught not to cry. However I cried inside and usually struggled to sit down for a couple of days.

The hustle and bustle of people was everywhere below us as we sat back against the chimney to consume our bun. It was about then that we heard lots of screaming and chaos coming from below. Looking over the edge I could see dozens of men on horses riding through the town. At first, I didn't know who they were until it struck me that this was a Viking raid. I turned to Egbert and told him what was happening, although he was already aware. He came and joined me at the edge where we both sat paralysed by what we were seeing. It was both thrilling and scary at the same time.

Vikings are massive men who wear metal helmets with animal horns or other figure heads on them. They blow horns to create confusion and have heavy shields and weapons which are designed to instil fear into their enemy. From my vantage point this imagery had a great effect.

The people below had dispersed with many taking to horseback and fleeing up into the hills. Others were locking themselves in buildings while others had run into the forest to find shelter and hide. The Vikings were cutting down any of the men who resisted them and had taken to burning all the timber buildings and structures. The flames and smoke only added to the confusion.

I noticed Sunngifu and her mother, Leofflaed, hiding behind a well in the market square. They were going to be discovered and from what I was seeing the Vikings did nasty things to the girls they caught. I pointed out Sunngifu and Leofflaed to Egbert and told him I was going down to get them. He said that it was too dangerous, and I reminded him that it was his sister and mother. He told me to hurry. Egbert was a good friend but sometimes a little slow on the uptake.

After scaling down the wall I ran over to the well where Sunngifu and Egbert's mother were hiding. Leofflaed had her arms around Sunngifu who was snuggled into her mother as much as you would think was possible. They both looked utterly terrified, especially Sunngifu. I wasted no time and told them that Egbert and I had a better hiding spot and that they were to follow me. All around us we could still hear screams of terror and the sounds of battle. Ignoring the sounds, I grabbed Sunngifu's hand and took off back to the forge and the back wall. Once behind the forge Egbert and I were able to help Sunngifu to climb the wall and up onto the roof. It had been very risky leaving the roof and it could have cost me my life. Thinking about this later gave me chills but also a sense of pride. The church tells us it is wrong to be proud although the feeling made me feel good.

Egbert's mother was grateful for our hiding spot, although she also looked a little cross at him as he was supposed to be doing chores and errands at home. Sunngifu was crying so I comforted her with a cuddle and put a finger to my lips to show that she needed to be quiet. Sunngifu is two years younger than Egbert and she looked terrified by what she had seen.

The raid went on for what seemed like hours although it would have been minutes. Vikings went from property to property plundering and taking what they wanted. Whenever they found men or boys hiding, they ran them through. Girls and women were either raped or taken as hostages. I had seen some of the other town kids get into the well to hide. As I was watching, a dozen of the Vikings gathered around the well. My heart was in my mouth, hoping that they did not hear or see the kids hiding there.

It seemed that some of the men had gathered and were starting to fight back. The Vikings did not stay around to fight but simply took their booty, including the female hostages, and rode out of town. As the Vikings left the people slowly emerged from their hiding places and the children from the well pulled themselves up and out.

It was carnage all around town with upturned carts, burnt out houses and bodies everywhere. Now was a time for tears as many had lost loved ones. There were parents who had lost children and children who had lost parents. Everyone seemed to have lost people who were close to them. Because we were a tightknit community, the losses would be painful. Everyone would pull together to help each other rebuild. As people came back into town the men gathered to discuss the raid.

Egbert's father saw us and rather than be angered he called us over and brought both of us into his arms. He thanked God that we were both unhurt before pulling back to embrace Sunngifu and Leofflaed. John then asked Egbert and I to race out to our farm and ask my father to come into town. The menfolk needed to discuss the raid and to bury the dead. I was not looking forward to this errand as I knew my father would then know that I had snuck away from the farm and my chores. There was no way out of this as I knew what I had just seen was serious and would change our lives forever. These were dangerous times and the fear had just come to Worchester and our own little patch of paradise.

We had all heard stories about the Vikings and their raids but they always seemed to be in a land and place so far away. Worchester is at the foot of the hills which lead up and into Wales. The land of the Angles is so far west, away from the Viking Sea, that I did not expect to be raided. Although there were always warnings from the adults, I thought these were just to scare us kids. The innocence of our childhood had now been shattered.

Egbert and I set off for my parent's farm which was up on the Malvern foothills. We were both fit and strong and could easily cover the mile without needing to stop. Once home we headed straight for the forge but before getting there my arm was grabbed from behind and I was yanked off my feet.

'Where have you been?' my father asked in a tone which gave me no illusions that he knew I had been into town and was about to give me a flogging.

'Father, Egbert's father has requested that you come into town for a gathering. There has been a Viking raid and many people have been hurt or killed.'

Before I could say any more my father cut me off and said, 'I knew you had taken off into town.' Then he stopped and looked at us both. 'A raid, you say.'

Egbert and I told Father about the raid and what we had seen. We walked into the house as we talked, telling Father everything we could remember.

Godiva was inside with Hilda, Cyneburg and Wassa. They were sitting around in a circle knitting when we entered the living room. Father told them there had been a Viking raid in town and that he needed to go into town to discuss what action there would be. Father told Godiva to take us up to the caves until he returned as there was nothing to say that the Vikings were still not around and raiding in the district. I began to complain when father put his finger to my lips and told me that my punishment was still to come. He told me that any word would only make the punishment worse. He said that he would take Egbert back into town with him. We all went outside where father jumped onto a horse and pulled Egbert up with him. I hoped that Egbert would get to listen in on the meeting so that we could hear what was going to happen.

The caves were another mile away from town and up in the rocky hills behind our farm. There was one deep cave which went a hundred yards back into the earth and another two smaller caves. We had explored the caves with candlelight. On one of our adventures, we found what looked to be evidence of human occupation with animal bones stacked in a corner and some primitive drawings on the walls and roof in that area. Our family plan had always been to use the caves as a place of sanctuary should we need to hide for whatever reason. There was no light at the back of the caves so unless torches were lit, we should be safe hiding there.

I had always been a little less certain of the caves as a hiding location as once you were in the cave there was no way out. I could see us getting trapped and having nowhere to go. For this very reason I had started an excavation further up the hills to create an exit location for the cave. I had worked on it for close to a year and was still no closer. However, I was determined and one day I would create a way out of our cave.

Father came up to the cave just before dark and told us we were safe to come home. As we arrived back at the farm Father took my arm and told me he had not forgotten my punishment. While Mother got the fire going in the house Father took me into the forge. He sat me down to talk before he told me I would have to be punished. He told me that forty-seven people had been killed in the raid and there were a further eight girls who had been abducted. It seemed that the Vikings had been raiding up the valley over the last few months but no one had thought they would come this far west, even though they had raided Worchester in years past.

This was an error by the council and one which was promised not to be repeated.

There was going to be a home guard trained in the art of war with the aim that this guard could be called on to protect the people of Worchester. Father told me that he was going to train in the guard which would meet three afternoons a week.

As Father would be away more often, I would need to do more work around the farm and in the forge. Father told me that he would now get me to start making weapons and mixing the metals. Up until now I had been the general hand who did all the errands and kept the forge fired. Although on many occasions I had watched Father work, he had never let me make anything as he had said that there was only one chance. If I made a mistake with the molten metal, then it could be fatal. Father always used to show me his missing finger and the deep hole in his upper arm to prove what he said. I knew it was hot as I had been working the fires for years. One thing for sure was that I had a healthy respect for what my father did and how dangerous it could be.

We talked for longer than Father or I had ever talked before. I even began to think that maybe he would not punish me for disappearing into town earlier. Father talked about the responsibility of the family and of how everything we did influenced those in our family and community. If one of us did not perform their role it meant that the family and community was exposed in the neglected area.

Father gave me some examples such as the mother and daughters weaving and knitting clothing for warmth and protection. 'If they said that they were bored and not interested in knitting, then what would we wear when the harsh winter snows come down from the hills?' Without the warm clothing it would not be possible to go out and gather food and firewood. The whole family would be affected from what was simply a feeling of boredom. Father said that sometimes he was exhausted and did not want to leave the house to make the farming equipment which he sold and swapped throughout the community. If he gave in to this exhaustion then there would be no money to get cloth, metal, clothing or food for the family. We would survive for a while as we had the animals and eggs, but we would soon struggle. Father asked me if I could see our roles, and the connection we had to each other.

At this stage in my life, Father told me that I needed to build my skills and strength. He told me that there was no harm in me starting to practise fighting skills. Firstly, father would teach me to build a bow and get me to make my own arrow tips. He told me he would help me to make my own wooden swords and show me how to make a proper sword. It was clear that I must work, work and then work some more so that I would be able to help protect our family and community once I was grown up.

As Father told me this I thought back to the horrific scenes from earlier in the day. I had seen people from our town beheaded and others run through the guts. The scenes of women being raped were still with me, along with the feeling of helplessness. Father's words resonated with me and I knew I had to strive to be the person he talked about. It felt like a defining moment to me and although still only ten years old, I felt like my childhood had just been left behind.

I asked Father who had taught him how to fight. Grandfather had been a blacksmith and taught Father the trade but I did not know he was a fighter. We had been on hunting trips together and Father was very good with a bow. Father told me that Grandfather had taught him how to shoot an arrow and wield a sword. He said that it was an Amity tradition for the father to teach his sons how to fight. 'One day you will pass onto your sons what I will show you over the coming months.'

As I stood to go into the house, Father halted me and said that I needed to receive my punishment. I mentioned the punishment was not necessary as I had understood all that we had discussed, and I had changed forever from what I had experienced. I also said that I would welcome punishment in any case as the punishment would help to make me stronger and be able to endure more pain. I could see Father smiling to himself as I told him this and so he gave me ten whacks with the rod instead of the usual five. I meant what I had said and although I was sorer than I had ever been I knew this was much better than the heartbreak I had witnessed earlier in the day.

Back in the house I was welcomed with a warm mug of soup and sympathy from my mother. Mother never questioned my father and his ways, just as Father never questioned Mother and how she ran the household.

That night we all sat around and discussed what had happened in town earlier. Father allowed me to tell the family what Egbert and I and seen and they were impressed to hear about the hiding place we had on the roof of Father's forge. I told them how we rescued Sunngifu and Leofflaed and brought them up onto the roof. Father then told us about who had lost their lives and those who were missing. We all said a prayer for those who were lost and then called it a night.

I struggled getting to sleep as I kept going over the sights and sounds from that day. My mind was racing with what I had experienced along with my conversation with Father. It felt like this was going to be a great period of change in my life.

Harvest was due to commence shortly which would take all our effort and time. Our harvest was modest as we only had a small wheat crop. We did however have to pick the apples, plums and blackberries before the weather really turned cold. Although a lot had changed, at the same time very little had changed, such as my chores.

Chapter 2 — Building Blocks

The next three years were as busy as I had thought could be possible. Father began training with the guard and helped oversee its growth from only a dozen members to well over a hundred regulars. Father was made a captain as he was one of the strongest in the guard besides being one of the founding members. The guard had continued to grow in strength and influence and although not being required to repel any raids the confidence of having them had begun to reap rewards for our community and throughout the region. The guards were known as the Angles, as our region and valley was known as Angles land.

Father put more and more time into the guard and seemed to revel in his training and status as captain. Consequently, I took over more and more of the blacksmith's work. I mastered making the farming equipment including all the rims and bolts for carts, horseshoes and bits for saddles and belts, hoes and harvesting equipment. However, I knew I had my father's enthusiasm for war and most enjoyed experimenting with making weapons. I loved playing with different metals to make swords although I did have many epic failures in this area. Father and I became very close through this period as he could see my love of his craft. Whenever Father got the chance to bring home new metals from Gloucester, he would present what he found as a gift. He was always interested to see what I had created, and we discussed different possibilities.

I did not disobey my father again with regards skipping my chores and sneaking into town. Egbert had taken to sneaking away from his chores and errands and began coming out to the farm. Together we relentlessly practised with our weapons which included the wooden swords and archery target practice. Egbert was good at both, but I was better. I had more opportunity to practise and used my time well when I was not at the forge.

The third activity which took the rest of my waking hours was the work up at the caves. I made myself a metal wheeled wheelbarrow and some heavy-duty pickaxes and shovels and was still madly working away at a back entrance. I really wanted to make this into a fortress.

The year before I finally found a way through to the back of the cave. By this stage I had created an extremely unstable excavation which was at risk of collapse. Since then, I had worked hard to shape stones and I had supported the access and made it into a stairway. Outside the stairway I reinforced the walls and filled in behind the walls with earth. There would only be a small opening on the surface which would be accessed through a secondary cave which I was in the process of improving.

Occasionally I would have the help of my sisters Wassa and Cyneburg who loved to get away from the farm and up into the hills. Mother would let them come with me as she knew they were young and just wanted to be free. The girls knew that one day they would be married and expected to raise a family so they wanted to make the most of their freedom while they could. Hilda was already sharing the key roles and responsibility of the household with Mother and was engaged to marry Egbert's older brother, Leofric. Our custom was that girls could not marry before their sixteenth birthday, so Hilda and Leofric must wait another year.

I liked the company of Wassa and Cyneburg and they were a massive help with positioning the stones for the secret stairway. Wassa was two years younger than I was at eleven and Cyneburg another three years younger at eight. Although there was an age gap Cyneburg was a tough nut and could keep up with Wassa in most things. Wassa was careful and thoughtful while Cyneburg was like a bull at a gate.

Every so often Tata joined us, and I put him to use. I usually gave him the special tasks of finding the exact rock I needed to close out a job. Tata was quiet, which I was told was unusual for a six-year-old. I thought he was wise because when someone is quiet it usually means they are listening. My siblings and I were all close and looked out for each other, from Hilda to Tata. Discipline in the Amity family, my family, was harsh but then it was not used very often as we children covered for each other and knew to do the right thing, most of the time.

My work at the forge had also begun to be well recognised within the community and demand had increased for the new swords I had begun producing. These swords were lighter but stronger and able to be sharpened more than the previous version. Likewise, my arrow tips were also stronger and sharper and able to keep a straighter line then the previous version. By the age of thirteen I had armed the entire Worchester home guard.

It was coming up to the harvest festival which coincided with Samhain, when we believe the souls of our departed return to their former homes and then head back to rest in peace. It marked the end of the harvest and the preparation for winter. Some called it the festival of the fire and others knew it as Halloween. To us it was Samhain and an occasion when families came together to be grateful for the year which we had just had. Fires were burnt around town and in the town centre there was a giant bonfire. I so much wanted to attend this year and practically begged Mother and Father for the opportunity to go along.

We had not been for five years and on that occasion, we only went in so that some extended family members could meet Tata. I was eight at the time and thus had a romantic view of the occasion as we were able to drink sweetened water and toffee apples. Everyone had seemed in good spirits as it was before the raid which came two years later.

I was told it is the year 857 AD and I knew it had been a good harvest this year. We were not the only family who had good rains and sunshine and a resultant bumper crop. We need to celebrate with the rest of the town, I told Mother. She looked sympathetically to my father who couldn't resist her charm.

Father said, 'All right, we can go, but not too late.' We all jumped for joy and since then we had been counting the days, hours and minutes.

The first thing I did when we got into town was to head to Egbert's home to try and find him. Leofflaed was there with Sunngifu. I stopped in and spoke to them for a while. All I wanted to do was head into the town square as that is where Leofflaed said Egbert was, but I was compelled to be polite. Sunngifu asked her mother if she could go into the town square with me. Sunngifu gave me a look as if to check and hope that I would be all right with this. Leofflaed asked me if this would suit me and I told her that it would. I liked Sunngifu as she was easy to get along with. Sunngifu did not talk a lot and when she did talk it usually made sense. Like my father always used to say, if they are not talking for the sake of talking, they are probably listening, and I thought Sunngifu was a good listener.

Sunngifu and I headed into the market square to see the big bonfire. We could see the light from the edge of town as it was just nearing the time of the setting sun. I found Egbert with some other kids from town who I also knew. There was Bran, Kelvan and an older boy, named Arthur. They were all chewing on toffee apples so I asked them where I could get one. Sunngifu left us as she saw some of her friends on the other side of the square. A few of the boys with Egbert teased me a little saying it looked like I had found myself a girlfriend. This made me blush a little which only gave them encouragement. I had not thought of a girlfriend as I was always too busy with the forge, cave and weapons practice. Egbert came to my defence and told the boys to leave his sister out of it. Fortunately, they backed down as Egbert had a reputation for being good with his fists and the others only needed one look to know that they did not want to fight me. The years at the forge, not to mention my other activities, had turned me into a powerful unit. Fighting, however, was a long way from everyone's mind as this was a night of celebration.

Arthur said he knew where we could get some mead if we wanted it and that sounded like the best invitation I had had in a long while. We all followed Arthur over to where his family was set up and we could see they had an entire barrel of mead. We were all offered mugs of it, for which I felt eternally grateful. I had only ever tasted mead on the odd occasion and knew it to bring a warm sensation after drinking it. Egbert and I spent the next couple of hours with Arthur and his family chatting about life and drinking merrily.

It was then that Arthur's father, Bevan, started telling us that there had been an envoy from Mercia sent by King Æthelstan. Æthelstan wanted to push the Viking army back and out of the land and had heard about our home guard and wanted them to join his men in an offensive to push the Vikings out of Mercia before winter.

This news shocked me as I knew there was not much time before winter, and I had not heard about this from Father. It disturbed me as Father had always said that nothing good comes from war and strength through preparations, wealth and technology would be deterrent enough to avoid war. Father had always put a caveat on his statement, saying that sometimes men had to fight and that I would know when that time came.

I asked Bevan if my father knew about this request, to which he replied that Osgar was aware of the request. That the guard had not already left for Mercia was due to the opposition of Osgar. 'He is a fine captain and warrior but he is still overly cautious,' said Bevan. Although there were some sniggers from the crew drinking mead, I felt proud that my father would stand up to the request from the king.

Worchester was officially part of Mercia but we liked to think of ourselves as being independent as we existed in the border regions between Mercia and Wales. Our isolation had been of great benefit to us during the bloody Viking wars, but now the war seemed to be coming closer and closer and it seemed inevitable that we were going to be involved.

I filled my mug and took my leave of Arthur and his family. I wanted to catch up with father to find out what he thought would happen. The Amity clan were seated not far away in the square and mostly staring in awe at the amazing bonfire. The bonfire had large figures of scarecrows burning in them like the festival of the burning man. Father and Mother were there with Uncle Arturo and his family. Uncle Arturo lived on the Welsh side of the Malvern Hills and usually came over to Worchester for Samhain day. This year he had brought his family over the hills to catch up. Uncle Arturo was quite a bit older than Father, so his children were mostly grown up.

Arturo and father were discussing the request from Æthelstan when Egbert and I came up to them. They stopped the minute they noticed us next to them. I asked them if they thought the guard should go and Father asked me how I knew about it. I told him we had just heard them talking about it. Father didn't question me further which was just as well as I didn't really want to put Arthur and his father Bevan in hot water if it was meant to be confidential. Father accepted my explanation and decided to share the situation with Egbert and me. Father also noticed that I was drinking mead which stopped him and made him momentarily speechless. I told him that Arthur's family had a barrel of mead and Father stepped aside and said, 'So do we.' I cracked up laughing, which was probably from too much mead, but this only kickstarted everyone else and soon Uncle Arturo, Father, Mother and Arturo's wife Mary were all bent over laughing. It was such a simple thing, but I think it was just what we all needed, a good belly laugh, about absolutely nothing. Hilda and my other siblings were just looking at us as though we were mad but I could see they were pleased that we looked jovial.

It was about then that I heard someone start playing the lute and pipes. The girls took off to the music to join in the dancing. They looked like they were all having fun which was the general atmosphere of the occasion.

Father started to tell us about the request to the council that the guard be sent to join in with the Mercian army. The question had divided the council with most wanting to march off to help. Father said he pointed out that they were a guard for defence and not offence. 'If we abandon Worchester,' he had said, 'then all that we love will be exposed.' His friend John accepted his point but Leofric, his son, jumped in and added that forcing the Vikings from Mercia would make Worchester even more secure, so it was our obligation to support the Mercian army to achieve this outcome.

I must admit I could see Leofric's point of view, which I conveyed to Father. He shook his head and said that from what he had heard Æthelstan was not
to be trusted and that the Vikings were too strong for the Mercians. He said that our only hope was to unite with the kingdom of Wessex and with their support the Vikings could be pushed back. Wessex was the kingdom to the south of us, ruled by Alfred the Great who was now an old man. Father said that Alfred had a son by name of Ethelred who was reported to be a ruthless commander who had won many battles against the Vikings.

Father went on for the next hour and it was evident that he was quite emotional about the discussion and situation. He said that the council was due to vote the following day and until the vote he had decided not to worry the family about it as it might be for nought. Uncle Arturo had the same view as Father and thought the guard should stay home to protect the valley.

I told Father I did not know what the right answer was. 'Leofric has a good point about helping our kingdom and gaining increased security by getting rid of the Vikings,' I said. I added that by joining the Mercian army our guard would get valuable battle experience and learn battle tactics. 'Our guard, including myself, had done hours, days and months of continuous practice without ever getting to see how good we were or if our techniques would work in battle.

This was met with laughter from my father. He called me his naïve little pup and said that only a fool sought glory through war. 'Fight when you must and if you lose you lose and if you win it is because you had to. To fight in a war, which you do not need to fight, and to see if you can fight, is just madness. If it turns out the other army is bigger, better or just better organised or led then you will be no more, and you will be none the wiser as you will be dead.'

I could see that Father was getting quite angry, which had not been my intention. Just then, Mother came up and grabbed Father to take him for a dance. Perfect timing, I thought as she led him away. Uncle Arturo put his arm over my shoulder and said that what my father said was true and wise. It did not sound right to me as I was still young and had not yet reached my physical limits. Arturo reminded me that my grandfather, my father's father, had been killed by fighting with the Mercians. Although a long time ago this was still fresh in my father's memory. I shook my head to my uncle in agreement and to show I understood. I had been raised to not only appreciate that everyone had a point of view and they may not be the same as mine, but also to respect the other points of view.

Egbert and I left Arturo and went to get our mugs filled again. My head was starting to get a little foggy and I could see that Egbert was further along the tipsy scale then I was. It seemed that Egbert had had a couple of top ups while father and I were discussing the Mercian request. Egbert and I headed to the music to watch the dancing.

It was past midnight when our family left Worchester and headed back to the farm. Arturo and Mary and their youngest son, Bran, came back with us and would stop the night. Bran was eighteen and very much like his father. He had spent much of the night with friends he knew from

Worchester. His three older sisters were all married with their own children or with children on the way. Bran also liked the idea of going to war against the Vikings.

The valley on the other side of the Malvern Hills was part of the Kingdom of Powys, ruled by King David. Powys was a region of Wales and due to its geographical separation did not get involved with the Viking's. Being land locked, Powys had not been affected like the Welsh kingdoms along the coastline, although Uncle Arturo did tell us that he had heard of Viking raids to the north of Powys.

Arturo and Osgar looked so different that they could not be picked to be brothers. Arturo was cuddly and boisterous while Father is all muscle and thoughtful. They seemed to complement each other and enjoy each other's company. Our families usually met up at least once a year and recently it had been my family who have travelled over the hills and into Powys. I loved the hills, so this had not bothered me.

The following day we said goodbye to Arturo, Mary and Bran and then Father headed off into town to take part in the vote. I trusted Father but I feared that he was not going to get his wish. If the council voted to send the guard to war, then there was a risk that some of the men would not be returning.

I was grown up enough to be aware of the consequences of this outcome. In fact, this thought made me feel a little foolish about my views from the night before. I had been fairly enthusiastic to go off and fight without thinking of the bigger picture. If Father was killed this would affect our family enormously. If John, Leofric or any of the others were killed it would be the same thing for their families and the community. I hoped now that Father would be successful and I found it hard to concentrate on my weapons practice. I also wished I had told Father what I thought, and I could have given him hope with my reassurance that he was right, in my opinion.

Father returned after dark that evening and he looked disappointed. Mother took off his boots and helped him to the chair in front of the fire. Hilda came in with his dinner and a mug of mead.

He told us how they had debated for hours but in the end John and Father had been outvoted, eight to two. This was a big blow as Father and John were two of the council leaders and the rest of the council had gone against their wisdom. Worst of all was that now the one hundred and twenty men in the guard would be leaving to join the Mercian army on the day after tomorrow. Father shook his head and said he had no choice but to accept the decision.

I tried to make Father feel better by telling him that at least he would be home before it started getting cold. He looked at me thoughtfully and thanked me for trying to cheer him up. He said he would need my help to prepare for his departure and he then took his leave and headed to bed.

The following day Father took me out to the forge and sat me down to listen. He told me that should he be killed it was my responsibility to provide for my mother and siblings. He told me to avoid going to war at least until they were all of age. I needed to give my sister Hilda away at her wedding and do the same for Wassa and Cyneburg after finding them each a good kind match. Father told me that I had strong leadership qualities and I should use them. The key to being a good leader is to be a good listener and Father told me this was who I was. He told me that I had unnatural skills with the bow and was stronger than any thirteen-year-old he had ever known. He told me not to throw away these skills and told me that we must get our defence right before we can attack. Father told me that he had thought that we should build a large castle with thirty-foot-high walls so that our people could always be protected, no matter the size of army which came against us. I was listening to every word but had to add in that I knew of a quarry where we could source the rocks for such a castle.

Father ruffled my hair and said that maybe on his return we could convince the council to start such a project. Father said that it could be built up the valley slightly where the River Severn came down out of the hills. By building it there the river could be used to form a moat around the castle giving it even more protection. It would simple be a matter of constructing the foundations and bridge and then digging the large trench around the western side of the castle and allowing it to flood. The castle would then be cut off. Father said we were getting a little distracted, which made both of us laugh. I reassured Father that I would look after everything until he returned.

The following day Father was to head off to Worchester to join the guard. The guard would then leave at noon, heading to Repton which was the current royal city for Mercia. Apparently, the royal centre or capital had moved around a bit, but I was told that Æthelstan's royal estate was at Repton. John and Leofric would also be going as members of the guard, leaving Egbert with his mother and sister. We all joined Father for the ride into Worchester even though I know he would rather have gone alone. Father understood that this was a big day for us and for our town.

I caught up with Egbert and Sunngifu waiting on the street which led out of town. The Worchester main street was cobbled, courtesy of the Romans. The rest of the streets were either stone, gravel or dirt which was quick to turn into mud when it was wet. Just add water and activity and you get mud.

The guard were punctual, leaving at exactly midday, or so it seemed by the position of the sun. There was plenty of emotion with the guard being clapped out of town to cheers and tears. We were a tough mob in the west, but we all knew what the consequences of war could be.

Our family went back to the Archers' house, which was John and Leofflaed's family name, to share lunch with them. Hilda was extremely worried about Leofric despite Mother's reassurance that both John and Father would do everything in their power to make sure he came back unscathed. I did not think that their reassurance did Hilda much good as she continued to fret all afternoon.

Egbert and I were both worried and discussed what we would need to do should our fathers be killed in the war. We both agreed that we would need to take responsibility for our families and that we would help each other. I suggested that they move out to the farm as it was more remote and less likely to be attacked. Our discussion went on for some while but rather than make me feel any better, it seemed to have the opposite effect. I was now feeling slightly down and just wanted to be alone.

I think Mother sensed the mood, so we left the Archers and went back to our farm. The weather was turning and there was a chill in the air. I worried about father as we got the fire going, knowing that we would be comfortable and warm while he would probably have to sleep on the roadside or in a tent once they got to Repton.

Around dinner I told Mother about Father's long-term plan to construct a castle upriver where we could protect our people and livestock from attack. By securing our homeland we could then branch out to free the rest of the people of the lands. Mother chuckled and had a glint in her eye saying I sounded just like my father. I felt a little affronted and insisted that it was a grand idea and should be commissioned without delay. Mother saw that I had taken it the wrong way and insisted that it was a compliment which made my sisters and Tata laugh.

I told them that I was going to be heading to a quarry I knew and would start quarrying rocks which could be used for the castle walls. I thought this would be a great way to take my mind off worrying about Father. All three of my sisters said they would help. Hilda said she needed something to distract her mind, which made me laugh and before long we were all sitting around the fire laughing.

The following day we packed up the tools onto a cart and hooked it up to Polly, our old draught horse, and headed to the location which I thought would make a perfect quarry. This section of the Malvern Hills had hundreds of yards of sandstone and limestone. The area I was interested in had sandstone which was fractured so I thought we would be able to chisel the fractures to create blocks. We would remove these blocks and stack them so that they were available for later use.

Egbert and Sunngifu showed up early on the second day and joined in the fun. I had to get additional tools but that was a small concern as this was a major project and many hands makes for lighter work. Egbert was also a strong pair of hands and a strong back, which would be more then useful.

So, as a crew, we worked like this over the next ten days. Mother, often with Leofflaed with her, would bring us lunch and water. They were also distracted and excited with our project and Tata liked being able to play around amongst the rocks.

Each morning I would practise my archery and fighting moves, maintaining the holistic approach which father had taught me. Father had taught me to not be all one thing as then we would be vulnerable from a different type of attack. Working in the quarry gave me time to think and I was beginning to realise that I had a very intelligent father.

On the eleventh day we received news that the guard would be heading home. The messenger said that there had been many casualties, which only helped to fill us with dread.

Chapter 3 — Upheaval

On news of the returning of the guard we stopped work in the quarry and waited. Each day we rode or walked into town to greet the return of the guard. For five days we were disappointed as the guard failed to show. Each time we left for home an hour before sunset as we needed to feed the animals and prepare ourselves for the evening. We knew, or thought we knew, that they would not be returning that late in the day.

Just after lunch on the sixth day the guard appeared on the road into town. They were walking along slowly with three carts carrying the injured and another with the dead, covered up. I only say this as it is as I later found out. The guard had four carts and looked to be less than half the numbers which had set off for Mercia.

My eyesight was good, and I could not see my father. There was silence from the townsfolk as they could also all see what I saw; there were not enough of them. We allowed the guard to pull the carts into the town square before those with loved ones, broke ranks and joined their families. John was walking and was fine while Leofric was lying injured on one of the carts. His leg had been broken when the horse he was riding was shot with an arrow and the horse fell, landing on top of him. I helped Leofric off the cart and onto a nearby seat. Leofric did not look well but now he was home he could be cared for and make a recovery.

I heard Mother ask John where was Osgar. There was silence as the girls had also heard the question and almost plea from Mother.

'Godiva, my dear, Osgar was killed by Æthelstan and his body is on that cart at the back.' Wassa and Cyneburg both burst into tears and this set Tata off.

This was when I cut in over the tears and demanded, with all due respect, to know how Æthelstan had come to kill my father. John shook his head and looked completely exhausted. Many of the other families were also now listening as John began to speak.

'I want you to know that we were fools to go to the aid of Mercia. There was treachery as we were not to be used to free our lands of the Vikings. Instead, we were to be used to defend Æthelstan against Wessex. It seems that Wessex and Mercia do not like each other, and Ethelred was marching an army to take Repton and create one strong kingdom with which to fight the Vikings. Æthelstan tricked us to get us to Repton. Once this became evident Osgar Amity was furious and told Æthelstan that the guard would be returning to Worchester. Osgar told Æthelstan that the guard had come to help free the land of Vikings. The Mercian army quickly surrounded us with archers and sword. At this point Osgar told them they were arseholes and turned to walk through the Mercians. This is when Æthelstan drew his sword and ran Osgar through. Another six of us from the front jumped in to help Osgar but these men were quickly cut down with either arrow or sword. The rest of us stopped as there was no use. Æthelstan had up to two thousand men and we numbered less than one hundred and twenty.

"We helped Æthelstan repel Wessex although I do not know for how long. We were forced to stay another week to ensure Wessex did not return. I do not tell you this story lightly and I feel shame that I should live, while my close friend with so many great qualities, lies dead on a wagon.'

With that John broke down and was inconsolable. I now had tears in my eyes and felt the same. I collapsed to the ground with my hands over my face. My God, what had happened? My poor father stabbed in the back by the man who was supposed to protect his people. It was totally heartbreaking, and I knew that I should be stronger, but I had never felt more hopeless and deflated then I did at that moment.

Egbert was the one who pulled me around. 'Godric, Godric, I need your help, my friend. Help me get your father off the cart and onto the bench where we can anoint him and give him a proper send-off.'

With that I came around and was able to stand and go over to my father. He looked so peaceful lying on the cart. I would like to think that he knew what was about to happen and that God had held out his hand and welcomed him into heaven.

We were not the only ones grieving at that moment as I now looked around. Mother was distraught but was dealing with my younger siblings. Hilda was also distraught and was holding and crying with Leofric and Sunngifu. Leofflaed was helping comfort others along with Mother. The rest of the square was filled with other families who seemed just as dismayed by the news which we had received.

All told we had lost thirty-five men of the guard and had a further thirty-two who were injured and had returned in a cart. The guard were all well practised and knew what they were doing. They told us how they were put on the front line against a shield wall which was not a style of fighting which we had been practising. We were archers and infantry who could all ride and work as a cavalry unit. Æthelstan had used us up to preserve his own army. On hearing this my anger just grew and grew.

While the women cleaned and dressed our loved ones, the men went about constructing thirty-five bonfires to send them off to the spirit world.

Some still believed in the old gods whereas most of us believed in Christian God and his son Jesus Christ.

I knew that Father was up there, and he would be guiding my actions. I could still remember him telling me to build my foundations and knew that now this was more important than ever. Æthelstan would be keeping an eye on our region now and would strike at the first sign of trouble. Besides the threat of the Vikings, we now had the threat of Æthelstan and possibly Ethelred and Wessex.

That night was a very sombre night for Worchester and the region. I had never seen so many people in our small town. It was a cold night for more than one reason. The cold broken only by the thirty-five fires built around the market square and down the main street. Our priest, Father Frank, prayed for each of the deceased and asked God to welcome them to his kingdom. I comforted my sisters and little Tata as Father's pyre was lit. I said a prayer for Father and thanked him for many things as we watched the flames take his body. I thanked him for teaching me to be a blacksmith, to build tools, to shoot arrows, to fight with my hands, sword and my mind, to ride a horse, for loving my mother, brother and sisters, for providing for us, the value of family and community and how to be a man. I wished him a safe journey into heaven and told him I would not forget his sacrifice in showing us the right and just way to act regardless of the consequences. I knew this was a lesson God wanted us to see and learn and it was unfortunate that he had used Osgar Amity to teach us this valuable lesson. At that moment I saw my father as a martyr.

Later that evening when we were nearly home, Mother thanked me for the kind words I had spoken about father. I looked at her and said that I thought I had said them in my mind. Hilda said they were spoken, spoken aloud. They all hugged me and again I began to cry. This time there was nothing which was going to hold back the tears as we arrived back at the farm. None of us could be bothered to get the fire going so we all went to our beds and cried ourselves to sleep.

The following day I did not want to get out of bed and the fact that I could not hear anyone in the house told me we all felt the same way. I shared a room with Tata now and I could see he was awake but did not want to move. I turned over and closed my eyes again. It was freezing outside the covers and I felt too sad to want to move. With my eyes closed I just hoped the previous day would go away. Unfortunately, it was not going to change which meant the source of my sadness was here to stay.

Sometime later I could feel Tata shaking my shoulder. 'Godric, I'm cold and hungry. Godric, can you please get me some food.'

I heard the words and thought of my father. I was snapped out of my depression with the realisation that I now had to be strong and be a father to this family, my family and Father's family. Up I jumped and gave little Tata a huge hug which put a smile on his face. This was just the tonic which I needed. I was still dressed from the day before so went into the living room and got the fire going.

I asked Tata if he could cut up some onions and mushrooms and told him I was going to make a giant dish of scrambled eggs. Tata was pleased to be given some responsibility and headed off to find the mushrooms and onions. Once he was finished with that task I asked if he could go and see if there were any eggs in the chicken coop. While he was doing this, I got the fire going under the stove and began to heat the frying pan.

Our movement brought out the rest of the family who all looked worse for wear but better than they looked the night before. That would be a day which we would never forget, the twenty second of November, 857 AD.

Over breakfast we spoke about Father and what he would have wanted. I mentioned to them some of what Father and I had spoken about. I told them about the castle which I believed the people of Worcester should build. Father wanted us to get our defence right so that we could look after ourselves first and foremost. They knew I had completed our cave retreat with the secret passage into another cave further up the hill. This had a secret room which was provisioned and would allow us to hide undetected. 'If we are threatened, we should go to the cave and hide until it is safe to come out,' I said. 'Our possessions do not matter as we can always make or get more. Our lives and our skills are what we cannot afford to lose.'

Everyone nodded and agreed.

'The guard must continue as these skills will be needed to protect our people in the future.' I told them I would be joining the guard and helping in this area. The women would have to assist with the work on the castle as we wanted it constructed as soon as it could be. Any response to Mercia would be through the council. However, I would recommend that we cut communication at this stage and do our best to avoid antagonising either Mercia or Wessex. The Vikings would remain our main enemy and our training and defensive work would be to ensure that we were able to defend ourselves and counterattack if necessary.

By the time we had cleared up after breakfast it was lunch time. We had chores to finish which had been neglected from the previous day but everyone now seemed determined to live up to the legacy which Father had left us.

Apart from one occasion when mother and Hilda went into town, we avoided anyone from town for the following week for no other reason than we wanted to grieve in our own way. By the time Egbert arrived we were all ready to re-join the community, which was not saying we were over the loss of our father. I think it was more about us realising we had to make sure Father's death was not for nothing. Getting back at Æthelstan was regularly on my mind although I instinctively knew that I had to be patient. Being a thirteen-year-old did not give me a lot of power even though I had now become the man of the house.

Mother invited Egbert in for a drink which he gladly accepted. Egbert chatted to Mother and me for a while and said that life back in town was starting to bounce back. He told us that Leofric's leg was getting better although he could still only get around with a crutch. Egbert told me that I had been summoned to a council meeting for the following afternoon, approximately an hour after midday. The council wanted to discuss the unfortunate events in Mercia and put a plan in place for the future. I told Egbert I would be there and that I had a few ideas.

After refreshments Egbert and I went down to the quarry. The girls were chipping away at their sandstone blocks. On seeing Egbert, Hilda came straight up to him to find out how Leofric was going. I told Hilda I was going into town the following day and she could come with me if she would like. This obviously pleased her as she had only seen Leofric on one other occasion since they had come back. Mother had taken Hilda into town to see how he was recovering and to help cheer him up. Egbert was impressed with the work we had been doing with the sandstone blocks. He knew about the quarry and our desire to build a castle, and had even helped to get us started, but he had not realised how determined we were.

The following day Hilda and I set off at midday to make sure I was not late for the meeting. I left Hilda with Leofric's and I went across to the town hall where the meeting was being held. The town hall was a small, single roomed, stone building, good for nothing except the odd town meeting. It was a cold day and thankfully the shutters were pulled and there was a fire going to warm us.

Looking around the room I could see that we were not the first but also not the last to arrive. John, president of the council, came over to Egbert and me and quickly took my hand and welcomed us. He asked how things were going on the farm and how my mother was doing. I like John as he had a good feeling about him. He was always kind to me and my family and seemed to be a man of honour who was respected throughout the community. Bevan and Arthur then came over and welcomed us and gave us their commiserations about my father. I told them it was tough but that I was determined to continue my father's legacy and honour his name.

The meeting started shortly after all the expected arrivals. In all there were approximately forty of us crammed into the room. It was not long before some of the shutters were opened to cool the room as it was quickly overheating. John called us to order and went through an agenda. Firstly, we were to discuss the campaign and Mercia and then we would open to new business.

After the campaign in Mercia was discussed, a motion was put forward that Worchester would never again fight for Mercia. There seemed to be unanimous approval, so I put up my hand and requested to speak.

'Shouldn't we add a couple of clauses, with the first being that we will never fight for Æthelstan, and the second being that we would only fight for Mercia should there be no doubt that it was in the best interests of Worchester and its people?'

I noted John's approval of my interjection as all in the room seemed to agree with my clauses.

With new business there were three of us who were officially welcomed to the council. Besides Egbert and me, there was also Wilfred who was the son of William, the town baker. Wilfred was a year older than Egbert and me and was a likeable young man.

New business went on for a while before there was anything of interest to me. The discussion moved to the selection of a new captain. There were two names put forward: John, Egbert's father, and Wulfstan, one of the town's stone masons. The vote was close and Ethelwulf was chosen as the new captain of the guard. I was not sure how Wulfstan would work out as there was no doubting his strength, but I did not see him as being a people person.

It seemed like new business was coming to an end and a few of the men were looking to get into the barrel of mead which I had noticed earlier. I still had matters I wanted to discuss so I raised my hand and said that I had some new business. I could sense some frustrated sighs.

I started off by telling them about how the death of my father had affected me and my family. Following on I told them how their loyalty and support had encouraged me about the righteousness of our guard and all its ideals. The guard was here to do what was right for the community and its people and this was unanimous. I then went on to tell them about my father's vision and how he had said we would never be safe until we had castle walls which we could flee to when attacked. Once we had a defensive structure, we could strike out to help clear the land of the

Vikings and any other people who showed themselves to be of low morals and values. This was a poorly disguised dig at Æthelstan and it drew approvals.

The room was still quiet, and everyone seemed to be listening intently. Most of the men knew who I was and were showing me great respect. With a few head nods, I was prompted to tell them more about my father's plan. 'Father identified a location where the River Severn drops down out of the hills. It is only two hundred yards upriver and on the western bank there is solid stone and clay platform. Once the castle walls are to a height of at least ten yards we can set to work on digging a ten-yard-wide trench on the western side of the castle walls. When this is broken through to the river this trench will flood and give us a moat. The castle must be large enough to house a population at least a dozen times the size of Worchester, along with our animals and stores. This castle will become a beacon of protection right along the valley and once people know where security exists you will find people migrating to the region.' Thus, the necessity for a large castle.

One of the men at the back asked where we would get the material. Wulfstan noted that he knew of some good quarries and I chipped in that we had a quarry on our land and had already commenced gathering sandstone blocks. This also seemed to impress the council and a motion was put forward to commence construction on the castle. The motion was passed, and Egbert and I were given the honour of pegging the castle location.

I did add that I thought the women should be engaged to help with the castle as time was critical and the weather was going to be against us. Without the castle our women were vulnerable, so they needed to be involved. I could see that this did not sit well with many in the room and consequently when it was added as a motion it was voted down. This was disappointing but I knew I should not get too far ahead of myself. They had agreed to the castle which was a big win. It seemed there was still a traditional view that physical work, such as fighting and construction, were the men's responsibility.

That night I told the family about the meeting and about how I was now a councillor. They were thrilled that the castle would be constructed. Egbert and I were going to peg the boundary in the morning. Plans were going to be drawn up by John as he was the most educated man in town. We all hoped he knew something about castles. There was a castle down in Exeter and another in Northampton but none of us had ever seen one, only hearing about them in stories.

The next few weeks took us up to the winter solstice which was another fire festival to ward off the demons and protect our community through winter. It was another opportunity to catch up with the other families in town. Once more we found ourselves with Arthur drinking his father's mead. Mother and my siblings were with John and Leofflaed and again seemed to spend most of their time dancing. Sunngifu came over and hung out with us for a while but I think she got bored of boy talk so went back to her family.

The following day we continued to load the sandstone blocks onto carts to haul down to the castle site. This was hard work as I was recovering from the worst headache. With everyone working it looked like an ants' nest with people busy everywhere sorting out the blocks. John had not yet finished the drawings, which kept us from not getting carried away. Given the weather we decided to take a two-week break to give John the time he needed. The snows had come in and we all felt like sheltering in front of the fireplace.

Knowing we had some time off I asked Mother if she wanted to go and visit Uncle Arturo and Aunt Mary. Mother thought it was a great idea although she was worried about the animals. I told her I had already checked with Egbert and he had said that he could look after the animals for a week while we were away. On hearing this Wassa, Cyneburg and Tata were all jumping for joy as it had been years since we had visited Arturo in Powys. We also needed to tell them about Father.

The following day we packed up a couple of horses and commenced our walk over the Malvern Hills. It would take us the best part of the day to reach our destination, but it felt great to be on an adventure. The snow was still light on the ground so our timing could not have been better. A couple of heavy falls and we could be stuck at Uncle Arturo's.

Chapter 4 — The Boar

Our aunt and uncle were surprised to see us and from the looks on their face it was evident that they were pleased by our arrival. Uncle Arturo had a sheep farm in a valley not far from Hereford which was the regional centre for Powys. It was going to be cosy in their farmhouse as my cousin Cafell and her family were also visiting. Cafell had married Evan and had two daughters, Ffion and Eres, who were six and four years old respectively, Ffion not being much younger than Tata.

It was always a special time when we met up with the family as we were all so busy and travel was not easy. Both of our families were farmers and always had animals and seasonal responsibilities. Arturo, Mary and the others all gave commiserations for the loss of my father, Osgar. It seemed unanimous that he was a great man and well respected. All this talk opened fresh wounds for my siblings and me, although I know I liked hearing talk of my father as for some reason it made me proud.

That night we stayed up late drinking and playing games. We were all dead on our feet by the time we bunked down for the night, a combination of the long walk and now the late night.

The following day gave us a good chance to split up into groups and for us children to catch up with our cousins. It was good seeing Bran so soon after their last visit to Worcester and it had been years since I had caught up with Cafell. Cafell was a beautiful and caring soul who had a knack of making everyone feel special. Her husband was the son of a farmer from up the valley closer to Hereford. Evan was six foot and looked to be a handy man to have in a fight. For all his size, though, he appeared gentle as he handled the young children.

Evan complimented me on my size and asked how old I was, thinking that I had come of age. Telling him I was only thirteen, I could see that he was genuinely shocked. I knew I was a good size and I also knew I was incredibly strong as I could easily out-muscle the boys from the village even if they were a few years older than me. I had always put this down to my hard work around the farm and working on the forge with Father. Now with the recent quarry work I was sure I was getting stronger still. I thanked Evan for the compliment, at the same time knowing that it had made me blush. I always blushed when I was uncomfortable, which was usually when I was being spoken about.

I was not the only Amity to be spoken about favourably as Evan and Cafell had plenty to say about the girls as Hilda was beautiful and only months from becoming a woman. As a woman she was going to be able to marry Leofric as they had both been promised to each other. Cafell took Hilda aside and they started talking marriage stuff and about how good it was to be married and to have their own family. Cafell's little girls were playing with Wassa and Tata. Wassa always had children hanging around her, which for me showed the nature of her heart. Wassa had a kind heart, always having time and energy for others.

I helped Bran with his chores, which included chopping wood, and asked him how the farm was going. He told me that the going was tough on this side of the Malvern Hills as everything had become a bit lawless. In the warmer months he would often have to stay out with the sheep as they were regularly stolen. In the winter months it was now too cold so although there were less thieves about neither his father nor he could stay out to stop them. His father had reported it to the sheriff but it had not changed anything. He told me that it was the sign of the times as there were more and more homeless people pouring in from the east with all the troubles with the Vikings. 'People are hungry and they must eat' he said.

I was silent for a while as I pondered the conversation.

The Vikings seemed to be everyone's problem. Something needed to be done about the Vikings so that the land could be at peace. Obviously, the Vikings would view things differently, but this was not their land. I said to Bran that we needed to build an army to force out the Vikings. He already knew about the guard but had not heard that we had started on our castle. 'Once we have the castle, we will build the army and force out the Vikings.'

Bran loved this and together we started plotting the downfall of the Vikings. We were two adolescent boys playing at war games. Engrossed in our plotting, we hardly noticed how the day flew by.

That night was livelier as we were less rushed now and had recovered from our walk the day before. Uncle played his lute and Mary sang as we listened at first and then one by one, we were all up and dancing. The mixture of family, mead, music and dance was intoxicating to us all and we finally let go of our grief from the death of Father.

The following day the family were all going into the markets in Hereford and we all agreed to tag along. Out of our family only Mother had ever been to Hereford and we all wanted to see what it was like. We all liked markets so were eager to set off early.

On the hour and a half walk into town it was evident that some of the farmers were struggling. I was not sure if this was a result of the refugees or general farming troubles. The roads got busier and busier as we came closer to town. Hereford was much the same size as Worchester and the market was really very similar. We split up and agreed to meet back at the sheriff's building in a couple of hours. I took off with Bran, Cyneburg and Hilda while Mother, Wassa and Tata stayed with Arturo and Mary. Evan and Cafell did their own thing with their children as they were not going to be travelling all the way back to the farm with us and they needed some supplies. Their property was halfway between Uncle Arturo's property and Hereford.

Coming back together I could see that the others had had just as good a time as we had. Everyone seemed to be smiling and chattering over the top of each other. We agreed that it was time for some lunch, so we purchased some ribs and baked swedes and found a spot in the sun to share the meal. The meal was washed down with a healthy sized mug of mead. The younger children had water as any age below ten was considered too young for mead.

We decided to head back home after the meal as it was getting dark early and we wanted to get home to check on the animals and get the fire going.

Evan, Cafell and their girls were still with us when out of the forest came a dozen armed men. They did not even try to rob us but went straight for us men in an attempt to cut us down. As already explained, I was not yet officially a man but looked like one, so I had a couple of them come straight for me.

Fortunately, we were all armed and given the times we lived in everyone knew what to do. The women all bunched into a circle protecting the younger children. They also had short swords should they need them. Due to the surprise, we were not ready, and while running through a shaggy looking bastard I saw that Arturo and Bran had both been stabbed and were on the ground curled up in pain. I took down another two attackers and in doing so also saw that Evan was doing nicely against them and looked in control.

It was then that I heard a scream from Hilda, I think. Turning around I saw that the women had been broken up and it looked as though Cyneburg had been stabbed. Someone was dragging off Hilda and Cafell. As I was distracted, I nearly lost my head but managed to block the thrust and stab the attacker. Evan had also been distracted and consequently stabbed through the back. We were losing the fight and all I could think to do was to get over to protect the women and girls.

At that moment a horn was sounded, and dozens of men came up the path and to our aid. It was just in time as we didn't have a lot of defensive moves or energy left. Fortunately, the riders stopped the muggers from getting away with Hilda and Cafell. The riders finished off our attackers and got down from their horses to see how badly we were injured. Cyneburg was already dead and Evan was not far from it. Arturo and Bran were both stabbed through, but it looked like both would live for the time being. All injuries were dangerous and prone to infection which could kill you a week or more after they occurred.

Evan was not going to last many more breaths, so we all gathered around to comfort him, Cafell and his girls. They were distraught, as you would expect. The others were all bruised and battered including Mary and Mother who had both been knocked to the ground with the butts of the swords and were sporting broken bones. This was nothing compared to my poor sister Cyneburg and the dying Evan. So close after Father dying, I was now distraught for my baby sister. Tears welled up inside me again and I was not alone. Wassa, Tata and the others were all in tears for the loss of Cyneburg and the renewed grief for Father. The scene was too much to handle but I knew I had to be the man now. Father would have stayed in control.

The riders who had rescued us stacked up the bodies of our attackers. They respectfully gave us some space to grieve before asking if they could offer us assistance. The men introduced themselves which gave me a surprise: it was King David of Powys and some of his guard. With him were his sons, Cadfael and Emrick, who both looked like they were aged between Bran and me.

Uncle Arturo said that we were heading back to the Amity farm down the valley. King David offered for us to go back to his property as it was much closer, and we needed our wounded tended to and we all needed a place to rest. None of us looked in such good shape so I was happy when Arturo thanked the king and said that we were honoured and appreciated the offer.

King David and his men assisted everyone onto horseback. The men without horses would strip the attackers of their belongings and wait for some of his guard to return. It turned out that there were fifteen attackers, so it was little wonder we had fared so poorly. The bodies of our deceased were carried back to the king's country estate. Here we were met by his family priest who said prayers over my sister and Evan as they were on their way to the afterlife.

The last couple of days had been the best for a long time and now we had this tragedy.

At the estate there were many attendants who helped those who were injured into clean clothing and washed and cleaned their wounds. Mother looked terrible and I would not have been surprised if she had a fractured skull let alone cheekbone. Mary looked just as bad as her nose was smashed in. It seemed that only the younger children and I were uninjured, although Cafell and Hilda's injuries were only bruises caused through the resistance they had given the attackers.

After everyone was cleaned up and given food, we were properly introduced to King David and his household. King David was at their country estate with his sons to do some hunting. They had been out to give the horses a run when they had come across us being attacked. I had done some talking to Cadfael and Emrick while riding back to the estate. As I had thought, they were not much older than me. Cadfael was seventeen and Emrick fourteen. They must have seen my grief as they gave me all the space I needed and only spoke when they saw I was ready.

Cadfael asked Bran and me if we wanted to see his sword collection which was an opportunity I jumped at. Emrick came with us as the four of us walked to the other end of the house. It was the biggest house I had ever been in. As we had ridden up, we had passed between stone walls which were almost ten metres high with cast iron gates at the entrance.

The boys told us how the problem of the refugees and consequently bandits, was getting worse and worse. I told them that it was all the fault of the Vikings and that we needed to do something to force them from the land. As I told them we needed to go to war I could see that I had struck a chord and that they were interested. We chatted like this for hours as we looked and were able to handle the most impressive sword collection either Bran or I had ever seen.

That night I cried myself to sleep and I knew Mother, Hilda, Wassa and Tata were doing the same as I could hear whimpers. Such grief was not unknown to us but still a bitter pill to swallow. Cyneburg was a dear sister and I was angry that I had not done more to protect her. I swore to become the best warrior that ever lived so that no other families had to feel the grief which I felt. Whatever it takes, is what I told myself.

Our injured party were worse than what we first thought so we were offered rooms at the estate and told we could stay if we needed. As I was in good shape King David invited me to go hunting with them which I gladly accepted. He asked what my weapon was, and I told him it was everything and anything, but I thought I was best with the bow. This seemed to make him chuckle as he asked his steward to bring me back a bow and full quiver. So, we set off on the hunt with King David and his men.

I rode along with Cadfael and Emrick and we spoke about weapons and techniques. Emrick told me that his father was impressed with me and thought that I had fought well. At that moment King David dropped back and caught the end of the conversation.

'I was very impressed with you, young Godric. You fought well and I saw that you cut down five grown men by your own sword. A heavy and cumbersome sword at that. Your mother tells me you are only thirteen which impresses me more. Where did you get your strength and learn to fight like you did?'

I thanked the king and told him about my work as a blacksmith from as early as I could remember. 'Weapons are something I have always practised at as we are always at risk of Viking attack. I want to force the Vikings from the lands so that the countryside may prosper.'

'You have spirit, young wolf, however vanquishing the Vikings may never happen as we see and hear about the damage they are doing with every arrival from the east. All I can suggest is to have the patience to become the master warrior you have the potential to become.'

I told King David that that had been my first real fight so I had not been aware of how well my training would go. King David then left us and rode back up to the front.

'I told you he was impressed,' smiled Emrick. It was good to be thinking of something other than our lost loved ones.

The hunting commenced once we reached the forests of the Wye Valley. King David had brought his hunting dogs which were to sniff out the wild boar. Once the boar was on the run this was when the hunt would commence in earnest. All boys loved hunting, and I was no different. There was an obvious thrill when one of my arrows hit its prey. I usually hunted rabbits and foxes. When they were about, I might go for deer, but this was the first time I had hunted boar. The Malvern Hills did not have many boars or deer left, or at least I had not seen any for a long time.

Once we entered the forest everything became colder and darker. We were surrounded by ancient beech and oak trees with dense fern undergrowth to either side of the path we travelled. The sunlight was all but blocked out by the canopy. If it wasn't for the thrill of the hunt and the company, I would probably have been spooked. Still I rode with Emrick and Cadfael and we all seemed to get along naturally.

There was a commotion up ahead and we could hear the dogs barking in the distance. King David looked back with a thrill in his eyes. 'It's on, boys.' He turned and kicked his horse into a gallop. I did the same, following Emrick and Cadfael. It wasn't long before we were off the path and heading deeper and deeper into the valley. Here the trees seemed to get even more ancient and more giant than before, if that was possible.

It wasn't long before Emrick, Cadfael and I were separated from the king and his men. We continued to push on following the sound of the group in front of us. It required a high level of skill to negotiate the rocks and the uneven ground through the thick undergrowth. I could tell my horse was not enjoying this ride as it was starting to resist my commands. This was part of the reason we had fallen behind, and I was feeling guilty that I was holding up the king's sons.

At that moment a beast — a boar — rushed at Cadfael on his horse. All our horses reared and Emrick's horse lost its footing, going down hard into a ravine. Emrick was momentarily trapped by the weight of his horse. The boar then attacked Emrick and the distraught horse. Instinct took over and within an instant I had an arrow on my bow and had released a shot; narrowly missing Emrick, it took the boar straight through its snout and head. The impact of the boar still hit Emrick but he had braced for the contact. None of us was sure what had happened or if Emrick was going to be all right. Cadfael was quickly off his horse and over to his brother.

The luck seemed to be with us that day as Emrick seemed practically uninjured. His shoulder was damaged where the boar had hit him with its weight. Besides that, he looked to have sprained the ankle which was trapped under his horse. Otherwise, it seemed that his pride was more injured than anything else.

King David and his men appeared on the scene just as Cadfael and I were getting to Emrick. Emrick's horse was back on its feet and Emrick was trying to get to his. Cadfael and I took a side each although as I reached for his shoulder he cringed in pain. Emrick's father was now with us and asking what had happened. Cadfael and Emrick gave the details to their father while Gethin, his steward, was surveying the boar.

'Sire, this is one of the largest boars I have ever seen. It will weigh anywhere between eight hundred and a thousand pounds.'

The men around us whistled as the steward went about taking off the boar's head. After surveying Emrick, King David announced that Emrick had a busted shoulder and the hunt would have to end. Gethin had finished cutting off the head and told me it was mine before stepping toward me to give it to me. On instinct I stepped back not really finding the massive bloody head appealing. The king and his men cracked up, laughing at my response, as it seemed that Gethin wasn't being serious and knew I would react the way I did. As this occurred, I began laughing also which set off everyone again, including Emrick who then winced in pain.

We all mounted back up and slowly made our way out of the Wye valley and forest and back to the king's estate. I rode with Emrick and Cadfael and we chatted about the hunt and the boar coming out of what seemed like nowhere. Emrick's left arm was bandaged up to take the weight off his shoulder. I could see that riding was difficult for him and he was doing well not to show the pain which I was sure he was in.

The boar was carried back on a cart and would make a fine feast that evening. Gethin told me that the boar head would make a fine trophy. It was one of the biggest he had seen, and it had large mature tusks. He said that the king would mount it in the hunting lodge at the estate with his other prize animals.

Back at the estate I caught up with the rest of the family who were still resting and recovering from their injuries received during the attack. I filled them in on what had happened with the hunt, downplaying my role in taking down the boar. They were relieved that we were all going to be fine and relieved that the king's son was not badly hurt. It was good to see Mother looking much recovered and Bran and Arturo with a bit of colour in their cheeks. I knew that Arturo and Bran were jealous that I was able to go on the royal hunt but this did not outweigh their grief for the loss of Evan and my sister Cyneburg.

Seeing their grief only reminded me of my sister and brought back the strong feelings of loss. My little sister Cyneburg was only eight. She was funny and caring and had an affinity with animals; just as Wassa was with little children, so Cyneburg was with animals. They seemed to understand her and were almost always calm when in her presence. I had also pictured Cyneburg marrying Egbert one day as I loved them both dearly It was something I used to tease Egbert about and he never denied it was a possibility. Egbert would be devastated and oh, it was too much to bear thinking about. I left the estate to find a quiet place on the grounds to be alone. I wanted to cry, and I didn't want anybody to see me do it. The only other time I had cried was with the loss of father. That day was still fresh in my memory and now with the loss of Cyneburg the loss of Father came back to me again.

I was in the grounds until just on dark when I knew it would be time to go back in. Cadfael found me as I came closer to the lodge. I guess he could see that I had been crying as he was gentle with me and said that they were all gathered in the hall to warm up and share company. He said that he had been out into the grounds looking for me but he had not found me. I told him where I had been and as it looked like he wanted more, I told him how I had recently lost my father and now my little sister had been killed. Cadfael comforted me and told me that it was still a cruel world. He said it was our duty to make the country safer so that others did not have to experience the same grief as I had. I agreed with Cadfael and told him that it was now my life's work to make the land safe, protect those who needed protecting and to force the Vikings off our island. Cadfael agreed and told me he would help me wherever and whenever he could.

Everyone seemed to be gathered in the main hall including Emrick, Uncle Arturo and my cousin Bran, who was propped up by cushions on a sofa. King David came straight over to us with a drink as soon as he saw Cadfael and me enter the room. It felt wrong to be served by the king. King David handed me a large mug of warm mead and turned to face the rest of the room. All eyes were on us as it seemed that many of the others had noticed the king serve me my drink.

Everyone in the room was silent as they waited for the king to speak.

'You are all aware that earlier today we went hunting down in the Wye Valley. The Wye Valley forest, is reputed to have the biggest and best game and today we proved this to be true.'

At that Gethin had a couple of men bring in the boar's head which was sitting on a board. There were gasps from the room, particularly from the ladies which included Aunt Mary and my mother. Seeing the head for the first time since being back, at the lodge, gave me a renewed impression of the size of it. My arrow was still sticking through the snout almost directly between the boar's huge tusks.

The king continued once the noise from the room died down. 'Tonight, we will feast on the boar and respect the creature for the magnificent beast that it is. However, tonight we grieve for the loss of two people who are dear to our guests, Evan of house Delwyn and Cyneburg of house Amity. For their loss we grieve, and I apologise to them that our roads are not safer places to travel. God willing, we will bring law and order to the land so that our families will be safe when travelling and when at home.'

We thanked the king for his kind words and took a swig of our drinks in support.

Following the drink, the king put up his hand for silence and then continued to speak. 'Tonight, I also want to publicly thank a young man who undoubtedly saved the life of my son Emrick. You can see the head of the boar, a boar which was heading at speed, from the undergrowth, directly at my son Emrick who was temporarily pinned under his horse.' There were nods of recognition from all of those gathered in the room. 'Everything would have happened in an instant and should this young man have delayed his shot for a second then Emrick would be dead. I believe this boar to have weighed eight hundred pounds, so this outcome is not unrealistic. The young man in question has acted on instinct and in an instant has drawn his bow, notched an arrow and fired it directly over Emrick's head. A lessor marksman could have put the arrow directly through Emrick's head, instead of the boar's. The arrow still sits where it struck the boar as a reminder of how miraculous this shot was.'

The room roared with applause once the king drew breath. This forced the king to pause. He was smiling from ear to ear as he looked around at me. Again, he wanted to speak so he raised his hand which was holding the mug. 'I want you to all bear witness to how grateful my family are that Godric of house Amity saved Emrick, my son. In the short time I have known Godric I have already noted his strength and leadership. Godric, you and your family will always be welcome in my house and on my land. If there is ever a need please do not hesitate to ask. Please raise your glass and drink to young Godric, boar slayer and saviour of the king's son.' Everyone cheered and emptied their mugs.

I was humbled by the King's speech and spent the next few minutes shaking hands and being basically adored. The king came up again, embraced me warmly and once again said thank you. He told me that he was going to hang the trophy, the boar's head, on the wall of the great hall as a reminder of this hunting trip. 'It will be spoken about and have ballads sung about it for centuries to come; such was the feat.' The rest of the evening ran along the same lines even after sitting down to enjoy the roasted boar.

That night I found it hard getting to sleep and once again I had drunk too much mead. It was funny how my mind was still racing even though I knew that I should be exhausted. I found myself thinking about Cyneburg and how fragile life was. We really did need to do something about the Vikings as their presence was having a cascading influence across the land. As ignorant as I was, I was sure that getting rid of the Vikings would fix everything. I needed to know all I could about war and continue with improving my skills. We needed to attract more men to our region so that we could build the army. The castle would do this, or at least I thought it would. Once we had the castle people would come to our region as they would know they had somewhere they could go and be safe when the Vikings came to raid. Then we could build the army and slowly but surely, we could force them from our land. In my mind this seemed logical and made the priority the completion of the castle.

Eventually I must have fallen asleep as when I woke up the sun was well up into the sky. Bran and Uncle Arturo were still asleep but Tata was gone, and I could hear lots of noise downstairs, so I knew I wasn't the first awake. As I got up Uncle Arturo woke also and we both went downstairs together. I was there to assist my uncle should he require it. Once downstairs there were greetings all around as all the girls were up and Gethin was organising breakfast.

Discussions over breakfast centred around getting Cyneburg back home to bury. The bitter, cold weather had set in and this gave us the luxury of time — as the body would not decay quickly in the cold — although the longer it was left the more likely it was that we would get trapped by the snowdrifts blocking the roads. The ceremony to bury Cyneburg really needed to be held back at home or in Worchester so that her remains could be at rest on the family plot. Evan would need to be taken to his family home which was on the northern side of Hereford. Uncle Arturo said that they would take Evan back to his family and stay with his second daughter Enid and her husband Dewi. Enid and Dewi also lived north of Hereford not far from the Delwyn family home. The king said they would escort them and assist with Evan's body.

The king offered us horses to help us across the Malvern Hills with Cyneburg. I accepted three horses, one for Mother and Tata, one for Wassa and another to carry Cyneburg's body. We had lost half of the daylight by the time these decisions were made so a plan was set to leave at first light the following day. The extra time would be beneficial to explore the grounds and for those who were injured to recover a little further.

The king and Emrick reminded me that they were forever grateful as we departed that following morning. I was reminded to visit often and to ask should I require anything. In a way it was a sad farewell, but it did feel good to be making our way back home.

Chapter 5 — Raids

The sun was low in the sky as the farm came into sight. There was no one at the farm when we arrived as Egbert had already checked on everything and fed the animals. Everything looked as we had left it, which was a good sign that Egbert had done a good job of looking after everything.

After unpacking the horses, I set about digging a grave to bury Cyneburg. It was tradition to bury our loved ones although Father's body was burnt on a pyre as was tradition for a chief or leader. All the bodies from those returned from Mercia had been cremated. The following day I would ride in to catch Egbert before he left home. I would tell him and his family about Cyneburg and invite them out for the funeral. I would then find the Worchester town priest and hoped he would be able to come out and give Cyneburg a Christian burial. We were all Christians, as was everyone I knew. We all believed in the afterlife and that our deeds in this life would give us a good place in God's kingdom. I hoped it was all true and that Cyneburg was now up there somewhere sitting with father and Jesus. I then reiterated my promise which was to see that our world became a better and safer place.

Egbert and his family were devastated to hear about Cyneburg and I felt terrible giving them the news. There were tears instantly from Leofflaed and Sunngifu. I had now had a few days to grieve and get a hold of my emotions but seeing them cry only set me off again. Sunngifu was like a big sister to Cyneburg and they had been good friends. Sunngifu took off in tears and her mother Leofflaed took off to comfort her although I knew she also wanted to be alone as she was also racked with grief. John told me that they would be at the farm by mid-afternoon and through watery eyes he embraced me and told me he was proud of how I was handling all the grief I had now experienced. He asked me if

I needed anything but there wasn't anything I needed now, other than the priest.

That afternoon was sad as I gave the eulogy. 'Cyneburg was one of the happiest people I know, and she would not want us to be unhappy. Yes, we are sad that she has gone to Jesus well before her time however she would implore us to not be sad on her account and she would see smiles on our faces.' This seemed to give everyone a little cheer, so we cracked open a barrel of mead and drank to the memory of Cyneburg.

The Archers and the priest all stayed with us on the farm which made for a homely atmosphere. It was nice spending time with Egbert as we were the best of friends. The Archers and Amitys were always close but that night we became even closer. John and Leofflaed offered to help with the farm and any number of things. Mother assured them that we would cope but thanked them nonetheless.

John told us that he had managed to finish the plans for the castle and asked that I go back into town with them the following day to view them. I had completely forgotten about the plans so news of them brightened my mood further. Now we could really hook into the castle using what we had already done with regards to preparations.

Hilda and Leofric's wedding plans were then discussed. It was to be a church wedding given that it was winter. I was to give Hilda away, as was tradition and it would have been Father's wish. John did offer but the priest said it was fine for the eldest male in the family to give the bride away. Hilda would arrive at the church in a horse drawn carriage wearing Mother's wedding dress. We prayed that it would not be a wet day as besides being bad luck, it could ruin Mother's wedding dress. The dress would be needed for Wassa at some later date.

To finish off the night Hilda insisted that I tell our guests about our adventure in Powys. They knew about Cyneburg and how she and Evan were killed but they did not know about the boar. Hilda gave everyone just enough so that they were on the edge of their seats once I started telling them about the hunting trip with King David. Even the information about meeting the king had impressed them all as we had not mentioned who the riders were who had saved us. We had only arrived home the previous day and had not had the chance for a complete reflection on the journey.

I told them the story as best I could remember, from the beauty and eerie Wye Valley forest to the eight-hundred-pound boar coming out of the undergrowth. They seemed amazed when I told them how I shot the boar through the middle of its snout and that the king was going to mount the head in his grand hall. It all sounded like make believe but Mother and the others vouched for me. I told John and Egbert that all the weapons training we were doing was working, as this trip was the first time I'd had the chance to test out what we had been practising, in a life or death battle.

The following day I went into Worchester with Egbert and his family. I was really looking forward to checking out the plans as this was a big part of our future. Egbert's father had a real talent for drawing as there were several plans showing the castle from different angles and different elevations. This was exactly what we needed to get started in earnest.

John was one of the only people I knew who had books. Books were rare so out of interest I enquired as to their content. He told me there was one about law and the office of notary. There was also two history books and a copy of the Bible although this was in Latin and few around here could read it. John told me he had been taught Latin by the old Worchester priest when he was a bit younger than me. Seeing that I was interested he asked if Egbert and I would like to learn how to read Latin. Egbert looked at me and I said why not, yes please. I asked him about the history books, and he told me that one was in French and the other was also in Latin. I told John that I wanted to learn about war and wondered if there was any information in the books about previous battles. John told us there was a lot of information about battles as most of history seemed to be made up with battles.

'There is information about all of Alexander the Great's battles as he took over Greece and marched his way through Persia, the Middle East and over to India.' Egbert and I were sitting there with our mouths open. Alexander the Great, I had never heard of him let alone the places Egbert's father had just mentioned. John went on. 'There is information about Charlemagne the king of the Franks, information about the Romans including their battles against the Celts including the Scots and

Queen Boudicca. There are many battles so if you want to read about them, you had best learn how to read.'

I told John that this was what we needed. We needed to learn tactics from the great wars. 'Tactics which have been successful in the past can be successful in the future.'

John looked at me and said that wars were dangerous and there were usually no winners. I had heard this before from Father and what good had it done him? Respectfully I told John that it was my life's mission to free our land of the Vikings, to bring peace to our roads and towns. John just smiled and said, 'So be it.'

Egbert's and my education started there and then. John started with the alphabet for Latin and commenced teaching us how to read and indeed write. Most of Egbert's and my days were taken up with chores and working on the castle, but in between and into the evening we both practised what John had shown us during the day. It did not take long for both of us to see signs of progress. The progress only encouraged us more and before long we were competing and pushing each other.

While this was going on the castle kept growing and growing so that by the time of the summer solstice the entire perimeter and foundations had been laid. Father used to say that the foundations are the most important stage of every building and John kept reiterating this message as the people of our town put their backs into building the castle. The stone was coming in equal quantities from the Amity and Wulstan quarries. Using both the quarries seemed to accelerate the work which made our successes more evident.

Before summer Hilda and Leofric were at last married. This was a big festival which was attended by most of the town. There were no invites as anyone could attend who wished it. This was the joining of Amity and Archer and thus a very special occasion for both families. Essential to the wedding was the handfasting ceremony which involved thirteen ribbons, each with their own symbolic meaning. The hand fasting ritual was a physical bond uniting a man and a woman when getting married. The thirteen ribbons were tied around Hilda and Leofric's wrists, uniting them physically, but also spiritually. Although we were all now Christian, we still retained a lot of our old traditions which had come down through the centuries. I walked Hilda down the aisle to Father Frank, where he and Leofric Archer my soon to be brother in-law, were waiting at the altar.

The party extended well into the middle of the night, so we all stayed at the Archer property as going back to the farm in the night was only inviting trouble. Leofric and Hilda had both agreed to move out to the farm as this would be a big help for us and Leofric did not have the money to go out on his own yet. I would enjoy having Leofric around even if just for weapons practice, although I thought I could probably get help with the forge also.

As summer came around news was filtering into Worchester from Birmingham and Coventry that the raids were getting more frequent and deadly. Worchester was welcoming the refugees as the extra hands were needed to harvest our crops and continue work on the castle. I had to stop work on the castle as my work at the forge kept me busy most of the day. I was grateful that the days were long as this enabled me to be a blacksmith, practise with my weapons and continue my education in reading.

One day there was a request which came through from Æthelstan that he needed men as the Vikings were starting to get on top of him. John and Wulstan told the delegation that we were too busy with harvest and could not spare any men. They told us that Æthelstan would be disappointed that we were not supporting our king and at this I know John would have struggled to keep calm after what Æthelstan did to us last time.

Our town guard now had over three hundred men who were all training together on three afternoons every week. From my short experience of a fight, I thought that as fighters we were all pretty good. Training was mainly archery as all the men were contributing to the building of the castle and did not need any work on their strength or fitness. The wooden swords did come out at least once every week.

I had taken on a role as captain of the archery and had commissioned four hundred bows from the town carpenters. These had to be to a certain specification to work with the arrows I was producing. My arrows had heavier iron tips and lighter rods which could travel greater distances and penetrate armour easily. I knew this as I tested many different options myself. Worchester was blessed with wealth having iron and tin mines, both metals being found in the Malvern Hills. North of Worcester there was a silver mine at Kidderminster which was thought to be exhausted of mineral, but I had heard that there had been a new silver find at the mine.

A week later and another delegation came from Æthelstan demanding that we take up arms to support our king. This time the delegation included two dozen fully armed men. The warning alarm had been sounded on sight of the armed men. This warning horn was a measure we had put in after the last raid back when I was ten. It meant that the men working on their farms around Worcester and the others on the castle could put down what they were doing and come to the aid of the town. As the delegation were starting to make their threats the number of our guard which came to meet them increased rapidly from half a dozen men to well over a hundred. Suddenly the thirty or so Mercians did not look, or I gather feel so tough. Again, they left empty handed and we all went back to what we were doing. By now Egbert and I were both fourteen and gaining more and more influence in the guard and around the town.

It was only two days after this that the alarm horn was signalled again. Thinking it was Æthelstan again I was loathe to respond but he might have arrived in force. I was at the forge at the time of the horn, so I made the forge safe and grabbed my quiver, bow and sword.

As soon as I left the farm, I knew this was something different. There was already smoke in the direction of Worcester and immediately I felt the adrenaline rush. This was it, I knew it, my first real battle apart from my skirmish over in Powys. At full speed I kicked my horse, which I had named Bolter, into action and we headed like a lightning bolt toward town.

Coming in from an elevated position I could see that there were hundreds of Vikings raiding Worcester. As I came into range I was in my stirrups and releasing arrow after arrow, taking down Vikings. I was not the only one as the guard from the castle and other properties began to arrive at around the same time. I kept Bolter at a safe distance as I continued to empty my quiver, arrow after arrow, attempting to do as much damage as I could. Eventually a lot of Viking attention turned toward me, and I had to draw my sword and fight hand to hand for my life and, I thought, the lives of my loved ones.

The fight went on for close to an hour and only ended when the raiding party had all been dealt with. When I mean dealt with it was when they were all dead.

I was covered in blood but thankfully none of it mine. It was a battle for the ages and although exhausted I was pumped. I didn't know how many I had run through, but I knew it was a lot. Yes, I was exhausted as I collapsed onto my backside too tired to hold my weight up any more.

John and Leofflaed were the first who got to me and I could see the concern on their faces. I told them that the blood was not mine and I was just exhausted. John helped me to my feet and said I would be better in a minute; it was the fatigue of war which I was feeling. Leofflaed gave me some water which helped me get my legs back. They told me that I had fought well. I knew I had fought well and wanted to have time to go through the battle in my head.

'How are Egbert and Leofric?' is what I first asked.

'Unhurt,' is what John told me. He asked me to come into the town square to clean up and get some food and drink. There would be a lot of work to do now. We would have to assist our injured and see to their wounds.

'That is being done' said Leofflaed.

I had not realised I had spoken what I had been thinking. So, I told them that we would need to gather our dead. 'Can I help with the gathering of the dead?'

Leofflaed told me that this had also commenced, and my assistance would be gratefully received as it was a big task.

For the next two hours those of us who were not injured were kept busy. We had to lay out our dead, see to our wounded and strip the Vikings of anything useful such as weapons. It was bloody and horrible work however I was now immune to the blood and the thought that these people were all alive a few hours before did not faze me. Father Frank presided over a service for our fallen and the Viking warriors. We had many dead including Arthur's father Bevan and our friends, Bran and Kelvan. Many women had also been killed such as the sheriff's wife Mildgyd and both Bakers daughters, Cyneburg and Wilburh.

There was much grief that afternoon as the miserable tasks were completed. Frank told me that he had counted two hundred and eighty-three dead Vikings. From his vantage point he did not see any leave the field of battle. Our dead numbered just over a hundred at a hundred and twelve, although forty-five of them were women and children. This meant that we had lost sixty-seven from the guards against the Vikings' two hundred and eighty-three and they had the advantage of surprise. Although there was a lot of grief in Worchester, I knew that these were significant numbers and pointed to the proficiency of our training in the guard. The knowledge that we were fighting for our lives and homes, was not lost on me. This had been a large Viking army, one that would have normally fought against Mercia or Wessex.

My mind was already racing ahead with thought after thought. It was clear that we needed to expand the size of the guard. The guard was working, and we were not even very sophisticated. I wanted to read John Archer's books on war as we needed to consider tactics. Defensive at first but then offensive tactics so that we could take the war to the Vikings. There would be Viking villages which would now be grieving and vulnerable as they had lost their men. This would be the perfect time to attack but I had no idea where these Vikings had come from or what really lay to the northeast.

This led me to the thought that we really needed to know our terrain. In my head I could see us leading parties into the northeast; not to raid, however, but to assess what our enemy was doing and how many there were. There was so much to plan for but for now I had to support the families of our town.

The following day at midday our council met which included Egbert and me. Bevan was the only councillor who had been killed so Arthur was welcomed to the council. We started the meeting with a prayer for our fallen citizens and friends. This was followed by a few speeches about the day before one commenting on how well we had all fought and especially me. I felt proud to be one of the guards to be singled out and knew the praise to be correct.

I had not slept that much the night before so I had sat up by candlelight and had written down what was going through my head. My quiver held fifty arrows, and only five were left when I gathered it after the fight. I did not recall any of my shots missing and in fact I could remember each shot. I was in the zone and it seemed like the battle and everything around me was happening in slow motion. Once I took to the sword, I could count a further twenty-three kills which brought my total up to sixty-eight Viking kills. I was exhilarated which was part of the reason I couldn't sleep. It was evident to me that I was made for war and this was my calling by God.

After all the speeches I put up my hand to indicate I wanted to speak. I agreed with the others that the alarm horn had worked well and that given the extreme danger we were all in the town and its guard had done an amazing job to defeat the Vikings. There was a real chance that Worchester and all its inhabitants could have been killed, given the size of the threat. I then touched on the success of the guard and how we had killed them at a ratio of at least four to one. In my eyes the castle was still our priority, however, we needed to start getting to know the Viking areas of habitation and even our surrounding towns. 'We need to send sorties out to the neighbouring towns so that they know they are not alone. If need be, we can support these towns and villages if they are under attack. Eventually men from these areas will then come to join our guard. The towns and villages will see how well we can fight and will want to learn our ways.' I went on to tell them how I thought that now would be the perfect time to launch a counterattack into the Viking areas but none of us knew the Vikings or their land.

They were all listening intently, and I could see many nodding heads.

'Our priority must be the castle but slowly we must increase our zone of influence.'

As I ended there was applause from the room. It was unanimously agreed in the council that on one training session each week we would ride out to a village or town in our surrounding community, to show support and let them know we had their back. Step by step this could be expanded while keeping our priority the building of the castle.

Out on the farm I started to think about weapons as I knew my sword was clunky. Most people fought with shield in the left and sword in the right. I thought about a design for a sword which could also be used as a shield. When turned flat against an attack the sword could be used to protect the body from attack. This would enable the user to wield two such weapons and attack with both left and right and defend with both also. One of the Vikings who I killed had a sword with a sharp point and then halfway down the blade the sword widened on both sides to a wide sharp edge. As this sword was wider across the middle this could be used defensively as required.

To perfect these swords, I needed to make them lighter. To get a lighter sword I had been playing with the process of using different quantities of coal, and cooling in the process. If I used too much carbon with the iron, then my sword was not strong enough to penetrate armour; however, not enough coal and it was too heavy. I was strong and did not mind heavy weapons but I had to be conscious of others who fought with the sword and the duration of battles. I could become fatigued even with all my natural and inbuilt strength.

Overcoming this problem, I felt like I had produced the perfect weapon for me and a superior sword for the guard. The weapon was lighter than the traditional sword, had three cutting edges and was versatile so it could be used defensively. I knew it would be no good for the traditional shield wall but in faster and more open battles would serve us better against the Vikings. Open battles would bring in our skill with horses through our cavalry.

News of the Viking raid spread through the district. With the news of the battle volunteers began to trickle into Worchester to join our guard. What started as a trickle became a flood within months. We now had close to eight hundred either full time or part time members which was a formidable force. I was still looking inward and patting myself on the back, not realising that we were getting to a size that was starting to get noticed by the big powers in the land, Mercia and Wessex.

Samhain came again and we rolled into winter. Winter usually meant that we were safe from raids but the attacks seemed to keep coming this year. The saving grace for us was that the attacks were minor compared to the major attack earlier in the year.

Hilda and Leofric were expecting their first child which was also exciting news for our families. This was going to be the start of the next generation.

In the new year the raids from the Vikings increased in frequency and size as the seasons moved through the year into spring. From our sorties out into the community it was evident that we were not the only ones being targeted. The Vikings were pillaging and plundering where they could and doing their best to avoid casualties.

A rider arrived in Worchester with news which made the incessant raiding make sense. At an extraordinary council meeting we were told that Wessex had taken Repton and that now King Alfred of Wessex ruled over Mercia also. We all wanted to know of Æthelstan as he was the treacherous bastard that we all hated. The rider told us that Ethelred of Wessex had cut off Æthelstan's head in an execution once Repton had surrendered. 'Most of the Mercian captains have sworn allegiance to Alfred,' he said. 'It appears this has weakened the Mercian lands against the Vikings, as they are growing very bold.'

The Worchester sorties consisted of twenty guard on horseback. As spring approached, the roads to Worchester became clogged with refugees. Sightings of Vikings were frequent however there were few engagements. When I was on sorties, I chased the opportunity to engage. The thrill of war had so engulfed me and at that stage I felt invincible. This aggressive attitude mixed with our results gave our sortie a much-respected reputation.

On one sortie we came onto the town of Meridan which was under siege. It looked like a hundred Vikings were around Meridan which had a small palisade wall protecting it. The wall had been breached in at least two areas and there was frantic fighting going on to keep the Vikings out. With a signal to the guard, we moved in close and charged our horses directly into the centre of the Vikings. They heard us coming but did not have time to take any evasive action.

Splitting the Viking party, we pushed on through them and once clear we turned and began taking them down with our arrows. The thrust through the body of their party had confused them and, in that confusion, we were finding it easy to cut them down. Our intent was to stay clear of them for as long as we could before engaging in hand-to-hand combat.

Although the Vikings were fierce warriors, we were finding that our guard were superior fighters. All the guard were involved in physical work which included working with stone while building the Worchester castle. Training sessions were a minimum of three times per week and these were very much about quality, learning and then practising the correct techniques. Our weapons were superior as I had put a lot of hours into perfecting all aspects of them, crafting them as best I could.

On this sortie we lost one of our guard, but the Vikings were defeated, and almost half of their number fled over the hills to safety. The town of Meridan opened their palisade gates and welcomed us as heroes. It seemed they knew about our guard and the construction of our castle which was now nearing the mid-point of construction. I told them that we were always looking for new members to the guard and that the castle would be a refuge for our entire district.

In this way Worchester was inadvertently becoming the centre of the old Mercia. Worchester was becoming wealthier, which was attracting more attention from the Vikings, and we were starting to get some of the problems that the bigger centres experienced with an influx of refugees. Problems which we were seeing included theft, violence, starvation and homelessness. These issues began to dominate our council meetings. Living out of town we became at increased risk of muggings such as the attack that happened when my sister Cyneburg was killed. Locks for our stores had become more important. To head off the problem of starvation, Worchester set up a soup kitchen to make sure everyone got at least one meal a day. Our thinking was that if everyone got at least one meal per day they were less likely to feel the need to steal to feed themselves or their family.

As winter approached and at the passing of our all-saints' feast, Samhain day, word reached us that a massive Viking raiding party had sacked Birmingham. It seemed that the Vikings were getting frustrated with our sorties and especially with our engagements. Our sortie group was known as the archers and we went out of our way to look for trouble. I had increased our sortie size to fifty men, and we rode the best horses by size and temperament. These sorties took men away from other tasks so although it felt good and gave us vital practice, it did come at a cost.

Birmingham was a similar sized town to Worchester so hearing that it had been sacked and most of its residents slaughtered came as a shock and sent fear through our town. How safe were we? Birmingham was only three hours north by horse and seven hours at a hard march. Birmingham did not have a castle and we had our castle, although it was not yet finished. The walls could already give us good defence but the moat and drawbridge were not complete.

Given the trouble we had been giving the Vikings we began to prepare for an oncoming attack. Palisade walls were erected around Worchester and we created a lookout post five hundred metres from town with instructions to sound two horns for suspicious activity and one loud horn if an attack was coming. Work on the castle also continued at haste with the wish to have most of the structure completed by winter. The finishing touches would take a year or two but we really wanted to have somewhere for the women and children.

Still the refugees continued to flood our town and I estimated our population was close to five thousand residents. I had heard that there was a city in the east called London which was so large it may have had ten thousand residents, but five thousand was the largest town I had ever been to or heard of. All the villages around Worchester were experiencing the same issues and most were large enough to be called towns. Although the castle was the construction priority for Worchester and its surrounds, there was other building going on everywhere. There was a real stretch on resources such as building materials, so the mines and quarries were now also busier than ever.

My blacksmith business was extremely busy with all manner of requirements from farming equipment and horseshoes to weapons and iron grills and fences for the castle and other buildings around the community. Leofric was now full time on the forge and Tata was our assistant, doing a lot of the menial tasks such as preparing materials and cleaning up. I started work on these menial tasks for Father, well before I became a blacksmith.

Leofric and Hilda had their first child which slowed the pace of life for a while as the baby required constant attention. Osgar, named after his grandfather, had the Amity nose and cheekbones with the Archer colouring which was slightly yellow. We all adored Osgar who seemed to lap up all the attention. I was sad that my father did not get to meet his grandson as I knew he would have been pleased. Seeing his grandson would have brought a smile to his face and reinforced his strong sense of purpose. It made me smile just thinking about it and I was happy I could still clearly picture my father.

Sitting around a fire we celebrated the birth of Osgar and reflected on how rapidly life was changing for us all. We were out on the farm and there were both the Amity and Archer families. The changes which we had experienced since the first Viking raid through to the present were incredible. John was thoughtful and suggested there had never been a period of such rapid change as what we were experiencing now. This made me laugh as although we were all busy, I suggested that our planet had continually gone through periods of massive growth and even destruction. It seemed like human nature that life ebbed and flowed the way it was doing for us right now.

This occasion was a night when I got to spend some time with Sunngifu whom I did not see much these days. Sunngifu and I had always been good friends with her being Egbert's younger sister. She was now a fine-looking girl who was looking more like a woman every day. I had the sense that Sunngifu liked me, so I took her hand and we wandered around the farm. She asked me if I could teach her how to shoot an arrow and I told her I would teach her anything she asked me to show her. This gave her a cheeky smile which I know had made me blush. She asked me what I thought the future held and I told her the stars were lining up and I saw a period of great prosperity for both of our families. I even told her that I saw a future for us and with this she squeezed my hand and smiled.

'Do you think my parents will agree?' Sunngifu asked me.

I was certain they would, and I told her as much. 'Would you consider being my bride and promising yourself to me?'

Sunngifu looked up at me and smiled and said she had never had any other plan. Wow, what a night it was for me. This was a night to remember and the worries of the world were as far from my mind as they possibly could be. Sunngifu and I re-joined our families back at the fire where the lute and flute had joined the party. Mother gave Sunngifu and I a knowing smile and looking around I could see that Leofflaed had the same look. I felt cornered and embarrassed by both my mother and future mother in-law. I should have known there were no secrets which we could keep from them.

It was early winter of 860 when the attack we had feared finally came. It was only a month after Birmingham had fallen so the Vikings were really coming with some momentum. The early alarm was sounded but did not give us nearly enough time, as we had hoped. We had more time than the previous attack but only a minute or two.

Leofric and I were both working in the forge at the time of the horn, Leofric tapping me on the shoulder to indicate that an attack was on. I was in deep concentration finishing off an intricate wrought iron gate. Within seconds I had downed my tools and given Tata the instruction to clean things up and head to the caves. Hilda appeared at the door to the forge just as we were leaving and we told her she should take Osgar, Mother, Wassa and Tata up to the caves. 'This could be the big attack we have feared so please do not come back until you know that it is safe.'

Leofric and I gathered our weapons and headed for our horses. Mother and Wassa already had them ready for us when we arrived at the stable. I kissed Mother before Leofric and I rode off to town.

There was smoke all over the sky and we could tell immediately that this was as bad as it could get. I was hoping that Sunngifu and Leofflaed and all the other women and children had made it to the castle. Although not finished it would be easy to barricade themselves behind the entrance. The walls were now too high for an attacking force unless they brought some heavy-duty siege engines or ladders.

In front of us we could see there were thousands engaged in hand-to-hand combat. I knew that Leofric and I had an advantage as we were coming in from higher ground and we were on horseback. A quick communication with Leofric and I knew he was thinking the same thing. We were going to harry their flank and keep moving back out of their way. Each of us had two full quivers, so a hundred of the best arrows. I have to say they were the best as I made them.

Leofric and I were able to be patient and kept at a safe distance until all our arrows had been fired. At this point it was evident that we had done serious damage so we charged the Vikings and cut down as many of them as we could before the fighting was too intense and we needed to dismount from the horses or sacrifice them for good. I was not ready to sacrifice Bolter as he had been very loyal to me and I was very fond of him.

Hand to hand combat was the part I loved as it really got my blood going, which I know is a weird thing to say as with the adrenaline of the fight already going through me it is hard to believe there was yet another level. I can tell you there was as I was in that zone now. Seeing everything in slow motion, it was like a dance as I went through my enemy.

It didn't seem like long before I heard a horn, and the few Vikings which were left fled back the way they had come. Exhaustion set in once again except this time I stayed on my feet. Leofric was down but still alive. He told me he was going to be all right, so I left him to his wounds. Looking through the mass of bodies I was concerned by the sheer numbers of the dead. There just didn't seem to be enough of the guard walking around to account for the destruction. I found Arthur and he asked me if I had seen Egbert to which I told him I hadn't seen him. Walking around town I came across John who asked me if I had seen Leofric or Egbert and I could tell him that Leofric was wounded but would recover. John told me that the women and children got to the castle. This news gave me some cheer although I was now worried about Egbert. Around and around, I searched until finally I came across Egbert, although he looked to be barely alive.

I dropped to my knees and cradled his head in my arms. Although still in shock from the battle, I had tears instantly. Egbert was seconds from death and in his last words he told me to look after them. Moments later and Egbert was then gone. My best friend and childhood buddy left this world. I sobbed into my best friend until the anger and thirst for revenge started to take hold. John found me shortly after Egbert passed and dropped to his knees and joined me. Together we shared this moment and although my father had been dead for years, I felt that John was as close as any father could get. Looking at John with tear filled eyes I told him, 'I will get Egbert's revenge, I will get my revenge and I will get Worchester's revenge.'

The battle of 860 was a major turning point for us Angles and the Vikings. They had thrown what seemed to be their full hammer down on us and we had shattered it. The battle was costly with us losing at least half of our one thousand strong guard. The Vikings looked to have lost twice that number which was a massive number of men to lose in a single battle. It was a bitter battle and one that would take a long time to forget.

After an hour or so I noticed the people re-emerging from the castle. The castle had worked, and we just needed one big push the following year to finish it off. It was sunset before we had finished dealing with the bodies and extinguished all the fires. As it was getting bitterly cold a decision was made to have the funerals on the following day. Our dead were going to be seen off in the old traditions with fire and not burial.

There hadn't been anyone come down from the hill road, not even from the adjoining farms so I was just quietly starting to worry. Leaving Sunngifu and her family I rode back up to the farm. Leofric had to stay at his parents' house as he was in too bad a way to travel. As I approached the farm some of my worst fears were realised. Our house was a smouldering mess with some flames to extinguish. Looking at the mess in front of me it was then that I noticed my mother's naked body standing upright with a stake from bottom to top. The look on mother's face was one of complete terror. I stood there in shock and slowly moved to remove the stake and cover her body. I said a silent prayer for Jesus to shepherd my mother and guide her to the gates of heaven where she deserved to spend eternity. The image in my head would probably never disappear. I had no more tears as they had all been spent earlier for Egbert. My poor mother had suffered a horrible death and for no reason I could make sense of. I whispered into my mother's ear, 'Now you can join your husband in the greatest place of all. Thank you for giving me life and guidance.'

With Mother in my arms is how Hilda, Wassa and Tata found me. They were distraught as I would have expected them to be. I was glad they had not seen her as I had seen her or there would have been even worse nightmarish memories. My revenge on the Vikings was ingrained in me and my feelings and desire to do them harm could not have been greater. This was not the time for revenge however one day they would know that they made a mistake crossing me. I was still an ignorant adolescent, but I was becoming a powerful enemy.

That night we all slept in the forge and probably would have to for a few weeks until we could rebuild our house. I told Hilda about Leofric and Egbert and this just opened everyone to further grieving. They were relieved that Leofric would be fine however Egbert was like a brother to us all and his loss was a devastating blow. Hardship and loss had become commonplace for the Amity clan, and I wondered what we had done to deserve such outcomes.

That winter felt even colder and more miserable than usual. There was a loneliness which filled my heart with the loss of my two closest companions. With help from neighbours and friends we had a new house in a little over a week. We were grateful for the new house but it did not feel the same without mother. Leofric was able to come home so at least Leofric and Hilda were back together. Hilda told us that she was expecting another child which was at least some good news to come out of those hard times. My determination with work had new meaning and became more frantic. I needed to be better but I also needed to know more about war. I doubled my time learning Latin and working on the history of war book which John Archer had lent me. The Vikings needed to be stopped and that required us taking the war to them.

Thankfully the long miserable winter began to morph into spring. The castle was at the point where we could commence the excavation for the second half of the moat. The River Severn ran around half of the castle so we only needed to divert some water into our excavation on the other half of the castle to give us a full-scale flowing moat. What a great defence this castle would have.

The other blessing over that winter was that there were no more raids on Worchester. It seemed that the battle had also taken the wind out of the sails of the Vikings which I had no doubt it would have. One thousand men is a massive army and a loss that they might never get over. This was my prayer although I knew that it was more likely wishful thinking.

Life was very different without Egbert and especially Mother. I felt the weight of responsibility for my family when before I always felt that it was my mother's responsibility. The only way I could protect my family was by clearing the land of Vikings.

Chapter 6 — Betrayal

Life for Worchester was never going to be normal again. The council met to discuss everything which had happened to our community over the previous two years. There had been many raids and still we had continued to grow our guard and build our castle. The problem for us had been the breakdown of Mercia and then the united defence of the land. Mercia had acted as a fractured group which was likely the direct result of Æthelstan and the way in which he ruled. We all hoped that Alfred would rule differently and bring the different regions together to fight the Vikings. Most of us had very little trust of people in power, however, we were willing to give working with Wessex a go for the sake of our families and the future.

It wasn't long after one of these meetings that a delegation came to us from Bristol, the seat of power for Ethelred. The delegation consisted of three men who were all senior members of Ethelred's army, as well as a young woman. Sigeberht seemed to be the man doing all the talking however both Oswald and Hereweald appeared to carry power as Sigeberht eyed them as he spoke. I was not sure why the woman came with the delegation as she was not introduced at first.

They told us that the work we were doing had been noticed and that Ethelred was impressed with our progress in what we had achieved. They gave us the speech about the Vikings and how it was Ethelred's, vision to have one united land with him as its leader. Ethelred was King Alfred's son and King Alfred was King of Wessex which now also controlled most of Mercia.

John told them of the betrayal at the hands of Æthelstan and that we were reluctant to commit to another leader without first knowing that they could be trusted. John told them that we operated as a council and usually voted on anything which could be contentious. At this point the young woman spoke up and told us that she was the sister of Ethelred. This was Aethelswith, Ethelred's younger sister. She told us that her brother had honour and was renowned for his battle prowess with many great victories.

I was impressed that Ethelred's sister had risked this journey to win our support. I was also impressed that our guard had developed such a reputation that they cared that we joined their army. This was a great sign and when a vote came as to whether we join the offensive with Ethelred my vote was in the affirmative.

The delegation waited outside while we took our vote. This was customary as decisions made in the council become the council's vote and not individuals'. The council vote was passed in the affirmative with only John Archer voting against the proposal. The delegation was invited back into the hall to hear our decision. I noted a collective sigh from them when we told them we were in. Were they really holding their breath that we would join? To me it certainly looked as though they were.

Sigeberht told us they were riding through in a week which gave us some time to prepare. The initial meeting location was to be Coventry. From Coventry we would be heading to Repton to destroy the Viking stronghold. It was now the council's turn to be shocked. Repton had been the capital for Mercia, surely it had not been conquered by the Vikings. Aethelswith confirmed that Mercia was leaderless and that the Vikings had taken full advantage. I commented that Mercia had been leaderless for years even though Æthelstan had been in the post.

Some mead was shared as the deal was struck. We would send the five hundred strong guard to Coventry to join with Wessex in a push back against the Vikings. Little did the delegation know that this was practically our entire guard since it was decimated in the raid late last year. We could not have committed any more to Wessex as this was a year's worth of hard work and team building just to have what we have.

During the sealing of the deal over a drink I had the opportunity to chat to each member of the group. Hereweald was of my late father's age and a similar build to me. He looked to be wise and thoughtful and gave me confidence that we were putting the guard into safe hands. Oswald was younger and seemed egotistical. I did not doubt his prowess in battle, however he didn't seem to show any respect to us. Oswald spent our conversation telling me how they had the biggest towns and the most men. I asked Oswald about some of the battles he had fought in as I genuinely wanted to learn more about battles and battle planning. It seemed that he thought I was questioning his credentials as he told me I was too young for the details and he was surprised that they let children onto the council. My elders had taught me to control my emotions so there was no way I was going to rise to Oswald's insults.

Hearing this exchange Aethelswith stepped in between us and took me by the elbow, steering me away from Oswald. Aethelswith was stunning and I guessed a couple of years older than me. She told me that she could remember coming through Worchester five years earlier when travelling with her father to visit King David. I told her I could not remember the visit as surely a visit like this would have been remembered. Aethelswith said that it was low key as these lands were Mercia and it would have been dangerous should King Æthelstan have realised they were here. It was her father's turn to visit King David to discuss the issues we were both having with the earl in Brycheiniog in the south. Brycheiniog was a region south of Powys and west of Wessex, across the River Severn.

'I cannot believe that this is the same town we came through as it has morphed from a small backwater town to a leading centre of commerce.'

I told her this was no accident as the council had planned to create a prosperous centre to provide security for the people. It all started with the construction of the castle which gave us a defensive position. Searching for security would bring people who would come and build in the community as they knew they would be safe from attack. The pace of change had escalated due to the problems in Mercia and with the Vikings. 'Refugees have been flooding the area for years now and this has only accelerated the pace of change. The castle will be finished within a year and the Vikings will hopefully be halfway back across the sea.'

Aethelswith seemed to think something I had said was funny as she had a cheeky but beautiful smile on her face. 'You speak with such love and passion for your town and its people. I do not smile to mock you, but your words bring me such happiness to see a leader who truly cares about their people. Love and trust are such priceless commodities, and in the world I come from there isn't much of either.' I could see that Aethelswith was also a romantic and idealist like me however in a world full of darkness sometimes it is hard to see the light. Aethelswith still had hope and still had a kindness to her, whether from her youth or resilience.

Our conversation was interrupted with Sigeberht saying that the delegation must depart. Aethelswith had captivated me and I felt a little empty once they had gone.

There was a lot of work to be completed to prepare for the coming war. Word was sent for the guard to meet an hour after first light on the following day. We were to meet to make plans and practise our weapons on the fields in front of our new castle.

The following day close to six hundred guard members arrived on the field fully armed. Our numbers were continually growing and within a year we were hoping to have a thousand guardsman.

Wulfstan spoke to the guard communicating the plan as agreed by the council. Wulfstan said that only five hundred had been promised so all the others, the newer members, would have the responsibility of defending the town and its people. Should the guard not return then the home guard should use the castle as defence and set about building up a new guard. 'Worchester and its people will endure, and the Vikings will be defeated.'

Taking over from Wulfstan I told the guard that we were not alone, and that Powys would also come to our aid should we need it. I then spoke about our battle formations and about some of the work I had been doing to understand past battles and techniques. 'We do not know what to expect and we will be fighting under the Wessex flag and their generals.' I explained how our archers had always been an advantage in all the battles I'd had with the Vikings and thus we needed to protect our archers with foot soldiers for as long as we could. 'Our bows are stronger than anybody else's and our arrows travel further and truer than any I have seen. Your swords are lighter and stronger which means you can kill quickly and maintain your strength for longer. It is these technical advancements along with your dedication which will see our land free and secure.'

There was a massive cheer from the guard which heartened all of us. From there we practised formations for the following hour and did so every day until our departure for Coventry.

Our departure was a big event for Worchester and its surrounding communities. Five hundred of our fittest and strongest men were marching off to war. These men were sons and fathers, brothers and even grandfathers. All of us had other roles in our family and communities and these families and the community would be hurt by each death. Given the times which we lived in there was no illusion that all of us would not return. We marched out of town fully equipped with our weapons and a day pack with food and water. We were cheered off by everyone who had come to see us leave. I felt emotional for several reasons but mostly because this brought back the memories of my father heading off to war five years earlier. That campaign had not ended well, which I hoped was not a premonition of what was to come.

Nearing Coventry, we could see Ethelred and his men. We pulled up short of the Wessex army so that we could keep the Worchester army together. Hereweald rode over to our camp and welcomed us. He asked me how many men we had and told us that they had about two thousand from Wessex. Two and a half thousand men sounded like a big army and given the setback to the Vikings the previous year, this should be all we needed to free Repton and do the Vikings more damage.

Hereweald took Wulfstan, John and me to meet Ethelred in the command tent. Ethelred was there along with Oswald and after greetings were exchanged, they told us a bit more about who we were fighting. Halfdan led the Vikings and they were settled across the north and in the East Angles which included the city of London. Halfdan relied on raids to gather his wealth but was also organised for large scale battles to increase their land holdings. This battle was critical as a win against Halfdan would be a big moral boost for us and greatly reduce the Viking ability to wage war in the south.

Ethelred looked to be ten years older than me and didn't seem to be in a good mood. Later I asked Hereweald about Ethelred and if all was well with him but Hereweald laughed and said, 'That is Ethelred. He can be miserable at the best of times and one wants to stay in his good books as he treats his friends well enough but hunts down those who displease him. Ethelred is a complicated character who takes a while to get to know.'

The plan was to set up camp to rest for the night. We would all march on Repton the following day, leaving at first light. Our Worcester units were to take the centre of the field with the Wessex forces on both flanks.

That night I don't think any of us got much sleep. It was unnerving to know we were going to be facing these vicious warriors again. I still occasionally got nightmares from the battle last year and especially seeing my mother's staked body. I had never told anyone about my nightmares as it was a private torture and I did not want to appear weak amongst my peers or family.

In the early morning the rain started coming down and it seemed to have set in. Lying in a tent listening to the constant rain made me miserable. My mind drifted to days spent with my family in front of the fire while it rained or snowed outside. The weather was a great excuse to spend time together playing games. As a family we never needed many excuses as we relied on each other and Mother and Father had always emphasised importance of looking out for family.

The rain was still pounding down when it was time to prepare to move out. It wasn't long before we were all drenched to the bone. Rain was running down my back and giving me a chill as the light came onto this miserable morning. Looking around I caught Leofric's eyes and could see he felt as miserable as me. John came up and placed a hand on my back and said, 'Let's get this over with as I can already feel the warmth of the fire back home.' This made me and Leofric smile as it gave us something to look forward to and made the coming war seem like a petty chore.

As the rain continued to penetrate everything the Worchester guard rode out of Coventry on our way to meet Halfdan and the Vikings. I hoped that they were just as miserable as us and an even greater hope was that they had decided it was not a good day for fighting and had retreated. The Vikings seemed to enjoy fighting, raiding and war, so it was unlikely they would pass up the opportunity that we were giving them.

There was a large open field on the south side of Repton with gentle slopes on both the north and south sides. With the rain the field looked to be waterlogged in the centre and lower areas. I could see the Vikings gathering on the northern side of the field in preparation for what was to come. Preparing to go into war was very surreal as this was the first organised battle which I had taken part in. All my previous fights had been without the knowledge that they were going to happen and thus I had reacted on instinct and fought for my life. Today we had a battle plan and had, in theory, prepared for what was to come. I knew to expect the unexpected but wanted this battle to be straightforward.

The command came through for us to move forward. The Worchester guard were all archers and were organised into two groups. The front group was on foot while the back group was on horseback. Sigeberht told us he was concerned that being on horseback would affect the accuracy of our archers however I convinced him that this was how we trained and that our accuracy and the courage of our horses would not fail. Thus, the guard moved forward just as the Viking mass moved down the opposite hill to meet us. On either side of the guard came the Wessex army, mostly on horseback with maybe a third as foot soldiers.

Vikings were fearsome foes and this army lived up to what I had previously experienced. Big men with head paraphernalia and carrying all manner of weapons from hammers to pikes, swords to spiked metal balls on chains. Head paraphernalia included spikes and horns to make them look more fearsome. With regards to numbers on the field, it looked as though they had a similar number to ours, a point which gave me courage. From experience I knew each of our guards was worth at least two Vikings due to our training and discipline. The Vikings looked and were fearsome but they also seemed to be careless which I thought was due to overconfidence in either their ability or their gods.

I had instructed our men to hold their pace so that they could let loose as many arrows as they could before engagement. With our increased elevation we should be able to keep shooting well into the fight, lifting our distance to ensure we missed our men and only hit Vikings.

Within minutes our two sides were engaged in full hand to hand combat. The fight had reached our back ranks and although still on horse I now had both of my swords out and was cutting down the enemy. Something made me look up and I noticed that neither of the Wessex armies on the flanks had engaged the enemy. What's more I looked ahead of us and it looked as though another even bigger army was coming over the distant hill to join the Viking army we are engaged with.

Without the Wessex army we were outnumbered five to one and with the additional Vikings looking to join our battle we were going to be slaughtered. I fought on while I digested what I was seeing. What was Wessex doing? Looking back out of the melee I saw Ethelred's Wessex leaving the field of battle. They had betrayed us and were leaving us to be slaughtered. Finding Arthur, I told him to sound the retreat. All men to flee the battlefield back to the trees, run for your lives. Three quick blows on the horn, was the signal to retreat. Those of us on horse needed to protect the retreat of our men on foot.

There were too few of us left on horse as most of the horses had been killed or the men had left their horse to engage hand to hand. It was no good as despair started to run through me. We were being slaughtered as I watched good men being cut down. The anger built up inside me and I felt myself step over into the zone of battle, what I later called my berserker mode. I put my swords away and with my bow I began to let loose arrow after arrow hitting Viking after Viking. Each hit gave one of our men a chance of making it back to the forest. Each hit gave us time so regardless of the threat, instinct was what was governing me now. I fought like a man possessed and in the following minutes most of our men were able to make it to cover.

There were still men fighting out in the field and that is when I noticed John Archer fighting for his life. He was surrounded and had no way of getting out or surviving. As I watched it looked like John was cut down. I directed all my rage to the attackers and spurred my horse into the battle. Pushing through the Vikings in my way I shot down John's would be attackers as I forced my way over to his position. Leofric was with him and fighting like mad for his and his father's life. Leofric was also fighting in a rage and looked like a man possessed but for how long could he keep it up. My arrows gave him some time and space to take a breath, but it was too little and almost too late.

As I got nearer, I could see that Leofric was injured and that John was still gratefully alive. Still in full engagement I jumped from my horse and told Leofric to get on. Leofric mounted the horse and I grabbed John and threw him over the horse in front of Leofric. Shooting off more arrows I was able to clear a path around us which Leofric took. The Vikings were on me, so I had to turn my attention to staying alive. I dropped my bow and quiver and engaged in hand-to-hand combat with my swords. Looking around it was then that I realised what a predicament I had put myself in. I was deep behind the Viking lines surrounded by hundreds of them. Looking up I could see that Leofric had got free and back to the cover of the forest. I also noticed Hereweald, Oswald and Ethelred up on the slope watching on.

That sight was enough to give me the strength to fight on. Still in the zone and possessed with the blacksmith's strength I cut down every Viking who came within my range. I kept moving so as not to get tripped up on the bodies which littered the field. It was then that I saw one of the Viking commanders maybe ten metres back behind half a dozen of his men. He was on horseback and instinctively I knew that this was probably my only hope. With everything I had left I made a bee line for this commander, swinging and cutting my way to his horse. I knew I had taken a few blows and had wounds, but I knew not to think about that now. Getting through to the commander with the energy I could muster I evaded his thrust, grabbed his upper arm and swung myself up onto the horse. With this momentum I had pulled him off the horse. There was confusion around us so without waiting a second and while the commander was still trying to hold onto the horse, I kicked the horse into action, holding on myself for dear life.

Using the weight of the horse I forced a way through the Viking line coming down the hill. At this stage most of the Viking army was between where I was and the safety of the forest. My only hope was to drive deeper into the Viking side of the field and into Viking held lands. Pushing up the hill I felt myself being hit by a couple of arrows. Although causing great pain I Ignored them and pushed the horse up over the hill and down across a river which looked to run through Repton. Somehow, I had been able to get clear of the army. I needed to push myself to keep going as I knew I was not safe where I was. After crossing the river, I headed off in a westerly, direction hoping to make a big detour around the battlefield.

It was a long day and it felt like I was only just clinging onto life with the blood loss taking its toll. I was so weak but I needed to push on. I had made it past Birmingham so knew I was only an hour or two from home. It was dark and the roads were deserted, I was not going to receive any help here. At least the rain had stopped although I could not recall when this had occurred. I think I must have slept for a while, hunched in the saddle, as I came to somewhere near the town of Ombersley, an hour from home. From there I must have passed out because it was daylight when I woke. I felt barely alive with my entire body racked with pain. The gods were shinning on me as Bolter was still by my side and had woken me by licking my face. With my last ounce of will power I pulled myself back onto my horse and we limped off in the direction of Worchester.

Crossing the River Severn into Worchester gave me one of the greatest feelings of relief I had ever experienced, even though I could not feel or sense much. For some reason I still thought I had a chance at life when I was almost dead with less than a small chance of living. As soon as I crossed the bridge I was noticed, and help came running.

I knew that I was alive before I opened my eyes. My consciousness had come back to me, but I wanted to lay there and feel what I could sense. I wanted to know how bad the injuries were. I felt my arms and legs as I slowly wriggled my fingers and toes.

Slowly I opened my eyes and was met by Sunngifu's smile. Sunngifu was up and shouted, 'He's awake.'

The next second, she was down on her knees next to my bed. I must have been in the Archers' house. I gave thanks to God as I knew that I should have been killed given my odds. I made a promise not to let God down as Sunngifu kissed my hand and cried. In came John and Leofflaed, both excited that I had come around.

They all went to speak at once when John finally said that I had given them a scare. Leofflaed said that I had been asleep for five whole days and they did not know if I was ever going to wake up. The first two days I had been fighting a terribly hot fever where they had worked through the night to keep me cool. When I had arrived, I still had two broken arrows in my back with some deep open wounds which were already infected. I had lost a lot of blood and in the end, they had expected me to die. They also praised God and John said that it was a miracle that I had survived. From what I was told I agreed that God had done a great job keeping me alive.

The battle was slowly coming back to me and I remembered that John had been badly injured or so I had thought. John told me that he had been stabbed however the wound, although deep, had managed to miss anything which was important. He had been in bed for days and had only been up for a day or two.

I couldn't talk for long as I was still feeling weak. Over the coming days my strength began to come back to me, and I was able to slowly put together what had happened on the day, who we had lost and the men we had left.

We had lost over half of the guard with a little under 200 of us surviving. It was a slaughter and the whole community was still in grief and coming to terms with our loss. This news devastated me however I knew that from the way the battle was heading we were lucky to have any survivors. It was a massacre and we were grossly outnumbered. Neither John nor I had yet raised the question about Ethelred and why he had not engaged the Vikings. Why he had left the battlefield leaving us to be destroyed. It would take years for us to build our guard back to when we had over a thousand soldiers. Our community has lost over three hundred backs which were needed for everything from farming, to building, defence and completion of our castle. Lying back in the bed my only thought was that Ethelred must have wanted us out of the way as he thought of us a threat. Rather than get to know us and trust his own people he has used our common enemy against us.

Broaching the subject, I asked John what he thought of Ethelred and the Wessex army. I saw something which I had never seen from John before. There was utter hatred in his eyes, and he stood and cursed and cursed the name Ethelred. 'What he did to us is the lowest act possible under the stars and may he rot in hell, rot in hell.'

In my head and heart, I felt the same way. 'For as long as I shall live, I will have my revenge on Ethelred,' I told John but said that now we would need to be smart. 'We are vulnerable to attack from Wessex and the Vikings. We need to build up our army as one day we may need to defend ourselves from an attack from our own people.' What a horrible thing to have to contemplate and say out loud. Ethelred was as bad as Æthelstan as he had also betrayed Worchester and our people.

I continued resting for the coming week as my strength got to a point where I could leave bed for hours at a time. My wounds were healing, and I would be right to go back home out onto the farm. I had enjoyed being looked after by Sunngifu and was looking forward to making her my bride in less than two years. Hilda and Leofric had been to visit me a couple of times and it was great seeing my little nephew Osgar and how happy he was. Wassa and Tata had also come on each visit and it was great to see the relief once they knew that I was alive. I told them I would be back to normal in no time so to watch out as I would have them back at their training harder than ever. Leofric said that the forge was still burning day and night with new business and he really needed me back to catch up with the orders. It felt like old times talking to my family again.

Arriving back at the farm gave me a sense of peace. It felt like years since I had been home although it had only been a few weeks. Part of me never wanted to leave again as I was immersed in the familiarity around me. The animals and their smells and sounds, along with the smell of the smoke coming from the forge, brought back memories of happier times when both my mother and father were still alive.

I was only back a few days when I received a visit from John Archer. He wanted to talk about what had happened at Repton and the guard. First off, he told me that Wulfstan had been killed at Repton so there was no commander of the guard. It was unanimous amongst the leaders that they wanted me, Godric, to be the new commander. I was listening however the little voice in my head was saying, but I am only sixteen.

John went on to say that what he and the others saw was a leader that they all wanted to follow. 'From the decision to leave the battlefield once the hand was played and we were left to be slaughtered to the selfless way you fought so that as many of the guard who could were able to escape.' I went to speak but John cut me off, putting up his hand. He was not finished so he continued. 'The courage and strength you showed entering deep into Viking territory to help Leofric and I was witnessed by most of us who survived. You took down dozens of Vikings with your bow and then the same with your swords. The way you gave

Leofric your horse and with ease you picked me up and threw me over the horse. I am heavy and I doubt any other could do what you did. That you survived and escaped the snake pit that you were in is a miracle, a miracle witnessed by many, including Ethelred and his cronies. We are God fearing men and the massacre which was Repton, and which you survived, tells us that you are the man to lead us. We need to rebuild, and you are the man who people will follow. The castle and the guard have been your idea all along and it is time you saw it through. I will follow you, Godric, and I would give my life if you asked for it.'

I had goose bumps once John had finished. It felt like a defining moment and difficult to believe it was me that he was speaking about. I didn't know what to say so I just hugged him and began to sob. What was our life but filled with so much sorrow and heartache? We stayed together in the embrace for a good while and I think John was also crying. Pulling away I knew I had tears in my eyes, but John was like a father to me and I just didn't care any longer. I was who I was, and I was free to express my emotions as I pleased. I had earnt the right to be Godric Amity, warrior and sometimes emotional.

John told me that there was to be a committee meeting the following day when the new council members would be sworn in. It was also when the new commander of the guard would be elected by the council. I told John I would be there and pulling myself together I felt honoured and said as much to John. I knew I had fought well however I was surprised that I was not killed in doing what I did. If ever there was evidence that there is a God, then this was all I needed. This faith made me feel invincible knowing that I had a higher purpose and that God was watching out for me.

Chapter 7 — Expansion

The following day I did become commander of a much-depleted guard. John was head of the town council and first up he welcomed the new members Ebert, Bran and Evan. I was flattered to be the commander of the guard and immediately felt the burden of the position.

On accepting the position, I told the councillors that there were three actions which I wanted to continue or put into place. Firstly, the castle must still be our priority and must be completed by the end of the year. Secondly, we needed to recruit members for our guard and that would only come by demonstrating our abilities by securing our region. We would ride our district to protect the outlying communities and we would raid into the Viking lands for plunder at any opportunity. With our low numbers we would beat them at their own game. Finally, we would commence training for war. What was evident from the battle of Repton was that Ethelred and his commanders did not really understand war and that their tactics were basic at best. 'We will commence proper planning for the day will come when we will take the fight up to the Vikings and possibly even Wessex.' I did add that our aim would always be to protect the lives of our people including our own. We would use strategies which gave us the greatest odds and even use negotiation if this was possible.

The council erupted in applause as soon as I finished speaking. John rose and put his arm around me, calling for, 'Three cheers for Godric.' This was as good a moment as any to open the mead and celebrate the new council and my position as commander of the guard. It felt good to have a purpose again.

Over the coming months Leofric and I employed two new apprentice blacksmiths and set about building a second forge out at the farm. We had the forge in Worcester however we found it difficult manning both as it was. Leofric wanted to be as close to Hilda and Osgar as he could be so did not want to be working in town. It made sense to expand out on the farm, so we built the second forge and some accommodation for the apprentices to live in. Hilda was well on the way with their second child which made it even more important for Leofric to be around.

As commander of the guard my time was busier than ever as I took over the completion of the castle and set about training new recruits. I appointed three new captains as one was killed in the Repton battle and I had been appointed commander. Aethelweard was appointed to be the captain in charge of archery, Deorwine the captain of sword, and I created a third position, captain of cavalry, which was given to Dunstan. All three had been members of the guard since it was first established and had earnt their posts. Their appointment was also celebrated as we needed to enjoy ourselves at every opportunity given the scale of the work we needed to accomplish. There was going to be a lot of sacrifice ahead of us and I wanted everyone to know it.

Emboldened by their victory at Repton the Viking raids continued through summer and into autumn. As the intensity and frequency of the raids increased, I was thinking about how this was assisting us in recruiting for the guard. Refugees continued pouring into Worchester and the surrounding district and news of our imposing castle gave families that sense of security. The outside walls of the castle stood at thirty yards high and the gates at the main entrance had been completed. Inside the castle buildings were eighty percent completed with enough accommodation to house five thousand comfortably and over ten thousand with a siege in uncomfortable conditions. There were enormous storage sheds and barns to house all the produce and animals. The women of Worchester had been working on everything from the fittings for the rooms including shutters and candles to pickling and building produce for the stores.

Like everyone I hoped that we would never need to use our castle in a siege, however, given the events of my short life I was very happy once the structure was completed. Work continued on the trench for the western half of the moat and would be broken through once the drawbridge was completed.

As summer ended, we commenced counter raids against the Vikings. This was to protect the community but also to show the greater region what we were capable of. The raiding teams contained warriors who were strong with the bow and sword. The intent was not to engage in hand-to-hand combat but to be prepared if there was no other option. Raiding parties took the best horses and contained thirty warriors. One of the captains would ride with each raiding party to ensure no unnecessary risks were taken. We needed to preserve our warriors now that we had been decimated at Repton.

The guard was back up to five hundred warriors by the end of the year with our recruiting and the influx of refugees. There had not been any news from Wessex, and they had not sent a delegation to deal with us. Worse was that they seemed to have abandoned Mercia to itself. The Mercian lords were left to struggle against a Viking push without support from their new lords and king. This was an opportunity for us, and we took it while we could.

We gave additional support to these lords whenever we could and sent warriors to Northampton when they were under siege by the Vikings. On this occasion we sent one hundred warriors but saw that a greater force would be required. Riders returned and I accompanied a further two hundred warriors of the guard to Northampton. The walls of the castle at Northampton were closed and Viking commands were stationed around the perimeter.

Our plan was simple: we would split into two groups and harass the Vikings until they abandoned their posts. We would not engage until the gates of the castle were open and the Mercians joined the battle. We would ride within range and use our archers to do as much damage as we could. We would also use fire arrows to damage their supplies and carts.

The battle went to plan, and we were able to do a lot of damage to the Vikings over the course of two days. At two days they seemed to have given up on their siege as they set about pulling back from the castle gates. On the third day the gates were opened, and Earl Evan of Mercia rode out with his warriors. On the signal that the gates were being opened we joined with Evan and made sure that the Vikings had no retreat. The battle of Northampton became a major victory of ours. The Worchester guard were treated like royalty and major celebrations were had inside the walls of Northampton.

Feeling most welcome we enjoyed the festivities of the evening. Earl Evan expressed his regret about Repton and hoped that I understood that he had no choice other than to obey Ethelred. I countered that we always had choices and I trusted that his decision was made in the best interests of his people and it looked like the best of two bad decisions. If he had have fought, then Northampton would have had a fate similar to or worse than that of Worchester. Our only chance on the day was full engagement and it seemed like Ethelred had never had this intention. So, I accepted Evan's apology and told him that we were only looking forward after learning from the past. I enjoyed the company of Evan in his court but was keen to get home as soon as we could as the snow had commenced, and the roads could become impassable any day now.

Riding back into Worchester we were greeted by most of the town. This time we could see smiles as they had already heard of our great victory. This was the first victorious return I could remember, and it felt good to finally have won a battle.

Elfin Archer was born that winter and was as strong as her parents. Osgar would have his hands full with his baby sister as she was born alert and with a strong set of lungs.

Sunngifu was growing into a beautiful woman and was busy helping with all manner of aspects in the castle. Our wedding was to be in mid-spring when Sunngifu would be turning sixteen. At that time, I would be a month short of my eighteenth birthday.

The castle was not completed by the year end although we were able to open the moat and a completed drawbridge on the first warm day in spring. It was a day to celebrate and although the water was freezing many of us jumped into the moat as part of the celebrations. We now had somewhere to keep us safe from attack. Work would continue inside the castle with fittings and stocking supplies in preparation for a siege. We at least now had a refuge if required.

My wedding day arrived and became a major celebration for the entire community. It was a church service in town, but people spilled out into the main street and afterwards the reception was held in the town centre. We had the wedding in the morning and had cracked the mead by lunchtime. Sunngifu and I did not stay for the whole event as we both rode out of town back to my family farm. Sunngifu and I would live on the farm and hopefully raise many healthy children. All my previous losses were forgotten that day as I became filled with joy at marrying my childhood sweetheart. I had lost my best friend and Sunngifu's brother Egbert in a raid years before. Both my mother and father and little sister Cyneburg had all been killed. The world could be so cruel but then deliver such amazing moments as I was experiencing now.

That night was my first night with a woman and as precious as any experience I had ever felt. Sunngifu and I were made for each other and that night coming together was a night we had spoken about for over a year. We both agreed that it was worth the wait as we lay in each other's arms deep into the night.

Life was bliss for the next few months and sure enough Sunngifu was with child which gave us added purpose to continue with the expansion of everything to do with Worchester and the community. Buildings were springing up everywhere our forge was as busy as ever. The apprentices were learning quickly and along with Tata were taking on their own work. I considered Tata to be a junior blacksmith now as he was a similar age as when I took over as blacksmith on the death of our father.

There were the usual council concerns with our residents about the refugees and the conflicts which seemed to arise. Given the purpose of our community there was little time for things to get out of hand. Everyone was so busy and in general those that joined our community pitched in and only added to what was being achieved.

Wessex sent a delegation late in the summer requesting support for a push into Repton. I was not in town that day but was out on the farm harvesting when I received notification. Annoyed as much as anything, Leofric and I both headed into Worchester to meet with the delegation. Oswald and Sigeberht were both in the delegation which included a guarded escort twenty strong. The last time Wessex sent a delegation there were only three plus his younger sister. There was a much different feel about this visit which was understandable, given what Wessex did to us last time.

Coming into the room I noted their arrival as well as I could with a nod and handshake. John told me that the meeting had not commenced as he had insisted that Leofric and I be present. I thanked John and noted that they came armed; when last they visited, they seemed less in need of protection.

Oswald responded aggressively, catching my drift. 'It is not us who keep to ourselves and spread discontent of the crown amongst our people. It is not us who have failed to send a delegation or pay our due taxes to Winchester and our king. You are lucky we have not arrived with the full force of Wessex to take what we are owed.'

Wow, I did not expect this response from Wessex and could see that the problems I had with Wessex were well and truly real. I did not know what their tactics were but I could see that they were unlikely to support us, or our community, should we need it. This reinforced that we were on our own, apart from a few smaller districts like Powys, and this made me a little frightened.

John jumped in to diffuse the situation as Oswald and I were squared off against each other. I had not realised how he had got under my skin and I was thinking how good it would feel to take off his head.

I asked them what they wanted now as the last we saw them was when they were running from a battlefield, leaving their friends to be slaughtered. 'What could you possibly want from us now?'

Sigeberht jumped in as I think he could see Oswald was also ready to make an attack. 'What happened at Repton was unfortunate for everyone. We received word that there was a trap and that the Vikings had a bigger army waiting to trap us all. The decision was made to pull back and messages were sent to the Worchester guard to pull back. For some reason your forces did not pull back and the result was their massacre.'

I was staring at them in disbelief knowing full well that I was accessible to receive messages and that I was the one who made the decision to pull back and only when it was clear we had been deserted by the larger part of our force, Wessex.

Sigeberht said, 'A new army is gathered and this time it is going to take Repton. Ethelred has four thousand men and is determined to take Repton and Torksey before the year is out.'

I looked across at Leofric and John before I spoke. I told the Wessex delegation that we appreciated the offer however we would not be sending a force to Repton to join in their battle. 'We are in the middle of harvest and we are busy preparing for winter. Our losses the last time we went to Repton have left us vulnerable to the winter and thus we are unable to help.' I could see that they had expected as much as they had a retort ready.

Oswald told us that we had no choice as we were to either fight with Wessex or we would be considered an enemy of Wessex. We were given a final opportunity to accept the terms or the army might decide to make a detour through Worchester to change the existing leadership.

There was a lot of tension in the air and I had to use all my will power to refrain from striking the man in front of me. I knew I did not want to antagonise them further, so I just said we appreciated their offer however the answer was still no. I told them that we would appreciate it if they could leave now and corralled them out the door. As they mounted their horses to leave, I could see them collectively look back up the valley at the Worchester castle in the distance. Sigeberht pointed out that we would not find refuge in that castle should they come for us. He told us that they had the best siege engines in the land and would relish tearing down those walls. With those final comments they turned and left.

I felt exhausted from the exchange and looked at the others from the council who also looked like I felt. There was no way we were going to send our boys off to fight for Ethelred and those bastards, after what happened last time and especially after the threats which were made to us today.

Back inside I turned to them and told them nothing changed with our priorities. I told them that I thought the threats were hollow and that we would continue to build, both wealth and livelihoods for the people. 'Our town and community will become the envy of the land and with that envy and wealth we will build an army big enough to defend against Wessex and to force the Vikings from our lands.' I reminded them that we had friends in Wales, especially in Powys, and that through our battle in Northampton we now had Earl Evan and some of the Mercian lords on our side. 'We are not alone, my friends, so let's keep on the path which God has set us.'

Due to that meeting it became clear that we needed to set up an early warning system again. We constructed a tower and gate house five hundred yards south of Worchester on the road to Gloucester and another on the northern road to Coventry. The early warning horn signals were to be used to warn of imminent attack. The other change we made was to reduce the number of raiding teams which would be out of town at any one time. Previously it would be three teams however we dropped this back to one to ensure we had the guard to repel any attack.

Wessex did not visit Worchester that year and we were able to keep building all aspects of our guard. By the time spring had arrived in 863 AD we had a guard of twelve hundred and were a formidable force. Any army which wanted to go to war against Worchester would now know that it would be costly. Other than the Vikings and Wessex our force would be the biggest in the region. As the weather warmed up, we continued to support the wider community, repelling the Vikings and making allies with the Mercian lords.

The thawing of the snow and the warmer weather brought a visit from our Welsh friends. King David and his sons Cadfael and Emrick visited bringing with them their wives, Queen Anwen and princesses Catrin and Hafina. They were welcomed as friends and allies and the castle had its first significant guests and warming party. The entire region was invited, and the mead and stores were opened for the celebration. It was great catching up with King David and his sons and it felt like we were family. They were sad to hear about some of our troubles especially with Wessex. Emrick commented that Ethelred would need to be wary if he thought to mount an attack on this castle, noting it as the finest he had ever seen. I was pleased with the praise and said that we would avoid war at any cost as the protection of lives was our priority.

I hastily organised a hunt for the following day. John, Leofric, Tata and I would hunt the Malvern Hills with the king and his sons. We told the king we were happy without additional guards but told him he was more than welcome to bring as many guards as he wanted. The king told me that he felt they were in good hands with us boys from Worchester having seen me fight before. He noted how he would love to see me fight now as he knew the fight in Powys was my first one and even that was impressive. I noted that it was my wish that the only animal we fought with would be a stag, fox or boar which brought loud laughs from those present.

The following day we set off for the Malvern Hills which gave me the opportunity to take the king past my farmhouse and forge. They had met Sunngifu, Hilda and the others on the previous evening however we still stopped for some tea and a look at the forges. One of the forges was still going and the two apprentices were making some simple objects such as horseshoes. The conversation was pleasant, and I could see that Sunngifu and Hilda got along with the king and his sons.

Mid-morning, we set off up to the caves which I really wanted to show the king. I lit torches to enable us to see as we moved further into the back of the caves. I told him this was our family refuge should our families be under threat of life and death. Cadfael noted that this was not the best hiding spot as there would be nowhere to go should the enemy come in after us. This was when I showed them the secret hidden door at the back of the cave. The door was on a stone block which slid across an opening when a pulley system was activated. The switch was hidden and only the Amity and Archer families knew where it was. Emrick pointed out that now the Aaron family also knew of the switch which made us all laugh. 'On the other side of the secret door is a set of stone steps which ascend to a cave which is not as deep and then finally to the surface where there is another hidden switch and door.' Our guests were impressed with our ingenuity and preparations. Later on, they promised to send some of their builders over to learn some of the techniques they could see we had used on the castle construction. This was a major complement coming from royalty as we were a backwater which was growing in prestige.

From the caves we continued off up into the hills and I hoped we came across some decent game to return the favour of the boar in Powys. Although this time the boar would not give us the adventure the Powys boar did, the head, I was informed, was mounted up on the wall of the hunting lodge. It was a pleasant afternoon even though the only hunt we got was for two scrawny foxes which managed to get away and a doe which the king shot. At least we had caught dinner as we lugged the doe home to be butchered and cooked. We all spent the night back in the castle where the king's men were stationed. I tried to hide my embarrassment about our lean hunting trip. I did not need to bother as our guests could see I thought they would be disappointed and went out of their way to show their pleasure over the day. I commented that at least it was good to see that some deer had returned to the forests.

The king and his men left the following day but not before we agreed to help each other should the need arise. King David was open with me and said that Brycheiniog was threatening his southern border however he did not see them requiring any support from us as his force was already three times that of Brycheiniog. King David knew of our troubles with Ethelred now and from Æthelstan years before. He told us that he saw us as the front line against the Vikings and that the work we did would and had helped to stem the flow of refugees into and out of Powys. Therefore, the king said that should we need the help of his army all we had to do was to send him a message via a runner. Shortly after they rode away to leave us pondering our good fortune to at least have one friend in this cruel dog eat dog world.

Our Worchester guard kept up on the plan of building our army and raiding and protecting the outlying areas in equal measure. With the heat of the summer the Vikings seemed to be at their most active. This increased activity seems to be balanced or even ineffectual against our growing guard and skills. The more we rode out and met action the greater our skills developed and the better our planning and knowledge became. As an added consequence this was going to be the best harvest in our region in at least a decade, or at least that was what we were told. With the security and Vikings being kept at bay the farmers had been able to plant more crops and see them to harvest.

It was not long after the royal visit from Powys that we received a welcome visit from the earl of Northampton. When out raiding we would often stop in at Northampton if in the area. To me Evan seemed like a good man who would do anything to bring peace to the land or at least his people. After our Worchester castle, Evan oversaw the next best castle in the region or the next best which I had seen. I had been told of great castles up north in Northumbria and east over in London. One day I planned to see these castles and make them a part of one united land.

Ethan had travelled with his father and they had a posse of close to fifty men. As I glanced at all his men, he noted, 'It pays to be careful these days.' The truth was that the roads were still very dangerous although the land between our two towns was safer, again in my opinion, than it had been for many years. Æthelstan, the old Mercian king, ruined everything when he began worrying about threats from within and turned his attention away from the Vikings. The lands of Mercia including Worchester had suffered ever since.

Evan told us that they had come to see the castle. They had heard that it was magnificent and from what they had seen riding into town what they had heard was correct. It seemed that everyone they encounter was talking about us and our castle. This news gave me mixed feelings as it could draw unwanted attention to Worchester, but it could also draw new fighters and families to settle in the area. It was good seeing Evan again and there was no time like the present, so I invited him and Ethan for a tour of the castle.

Just as King David had been, Evan and Ethan were also thrilled by the view from the parapet, a view down the valley taking in the River Severn and town of Worchester. After walking around the castle for the afternoon I invited them back to the farm for a meal and offered for them to stay with us for the evening. They agreed at once and we went back into town so that they could grab their things and tell their men what they were doing.

Out on the farm I introduced them to Hilda and the children. They knew Leofric who was still at work in the forge so Leofric stopped to catch up with them. This was where I also found Tata and Wassa whom I also introduced. Immediately I could see that there was a connection between Ethan and Wassa however I restrained myself from commenting. We went back to the house and I poured us some drinks. It was nice to sit down and relax with like-minded people. I didn't have to think about what I could or couldn't say and they just understood the problems and dramas of the day. The issues which they had in Northampton were like the same issues we faced.

It was in this easy state of mind that we all relaxed into the evening, with Leofric and Tata joining shortly afterwards. Wassa helped Hilda prepare dinner and we all joined them at the dinner table. Sunngifu came out of our bedroom to meet the guests. Sunngifu was ill with morning sickness so had been in bed for most of the day. Evan told her that she was blessed as morning sickness was a good sign that she was carrying a strong health baby. He told us this was a story passed down from the elders back in Northampton.

It was a joyous night as Leofric got out his lute and Hilda blessed us with her voice. Leofric and Hilda were great to have at a party. After Sunngifu went back to bed the rest of us got up and did some jigging to the music. Wassa and Ethan enjoyed each other's company and danced right up to when the music stopped.

The following day Ethan caught me as I was out milking the cows. He told me he wanted to marry Wassa as he could tell that she was the one for him and he just loved her. Ethan was eighteen and Wassa had recently turned sixteen meaning there was no age restriction. I asked Ethan if he was sure as they had only just met. He told me he was sure and would know it was right if Wassa agreed. 'You have my permission to ask Wassa if she will marry you.' I told him that I wanted to speak to Wassa afterwards but with my blessing he was already off and not listening to me.

Coming in for breakfast I could tell that Ethan had asked to marry Wassa as everyone was in good spirits with broad smiles on their faces. Calling Wassa aside I congratulated her but asked if she was sure as she had only just met Ethan. She told me that she thought she loved Ethan and that as I had given him permission that she trusted my judgement also. I had tears in my eyes, so I just hugged my little sister. Ethan was a good man as far as I knew. I had known him for a year or two and we had hunted and raided together. He was a good brave fighter who was respected by his community. As far as I knew this was a good sign for any man. We hugged again and went back out to the others.

This was another joyous occasion and would link our family with a powerful ally in the east. The rest of the day was spent organising the wedding which it was decided would be as soon as was possible. As the community was busy with harvest it would wait until after harvest. The week before Samhain day was chosen and it would be in Northampton. Wassa had never been to Northampton and was dying to get over to her new home. I told her to be decent and respectable and that she would have to wait.

Our parties departed the following day after what had been another welcome visit. I knew our good fortune could not last for ever and spent some time contemplating where and when the danger was going to arrive. Evan, Ethan and their men went back to Northampton to prepare for the coming wedding.

Mid-autumn we were visited by another delegation from Wessex. This time it was Hereweald and Aethelswith along with six guards. The guards looked every bit as fearsome as any Vikings which is probably why they only had six. Deorwine arrived out at the farm to inform Leofric and me that the delegation was in the town hall. We put down what we were working on and headed back into town.

I was surprised to see Aethelswith and once again I was struck by her beauty. Aethelswith had very soft gentle features with thick flowing dark red hair which looked well cared for as it hung tied back over her shoulders. She was of medium height with great proportions and would turn heads wherever she travelled. Hereweald had been the quiet member of the command when we had previously met. Oswald and Sigeberht had done all the talking and seemed to like the sound of their own voices. I was pleased that I did not have to listen to their poison again, at least on this visit.

Greeting Aethelswith I kissed the back of her hand and followed up with shaking Hereweald's hand. They had been waiting at the hall table for our arrival. I invited them to take a seat as Leofric, Deorwine, Dunstan, Aethelweard and John also took seats. 'To what do we owe the pleasure of your visit?' I was asking when cut off by Aethelswith.

'I know this is not a pleasure for you and why should it be,' Aethelswith questioned. 'My brother betrayed your community which led to the loss of many lives. Please accept an apology on behalf of Wessex from Hereweald and me. I told you that my brother could be trusted and for a time this is what I believed. I grew up idolising him and I now know my faith was somewhat misplaced.'

'Your brother's actions are still fresh in my mind and the minds of the people of Worchester. His actions can never be forgiven. While he represents Wessex, we are not able to forgive Wessex. As you have pointed out we lost many sons, brothers, fathers and friends because of his deliberate or cowardly act.'

It seemed that they had come to convince us to ride with them to fight against the Vikings. Hereweald told us that they wanted Repton before the year was out and thought now was a good time to hit them. They told me that Northampton and the other Mercian lords were committed so this time the army would be much better equipped. Hereweald told us that Ethelred would not leave us alone for long if we did not at least commit some force to this cause. The discussion went on like this for some time. The day was getting late so in the end we invited them to stay for the evening and said that we would at least discuss it amongst the council.

Aethelswith and Hereweald were shown the castle and given quarters inside the walls. I could see that they were impressed and Hereweald, who would be my father's age, told us that it was the best castle he had ever seen. I still did not totally trust them, so I did not give them the grand tour or tell them too much about how successfully we had grown our guard.

Leaving the guests to freshen up we made our way back to the hall to discuss the proposal. I was pleased to see that the council thought the same as me and a decision was made to reject the request from Wessex.

That night the council dined in the castle with our guests. After dinner I asked Aethelswith if she wanted to take a walk up on the parapet. From the parapet we had a great view of the River Severn as it wound its way through the fields and Worchester. It was a full moon, so the valley was lit up and the moonlight was reflecting off the river. I asked her what Wessex was really like and if they would ever unite the land to force the Vikings out. Aethelswith sighed at my question and said that she feared that a united land may not be possible under her brother. She told me how her father Alfred had once united the lands of Wessex, Mercia and Southeast Angles but her brother only seemed worried about keeping the lands. Ethelred distrust's his lords and this was tearing the lands apart and leaving us vulnerable to the Vikings. She told me that there was no love between her and her brother and that they had come here out of concern for what her brother might do if we refused to join his fight.

I pointed out that her brother had not seen our castle and that might give him cause to think twice.

'My brother very rarely thinks,' she told me with a smile.

Aethelswith asked me about Sunngifu and the baby which was on the way. She told me that it was her wish to one day have a family but she had been told that she would only be allowed to marry someone who helped expand the kingdom. She was resigned not to marry for love and was now getting worried that it may

not happen at all. I thanked Aethelswith for coming and giving us the warning. The decision had been unanimous for the loss last time was too great to forget. 'We currently watch our backs against Wessex as much as the Vikings while doing what we can to protect Mercia.'

Aethelswith said that word was that we were holding back the Vikings and protecting the lands from Coventry to Northampton. 'This only enrages my brother further as he sees your influence grow.'

I thanked her once again and we walked back down for further drinks.

Our visitors left the following morning and Leofric and I went back out to the farm. Sunngifu wanted to know all the details of the visit. I don't think that Sunngifu was jealous as I do not think I would or have ever given her reason to doubt me but she was heavily pregnant, and we all know that women tend to act unpredictably when pregnant. I told her the details as neutrally as I could, not wanting to cause myself any trouble. I didn't realise that talking about her beauty was a big negative and consequently I had to beg forgiveness just to be allowed to share her bed that night. She was sullen for a couple of days and then seemed to snap out of it and act as if nothing had ever happened.

Autumn was coming to an end and Wassa and Ethan's wedding was very close. The wedding almost coincided with the birth of our son whom we named Egbert after my best friend and Sunngifu's older brother. Egbert was healthy and loud and immediately kept us both busy. When not working Sunngifu would hand me Egbert as she was exhausted and kept telling me it was my turn. Wanting to stay in the good books I felt as though I was pulling my weight, but I was getting exhausted.

The Amity's and Archer's all set off to Northampton ten days prior to Samhain day. Wassa was like a kid with a new toy and had done most of the packing herself. We had a cart full of her possessions as Wassa would be moving into Northampton with her husband. We took a guard of twenty men with us as most of us were seasoned fighters anyway with Leofric, John, Tata and friends Arthur and Dunstan. Our Worchester priest Frank also travelled with us and was going to perform the ceremony to link Wassa and Ethan. The journey was pleasant and without incident. We arrived just on sunset, a full day's travel after setting off at sunrise.

Sunngifu struggled on the trip as Egbert didn't settle and Elfin and Osgar were not much better. On arrival we were greeted at the castle and invited into some magnificent rooms with a wash basin to freshen up. Downstairs we were given a delicious meal of hare and venison. Sunngifu and I retired for the evening as we really wanted Egbert to sleep. Sunngifu and I were both exhausted with the process of packing, having a newborn and getting the farm ready for our departure. The two apprentices, Bevan and Bert, were going to look after the farm and the animals while we are away.

We had a day before the wedding which was a good chance for us to relax and freshen up. Northampton looked overcrowded and I was told as much over lunch. It didn't matter to us as it was a great chance to show Sunngifu and Wassa around the castle and to introduce them to the rest of Evan and Ethan's family. Walking the streets people frequently stopped to say hello and meet us, including little Egbert. There are many great things about babies however one thing is that they sure know how to pull a crowd. It did not matter where we went as everyone wanted to get a closer look at Egbert. Some in the crowd thanked me for the protection I had been giving them. I would be lying if I didn't say that this made me feel proud in front of Sunngifu. I knew this was a sin but sometimes it is good to feel appreciated in front of your dearest.

The wedding was another beautiful occasion, linking Wassa and Ethan and uniting our families. We were slowly becoming united in the vacuum left by Ethelred and Æthelstan's feud. We did not know what the future held however it felt great to have friends. Evan and his family were like-minded people who had a similar vision to me around safety and peace. Together we might one day achieve our dream. The church was full of friends and family and Father Frank gave an impassioned account for the couple, but especially for Wassa as he had watched her grow up from being a little girl. Ethan was a popular figure in Northampton and people seemed genuinely happy that he was linking them with Worchester. Word of mouth is important and again I was pleased with how we the people from the west were being viewed.

At the reception I offered to start training some of Ethan's guard in our modern battle techniques and to have them start using our new longbow. He had seen my bow and commented on its size and obvious power. I told him I would give him a demonstration the following day if my head recovered from this evening.

We had a wet nurse look after Egbert once the dancing and music started. Now Sunngifu and I could enjoy the evening without having to worry about the baby. Sunngifu looked worried and exhausted anyway however I pushed on and after a few songs it looked like Sunngifu began to relax. It was a lovely evening which reminded me of our wedding night. Wassa looked so magical and in love, a great feeling, as I could remember it well. Father and mother would have been happy as surely happiness and love are two of the most important qualities a parent could want for their child. Wassa had been my responsibility and saying yes was not easy because the romance had been instant and secondly because of my responsibility. Looking on from the dancefloor I was glad my decision had been easy and that it seemed to have been the right one.

The following day I gave Evan and his commanders a demonstration with my longbow and offered it to some of his archers to have a go. They all agreed that it was far superior to the bows that they used. I told them that it had two secrets: first was the timber from the spruce tree and secondly the lead tips which were weighted to perfection. They told me they would take as many as they could afford. I told them I would give them a hundred as a wedding gift from Wassa and her family. This pleased Evan and we opened another barrel of mead and commenced drinking even though it was before eleven o'clock.

As with all good things we knew that we had to get back into life and head home. It had been nice to be away from home and thus without any true responsibility. Samhain day was on its way which was an important and joyous occasion for Worchester, so not to be missed. That evening we said our farewells to Wassa and Ethan. We thanked Evan and his family for their hospitality and friendship. We told them we would be leaving at first light the following day. The weather looked good for travelling and we wanted to get the children home.

At sunrise we set off from Northampton to the music of a screaming baby and tears from Wassa. I could see she was sad but compensated as she was so much in love with her new husband. Our little holiday was over and I was looking forward to getting back into the forge to keep experimenting with our weapons.

It was two hours into our journey when I sensed something was wrong. The horses started to become a little skittish which was a sign that my instincts might be right.

Out of nowhere we were hit with a volley of arrows. Riding out front I was able to just get my shield up to deflect the arrows as they were about to strike. Hearing screams I turned to see my beloved had fallen forward in the cart so I dropped back as quickly as I could while Dunstan called everyone back to bunch up and protect the carts.

Arriving at the cart my heart immediately sank into my stomach. Sunngifu had taken an arrow through the neck and was lying there dead. I jumped onto the cart and hugged her close, but it was too late. Leofflaed had baby Egbert and on seeing this my anger became uncontrollable. Leofflaed and I locked eyes and she immediately said, 'Godric, you cannot bring her back. You have a son who needs you.'

Another volley of arrows landed on our position and I was able to shield Leofflaed and Egbert. 'Get under the cart,' I told them.

It was too late for me to calm down as I left the cart and was back on bolter in an instant. The attack by the Vikings came at us then and it looked like a raiding party with as many as a hundred men. As far as I was concerned it could have been two thousand men. I wanted revenge and I wanted to extract maximum pain on the animals who had killed my Sunny.

Riding out to meet our attackers I began with my arrows cutting down as many as quickly as I could. I kept clear of the enemy for as long as I could as I fired arrow after arrow. The only thing which stopped my onslaught with the bow was when my brave horse Bolter was eventually cut down. As the horse fell, I was able to jump free and now the fun would begin.

It was early and I was well rested and nourished from a wholesome breakfast. My weapons were sharp and ready for blood and blood is what I gave them. I do not recall much of the next moments as I seemed to slip into a blind frenzy. The fight was vicious and to the death and only ended when the remaining Vikings withdrew, fleeing for their lives. I tried to grab a horse to chase them down but was stopped by John.

Pretending that I was calmed I waited until I had some space then grabbed a horse and sprinted after the fleeing Vikings. Catching them I was once again in the zone of killing and I set about making sure there were no survivors. They fought hard, once they realised they could not outrun me. Numbers did not worry me as I sought their destruction. For some reason I still felt fresh and on noticing who looked to be their leader I made sure he was one of the Vikings I killed.

Leofric, Dustan and some of the guards caught up with me just as I was getting near to the end of my killing spree. They helped to finish off the few remaining Vikings and at that point I collapsed off my horse and to the ground. I was not hurt but for some reason I was now exhausted and unable to stand. I closed my eyes and sobbed for my little Sunny. Our long life together was no more, and little Egbert was now without a mother. I put my hands over my face as I sobbed. John was by my side while the others stood guard to make sure there was no other surprise attack.

John helped me up and I can remember him soothing me like the father figure he was. Arm in arm John guided me back to the carts.

There were eleven deaths from our journey group. We lost Sunngifu and ten of the guard.

John told me the attack had been well planned and that we were obviously the target. The Vikings knew that the leaders from Worchester were attending this wedding and that there was all likelihood that we would be travelling back along this path. They could have been waiting days for this opportunity. Such a large raiding party deep behind the safe zone we had cleared showed us that they had a purpose. The Viking party numbered a hundred warriors so we were lucky to have survived given the difference in our number.

I had Sunngifu in my arms and could see that I was not the only one grieving as Leofflaed and John had lost their daughter and looked grief stricken. Closing my eyes, I sobbed some more and did not want to move. We were all close in our community and again all the pain of loss from this attack and the past attacks was brought upon us again. Egbert was crying for his mother but we all ignored him as the pain and wounds were too fresh. John asked if the guard could load the bodies onto the back of the carts. I knew we would have to keep going so I picked up Sunngifu and placed her in the front of the cart with her mother and Hilda. The arrow had been pulled out and I used a blanket to cover her. I could see little Osgar and Elfin were terrified and unsure what to think.

Father Frank came over after finishing blessing and saying final words over the dead from our guard. I allowed him close to Sunny so that he could bless her soul and send her to the angels in heaven. Father Frank was special to both Sunngifu and me, and his own grief was also evident as he struggled to keep the tears from choking up his speech.

The guard did a final check over the field of battle and gathered all the weapons and valuables which they could.

We set off cautiously for Worchester and John commented that it would now be after dark before we arrived home. With tears in my eyes, I no longer cared and sat sullenly upon my horse as we plodded along. I did not fear another attack now as I had worked out that from the size of the force, it was unlikely they would have split it into two separate forces. They had expected success and in my eyes the death of Sunny was success for them. Oh, I was so angry but with nothing left to take it out on. I sank into a state of depression as we continued home into the early evening.

John and the others left me be which was either because of their own grief or because they were wise enough to know that intervention would do no good on me.

We went straight out to the farm and lay Sunngifu on the bench in our room. We would have a service and bury her the following day. Father Frank and the others all stayed with us on the farm as we opened some mead and drank to Sunny and her life.

Being exhausted I did not remain up long and was soon in a deep sleep on our bed.

Waking late the following morning I jumped up when I realised it was light. Being close to Samhain day I knew that daybreak was getting later so I had really slept in. Rolling over I remembered Sunngifu and again my grief came back. First my father, then my sister, my mother and now my wife had been killed if not directly by them then at least because of the Vikings. With each wound my commitment to their removal from our land became more and more resolute.

I got myself up and walked over and pulled back the blanket to my Sunnies face. She was like a little Angle, way too young to lose her life. I felt all teared out and could feel determination and strength returning. I gave her a kiss on the forehead and covered her face with the blanket.

Leaving the bedroom, I could smell the bacon and eggs and hoped that there was some left for me. Entering the kitchen there were many faces all turned to me to gauge how I was. I told them that I was better for the sleep and that I would seek revenge against those who had taken Sunngifu's life. Leofric said that it was good that I had my strength back however he said that I most certainly got my revenge yesterday with the slaughter of their raiding party.

'Yes, I know, but that raiding party must have come from somewhere and was following someone's command.'

As I sat down to a hearty breakfast of bacon, eggs, sausage, chops and black pudding John went on to discuss the raid. He told me that he had only ever seen one person fight like he had yesterday and never from anyone other than me. He said that when I had the blood rage it was like I was being guided by the hand of God. There were a hundred dead Vikings yesterday and over eighty of them would have been killed from my bow or sword. Leofric then asked how it was possible. 'How can one man, grief or anger besides, kill so many in such a short time?' John continued, saying that it was like I had been slaying children and not blood thirsty warriors.

I told them it was like a frenzy which I did not have control of. Even though I knew it was happening I just let myself go and my fire took over. 'If I can do that and even if I can teach others to reach for their fire, we could be unstoppable and can at last create peace where our children can grow up and not be slain.' They all agreed and said that once I found the secret, I was to teach it to them all. I told them that I knew it as my berserker mode.

After breakfast we went to the family burial plot and dug a deep grave for Sunngifu. It needed to be six-feet-deep so that the dogs or wild animals did not dig it up. While I dug John and Leofric made a coffin for Sunngifu. Hammering at the dirt with my maddock and axe was therapeutic and by the time I was finished I was sweaty all over but healed of my grief.

The service was small and private but all the important people in Sunngifu's life were there. Father Frank shed another tear as he threw the first dirt onto the coffin and I said my own private prayer for Sunny. Afterwards we ate and everyone stayed around for another evening to share stories but mainly each other's company.

John and Leofflaed needed to head back into Worchester to help prepare for the Samhain festival so they left first thing the following day along with Dunstan who was the captain of the cavalry. Hilda said she would look after Egbert and care for him as though he was her own.

Hilda told me that she knew how busy I was and that my destiny was to free our land. Family was important to all of us and I was grateful for the family I was born into. They would do anything for me, and I knew that I would do anything for them.

At that stage I hadn't even thought to send a message back to Northampton about the raid and to let Wassa know that Sunngifu had been killed. Raising this with Hilda she said that John had sent two men from the guard back as we had set off. As we were travelling at the speed of the carts, they were able to catch up with us after delivering the message.

Chapter 8 — Revenge and Power

Word of our ambush by the Vikings was already through the community by the time our family arrived in Worcester for Samhain Festival. With regards the weather we were lucky as the real cold had not yet come down from the hills. Mild weather brought the crowds as this was usually everyone's last big social event until winter ended.

I received condolences from all the people I spoke to and I could see there was plenty of awe around what I did to the Vikings. I sensed the admiration and came across more than one conversation where my feats were being discussed. As the drinks flowed and people loosened up, I started getting toasted which only added to the atmosphere and drunkenness.

These evenings were long, but I was not in the mood for drinking and making it a late night. My mind was already on battle plans and training the guard to be much better than we already were. I was also sad that Sunngifu was not with me to share the occasion.

My battle frenzy had shown me how good we could all be if we had the mental and physical toughness. I wanted a project to build endurance and strength with the guard now that the castle was complete. Building the castle had made us strong and given us a goal to strive for. Most of us were farmers and had a natural strength however I wanted us to get to the next level. A project would also bond us and give us added passion as we fought.

I thought of Sunngifu and Jesus and came across the idea of building a massive cathedral, the scale of which no one had ever seen before. I also thought to build a stone embankment and docks along the River Severn. Both projects would require large quantities of stone from the quarries and iron from the forges. The entire community would see these being created and share in the benefits.

Hilda and the children left the celebrations early while Leofric stayed on saying he would keep an eye on Tata. Tata was now twelve and allowed to drink mead. Being so young he would be bound to get himself into trouble if not watched by one of us.

The following day I went back into town and spoke with John about my building ideas. John thought they were great and said that he would organise a council meeting for the following day. Most people were less than their best the day after Samhain, so it was best to give everyone the chance to recover. I agreed as I really wanted everyone to hear and understand my plan.

I put the ideas to the council and they unanimously agreed with the benefits of the scheme. The guard had continued to grow, and we needed the discipline which a major project could bring. Father Frank was over the moon with the idea as this would give him a great chance of promotion in the church and the church was not having to pay anything toward the project.

Over winter we worked as hard and often as we could. There was nothing in the fields and the chances of us being raided during winter were also slim. This extra time gave us an opportunity to lay the foundation for both projects especially given we had over a thousand of us working on them. Between the quarries, the construction, weapons practice and the forge I was as busy as at any time in my life. Fortunately, Hilda was taking good care of Egbert as I appeared to have no time for him. He was a newborn so I hoped that I would get the chance to bond with him as he got older.

Being busy helped me forget my grief and was probably why I relished the challenges.

By the end of winter, we had cleared the footprint for our new cathedral and excavated the foundations. We had even laid the foundation stones and were well on our way with the cathedral. We had made similar progress with our riverside quay and stone embankment. This started with us reclaiming the edge of the river with stones before construction could begin. Before we knew it, the birds were out and about, the days were getting warmer and there were shoots on the fruit trees.

The year was now 864 and I would be entering my twentieth year of life. I was sitting and enjoying a drink with John and Leofric when John told me that he thought leadership sat well with me.

'Where does this come from?' I asked. He told me that he was just thinking about how young I still was and how I had naturally fallen into leadership especially after the death of my father. It was so natural that no one seemed to notice it happening and thus nobody put up any resistance. John said that quite often there were political games and a lot of people talking behind people's backs. Normally there was a gathering of numbers to shore up one's position however with me there was none of that.

I told John that I didn't think of myself as the leader except for maybe the guard and even here I was in charge because I was asked to be in charge and in a way, we were following my vision.

'Agreed,' said John and Leofric together. The timing of the responses made us all chuckle.

John said that humility was my endearing quality. I did not assume leadership or seek it but was given it freely. Leofric then told me that the guard would follow me to the ends of the earth if I were to ask it.

John added that Worchester and the entire community would do the same. 'I may be the head of the council, but everyone looks to you on that council and they listen to your word.' I was a little stunned. 'Haven't you noticed?' said John. 'Of course, you haven't,' he answered for me.

I guessed they were right but, as they said, I had not sought any position or allegiances.

'I tell you this not to mock you but to make you aware of the power you have. With this power comes great responsibility as the people of this town and region rely on you. If you ask them to go to war, they will go and gather their weapons. If you ask them to build or to sow crops they will build or sow crops.' 'Thus, it is important that the decisions which you make are the right ones. Consultation with your friends, family and the council will help to keep you grounded and the decisions benefitting the community'.

Wow, I had never thought of my relationship with them in this light. John told me as much and was telling me now as I guessed he trusted that I would not abuse this freely given power. Worchester was my home and my dream was for everyone to be safe and to live at peace. I was adamant that the only way this could be achieved was to force the Vikings from our land and off our island. I could see the green shoots of this plan and I knew that it could be achieved.

Although our list of allies was growing, trouble was never far away. We had to stay focused and committed to achieving our goals.

It was early spring when a large force was noted marching toward Worchester. The force was spotted from the castle and the warning horns were sounded. It was not known if they were friend or foe even though they were coming from the south and the Wessex direction. Given their size they were a major threat to our community.

Given the warning the people of Worchester gathered their valuables and families and headed for the castle. Initially it appeared as though the castle was going to be tested for the first time. Aethelweard gathered the guard and had them assemble at the south side of Worchester on the road into town. The guard was now more than fifteen hundred men and eighty percent of these were battle ready and skilled in their disciplines. John later pointed out that the problem was that the army coming toward us was six-thousand strong and they also looked like seasoned warriors.

At the time this was all happening I was hunting out the back of our farm in the Malvern Hills. I was with Tata and Leofric and we had already caught two hares and a fox. Tata was quick and already a competent hunter. Tata also had better hearing and said that he thought he heard a horn.

'Was it long or short, one, two or three?' I asked him.

'One long one I think,' said Tata.

Leofric and I both swore and moved as quickly as we could back toward the farm and town. One long horn signalled that Worchester was under attack. This time of the year was still usually safe from attack and thus we did not consider a hunting trip being an issue. The guard was now big and strong so should be able to deal with any raid or threat. I had three competent captains who would do everything in their power to keep Worchester safe. It took us an hour to reach the farm and by this time there was Dunstan with a couple of men waiting for us.

Dunstan said that there was trouble in town as Wessex had shown up in force. We gathered our horses and prepared to join Dunstan. Tata had grabbed his horse and I was about to tell him to stay home to protect the girls when I thought twice about it and gave him a nod. It was easy to forget that Tata was going to be thirteen this year, old enough to join the guard if I allowed it. I did not have a good feeling about the situation, so I spoke to Hilda and suggested that it was probably best if she took the children up into the caves. Hilda agreed and gave both Leofric and I a kiss before we left, telling us to be careful.

The three of us joined Dunstan and the guards and headed into town. It wasn't long before we could see the enormous force gathered to the south of Worchester. Their entrance was blocked by our guard which I thought looked impressive albeit smaller in size to Wessex.

Dunstan told me that Ethelred was at the head of the army and he was demanding to speak to the leader of the guard and or town. Everyone had apparently deferred that authority to me which had led to a mini man hunt to find out where we were. Hilda was able to tell them that we were hunting in the hills and may not be back for hours. Thankfully with the help of Tata's ears we were aware of the threat and had hurried back. I was now getting extremely nervous as one mistake here could cost all of us our lives.

The guard made space for us when we arrived at the standoff. I saw that John, Deorwine and Aethelweard were on the Worchester side of the road and Ethelred, Sigeberht, Oswald and Hereweald on the south side, on the road to Wessex.

Joining John, I turned to look at the Wessex delegation. I was tempted to speak as everyone was quiet and I thought they might have been waiting for me to say something but thought that as Wessex had brought the army to our gates, they may have something to say. I was armed as it was unknown if Wessex was friend or foe.

While this was taking place the town and region had filled the castle and lifted the drawbridge. All the best spots on the parapet had been taken up. From the parapet the meeting of the guard and Wessex could be clearly seen. I could imagine that there would be great suspense with the townsfolk as it would be clear that we were outnumbered. We were their family and without us could they defend the castle against an attack? If we were attacked the plan was to send riders into Powys to request help from King David. King David had said he would come if we asked. The request was only to be sent if those in the castle were sure that we were being defeated and consequently they were or were about to be under attack. Meanwhile, they watched on as our two groups eyed each other.

Eventually Sigeberht stepped forward with a couple of demands. He said that he was the spokesman for our prince and future king. We were to give up possession of our castle and the guard was to join them on campaign to take Repton back. The last demand was that Godric of house Amity was to be forfeited to judgment by Wessex on the charge of high treason. After making these demands there was silence although I thought there would be more. We all knew what the charge of high treason brought and that was certain death.

I could sense the tension from John and the men behind me. Wessex was requesting that we hand over the product of all our hard work, work which took the best part of seven years to complete. Our castle was our protection from raids. Our castle was our insurance against attack from friend or foe such as the ones who stood before our gates. The request also meant siding with a people who saw us as less than them. The alternative seemed like a battle and a battle we were unlikely to win. A battle could cost our entire community if we lost all or most of the men in the guard. I now felt the tension and was extremely nervous.

Thinking as quickly as I could I knew I wanted to avoid an open battle as we would surely lose, and it would be a blood bath for both sides. Wessex and more importantly Ethelred could not be trusted. He was as bad as Æthelstan and his actions had led to the death of many Worchester loved ones.

With a little bit of outrage, I asked them why they thought we would fight for them when we were left to be slaughtered in the battle for Repton. Sigeberht shouted that we would fight for them or we would all die here and now. He said that the option we chose mattered not to them. However, he added that it was our duty to fight for Wessex as Ethelred was our liege.

I told them that this castle was not ours to give as it was owned by the people of Worchester and our surrounding communities.

'Then we will take it if it isn't any one's to give,' shouted Ethelred as he stepped forward.

'It may not be ours to give but it is ours to defend and defend it we will.'

Ethelred saw his opportunity and pounced. 'It sounds like you are threatening your sire and have thus put your life in my hands. The castle is mine and now your life is mine also.'

Taking the opportunity, I baited him; 'I see you as a coward and don't think you would be man enough to fight me.'

In his outrage Ethelred stepped forward and shouted that he would teach me a lesson in warfare. Oswald and Sigeberht quickly jumped in front of Ethelred and whispered into his ears. Ethelred stepped back and said that I was trying to bait him. 'I only answer to my father, so I certainly do not answer to you. Your castle and your guard are mine and your life is forfeit. If you beg forgiveness, I will grant you a quick death by taking your head otherwise a confession will be tortured out of you.'

All I could do was smile as I knew that he was only minutes away from dying. My nerves had slipped away and changed into a calmness which I now felt. I could feel the power inside me surging. The power reminded me of that day my beloved Sunngifu was killed. Nothing was going to stop me getting vengeance. I had to avoid a battle as all the hard work to build the guard could be lost. All those people back in the castle who relied on me could lose their loved ones and later possibly their lives. I did not worry about the pressure of responsibility as I was frantically worked out a plan and put it into play.

Behind me Leofric, John and the captains were close by along with my little brother Tata. Oh Tata, why couldn't he have stayed at home?

'You want my life, you dung heap, I will let you come and take it along with five of your best heroes. If the six of you can kill me the guard, castle and Worchester will be yours.'

'It's a trick,' shouted Oswald.

As quickly I retorted; 'On my word and in front of all these witnesses, there is no trick. You can select any five warriors of your choice however they cannot be from Worchester or the guard.'

Ethelred was goaded so he scoffed at me. 'You think you are that good, you whelp. Oswald and Sigeberht, draw your blades and bring your three best men.' Ethelred drew his impressive blade and began to step from side to side as he seemed to be preparing for the fight. Oswald returned with three giant men. Each of these warriors was a head taller than me and as wide across the chest. I was not a small man so saying they were as large as me and taller than me is saying something. Everyone moved back a little to make way for the fight. I had not yet drawn my swords but again I started to laugh.

Outraged, Ethelred demanded to know what I laughed at. I apologised and said that what was about to happen was no laughing matter and I should be more solemn. Six men were about to lose their lives and hopefully God would take them into the kingdom of heaven.

Ethelred charged at me while telling me that God would not be taking me into heaven. Stepping aside I was able to leave my leg out and trip him so that he fell to the ground, humiliated. This prompted the others to step into the fight.

Turning toward Oswald as he and the others came at me from behind, I parried his elbow, ripped his sword from his hand somersaulted over their forward advance. As I landed, I quickly put the blade through the backs of two of the warriors and then Oswald's middle as he turned around. The third warrior and Sigeberht came at me however within seconds I had run through the warrior and taken off Sigeberht's head. After taking Sigeberht's head I threw Oswald's sword on the ground and pulled out my impressive twin blades. I knew they were impressive, and this was the look I was after as I went after Ethelred.

Now Ethelred was scared, and he ran to Hereweald and demanded that he protect him. Hereweald did not move and said no, crossing his arms. He began pleading with the men behind Hereweald but Hereweald held out his arm and blocked Ethelred. 'You had a fair deal, five men of your choosing and yourself against Godric, commander of the guard. The ledger is now even, one against one.'

'I will be your king,' shouted Ethelred.

Attempting to goad Ethelred further, I told him he would never be king but was rather a weakling and coward. This was all it needed as he turned and charged at me. With quick work I had separated Ethelred's body and head. His body dropped to the ground as I held his head aloft, blood spurting from the body as it convulsed while the head dripped blood and the eyes still looked at me in shock.

In my mind I was thinking what would happen next. The way which I figured things out it could go one of two ways. First there could be war, a war which would cost thousands of lives and destroy the guard. This was a worst-case scenario. However, Wessex and their warriors had just lost their famous prince. Some of them would think it only right to seek revenge even if it was only to make them look good amongst their peers.

The second, more likely and the preferred option, would be for Hereweald to take charge and to lead this army away from our town and castle gates. I had seen that Hereweald was a good man and he proved it again by keeping the fight fair. Hereweald could control this army and go and explain to his king what had happened here today. This would be the right thing to do.

I threw down Ethelred's head as it repulsed me, and I did not want to see it again.

What happened next surprised me as it was not one of the two options I had considered. Hereweald stepped forward with his sword and stabbed it into the ground in front of him. He knelt on one knee. 'Godric Amity, I, Hereweald of house Darlo, pledge my service and sword to you, my commander, if you will take it?'

The events of this moment were witnessed by our guard and its leaders and by much of the town from on the castle walls. One by one the warriors in front of us took a knee and pledged to us. Within moments the fields in front of us were filled with kneeling warriors. This was a very surreal experience and I had to snap myself out of what I was witnessing and seize the moment.

Seeing some stones nearby on the side of the road I strode across and climbed to the top. This was going to give many of them a view of me and hopefully they would hear what I was going to say. What I was going to say had not yet occurred to me however I knew something had to be said and I expected that it would come to me once I started speaking. I gathered myself and with my loudest voice I started addressing the armies around me.

'Fellow Angle landers, we have been freed from the oppression and limited future which was life under Ethelred. He was not a good lord and could not be trusted. Ethelred is responsible for many hardships and heartbreaks in our community and I have no doubt that ours in not the only community which feels this pain.

'Please stand up, Hereweald, for you do not need to lower your head to me. The day Ethelred betrayed our people I looked into your eyes and saw the disgust which you felt and the shame his actions gave you. It is very hard to stand up against a despot who has assumed total power. Please stand, everyone who has taken a knee. Your allegiance is most welcomed and will be honoured. Your lives are worth everything to me and the fact that you put them into my hands honours me beyond belief. Know that I will not treat your life lightly and will use it to seek peace and prosperity for all of us.

'Forcing the Vikings from our island is the only way that I can see us being sure of peace. It has been my goal for many years to defeat the Vikings and to force them from our lands. With your support we can see this dream fulfilled and we will see peace for our families and communities.'

With that the gathered warriors cheered and cheered. My voice was starting to break up as my throat was dry and I had been shouting at the top of my voice.

I told those gathered that I needed a drink as my throat was dry and I welcomed them to come and share a drink with us and to enjoy the hospitality of Worchester.

It was a big overstep of my authority as we would have to break the stores that we had put aside in the castle to feed and satisfy such a large number. However, with another six-thousand warriors at our service our security was probably greater than it could have been. We did not know how King Alfred would react and there was every chance he had an even bigger army ready to march on us, however, that was thinking about moves too far in advance and beyond what my understanding of what the resources and powers in the land were.

I had only ever bothered about what I could see and control although I was beginning to see how blind this was leaving me. I knew nothing about Wessex or the East Angles and only slightly more about the Vikings and the north. Assistance was what I was going to need if I was going to survive in this bigger pond which we had all just entered. For now, I needed to seal this day and what better then food and drink for empty stomachs.

Hereweald and Morgan, who was Hereweald's second in command, joined us for a meal of chicken washed down with mead. Hereweald told me that he had always admired me since that day at Repton when I had ridden into the Viking army to rescue my men. I mentioned that they were not my men but my friends and fellow soldiers from Worchester. It was our duty to look out for each other and I had been outraged that we had been tricked into such a sacrifice. Hereweald agreed that it had made him sick following the command of his lord and not a moment has passed since that day that he has not wished he could have acted differently. He went on to say that the wrong of that day was corrected today with the removal of the bearer of that evil. We all drank to that and continued with stories well into the afternoon. The weather was good so I suggested that half of the men should sleep in the castle and the other should sleep out here under the stars and with their animals and possessions.

As the mead flowed the discussion moved to what we should do with the army. I suggested that we put it to good use as an army of this size was difficult and costly to put together. Everyone agreed with what I was saying as I could see the light in their expressions. Encouraged by their body language I suggested that we should ride on Repton and take back that cursed city for us Angle landers. This idea was unanimously accepted before I had a chance to change my mind. It was agreed that the following day we would move out and head to Repton. We would only bring the supplies we required for two days so that we could travel light. Worchester could be used as a base and Repton would be ours within a couple of days.

Word of our plans spread throughout the camp and you could hear the excitement from pockets around the mass of men. Something good had already come from this day and this situation was only getting better as us leaders got along and worked on our battle plan. Most of the council were with us but I made sure those who weren't were also in agreement with the strategy. It seemed that they all were so we were to march to war the following day.

Hereweald and Morgan were both experienced in war and had been to Repton and Torksey and even further north to York. The Vikings had first taken York as they moved inland from the coast back when Hereweald and Morgan were my age. Northumberland had fallen a decade later and since then the Viking commander Halfdan had been pushing further and further south, plundering as he went. He ended up with all the East Angles and had London and most of Kent. There was word that a larger force was gathering which was going to clear the land of Anglo Saxons and make the land all under Viking rule and law.

We discussed plans much later than was wise but it was great to have commanders who were enthusiastic about my ideas. Since reading John's war books, I had put a lot of thought into different battle techniques and I was enthusiastic to give them a run. It was not that I wanted or looked forward to warring as I knew that people died in wars and they created much suffering. However, when you put so much effort into something it was good to see that there was a result or purpose to that effort.

The following morning, we rode north for Repton with the excitement in the air of young children heading off to the fair. There was enormous optimism amongst the guard and the Wessex army, and it had not taken long for both groups of warriors to connect and appreciate each other. I could hear some of the comments about the guard's weaponry and I told Morgan how we had redesigned the long bow and improved the strength and weight of the swords. They were thrilled when I showed them some examples, so they put in an order there and then for ten thousand of each item and ten times that many arrows. Telling them they would be ready on the morrow they all burst out with laughter. Our laughter drew attention from all around as people looked on with smiles. I think that they enjoyed seeing their commanders getting along and sharing a joke. I was not sure how often Ethelred joked with his commanders or men.

We rode straight past the outskirts of Coventry and were cheered on by the townsfolk from behind their palisade wall. Coventry was a big town and had been on the front line against the Vikings for years. Over the years we had spent a large amount of time riding to their aid and protecting them from numerous attacks. Worchester and Coventry were good friends, so we accepted a delegation from the town as we were heading past. They wished us God's grace and asked whether we needed their guard for this battle. I thanked their commander, a short man of the name Owen. 'Vikings are cunning, and they always lay traps. Keep your men behind the walls until we have secured Repton. Put together a group of your best men as these may be required to rebuild defences at Repton as Halfdan or other Viking forces may try to take the town back.'

Owen seemed pleased to have an important mission as he rode at the head of his delegation with speed back into Coventry. They were good people who had been terrorised for way too long.

Our force pushed on to Repton as we wanted to secure the region before night fall. As we approached the site of our battle four years previously, I felt a little reticent. My horse must have sensed my feelings as it also became a little skittish. I have always been fascinated by how astute horses are at understanding their master. The first Repton battle was a forgettable horror while this time we would call the occasion the second Repton battle. I hoped for a better experience this time although that would not be difficult, given the previous failure.

Moving out into the clearing we could not immediately see any of the Viking forces. To make sure this was no trap we sent riders to the distant ridge to survey the scene. They returned shortly afterwards and told us that there was a Viking force camped on the south bank of the River Trent. The force was estimated to be two thousand which was much less than we had expected.

The plan was for a sneak attack as it appeared that they were not aware of our presence. Only a third of our army were cavalry and we could close the distance from the ridge to the Vikings in minutes. We would hit them hard with the cavalry and give our infantry time to cover the distance and finish off the survivors.

Although not a sophisticated plan it sounded like a solid plan which we all agreed to. I was disappointed that I couldn't use any other ideas however Repton and minimal deaths was our goal. There was no chance of an ambush as we were south of the river and we could see the fields on the other side of Repton and the river and unless they were fish the area was clear. Repton had a couple of Viking boats moored in it however even if loaded two boats was going to be no match for over seven-thousand men. Despite our advantage I was again nervous for a good outcome. Responsibility was on my shoulders and I could not afford to get this wrong.

The battle commenced and played out as we had expected. I rode with the leading group as I thought this showed confidence and gave confidence to the men. Standing in stirrups as I rode, I shot down half a dozen men before clashing with their counterattack. My swords came out and I had the thrill of battle and systematically cut through man after man. It was a blood bath as although they loved to fight and were fearsome, they were in disarray, unprepared and separated. They had no chance of forming a shield wall for protection and by the time our infantry arrived the battle was effectively over. A few tried to flee to the river and the boats but they were easily run down by the cavalry and killed.

With the success still fresh we entered Repton to reclaim it for Wessex. It had been a good day as this was our first victory as a combined force. Cheers went up around our group as we tasted the success of our win. Repton was less than half the size of Worchester but it sat on valuable farming land and a strategic location on the river. The town was empty apart from some slaves and Viking merchants. Although there was support for me to run these people through, as payback, Hereweald and I stopped them and told them we were building a better land for all.

I spoke to the merchants but I could not understand what they were saying when they spoke back. One of the slaves told us that the merchants would leave if we allowed it and I smiled and nodded my approval. There were some grumbles from some of our men but most respected my decision. As a reward for letting them leave one of the merchants had the interpreter slave tell us that the main force had gone to battle Northampton. Halfdan was not amongst them but he had commanded that before summer he wanted Northampton to be his.

We had a decision to make and it seemed that everyone was deferring to me to make this decision. We could push on to Torksey, make our way to Northampton to give them our support or end our campaign and head home. I would have loved to have headed home as this was all starting to make my head spin. I wanted some time out on the farm to figure everything out. I also wanted to celebrate the victory with Worchester.

Northampton had an impressive castle, almost as strong as the castle at Worchester. My younger sister Wassa was in Northampton but I did not want to make my decisions based on emotions. Torksey would be a real prize and now that we were through the outer skin of the Vikings it was a prize worth taking. Pushing deeper into what was now Viking territory would have some risk depending on whether we believed the merchants about the army being at Northampton. Another advantage of pushing forward was that our army in Viking territory might draw away the army from Northampton.

With so much to consider I shared my thoughts with Hereweald, John, Leofric and Morgan. I told them my preference was to push on for Torksey and listened to their thoughts. As they agreed with my thoughts, I made the decision that we would push on to take Torksey. How I prayed that I had made the right decision although everyone seemed in agreement with what we were doing.

The message was sent through the camp and as it spread the excitement of an army on the move once again took over. This was a massive force and morale amongst the warriors was high. Yesterday's victory was decisive, and it was amazing how quickly the confidence had grown. It was easy to get caught up in the almost unanimous enthusiasm. I reminded the men I saw to keep their wits about them as we could be walking into a trap.

Torksey was not far from Repton and was still on the River Trent. Apart from the odd merchant or traveller there was no contact with the Vikings. Before midday we were looking up at the town of Torksey. It had two rings of palisade defences surrounding it but we could see that the gates were open. Taking a chance, I ordered Dunstan to take the cavalry to secure the gates. We would follow at a distance and provide cover should they have archers on the town's towers. The town was ours within an hour although there was some resistance. It was obvious that they felt secure and thus did not expect an attack.

Securing the Torksey town centre I felt great relief inside. However, the next move was more uncertain. Did we wait and secure Torksey against the Vikings attempting to take it back or did we now ride for home, splitting the force and leaving some behind to keep the town? I did not like the idea of leaving men behind because although there were walls, they were only palisade and it would be easy for a larger force to overrun the position. Palisade walls were wooden walls constructed out of small logs being fastened together. They would halt an army advance but given time a force of decent strength would be able to get over or through it. It would be a death sentence for whoever was asked to remain behind. The decision was made to spend the night in the town and decide the following day.

The attack came some time through the middle of the night. Fortunately, we were woken before it really hit, however, we were still unprepared and had not been aware that a large force had been on our tail. Horns were now going off all around Torksey as the town was lit up with fire arrows. There was chaos as we all prepared for hand-to-hand combat. The captains did their best to keep the calm but with the dark, fire and noise this was almost impossible. In the resulting mess there were many casualties.

This was the longest night of my life as we held on and prayed for daylight. The only light we had was the light from the fires as the clouds eliminated any chance of light from the moon. Outside of the palisade walls we caught glimpses of our enemy but they moved into and out of range as they hurled rocks, spears and other objects at our men. The best we could do was to take shelter as the arrows and objects kept coming and we kept losing men. Every now and then we would get a group who would charge the wall and attempt to break it down. This was our only chance to do some damage to the Vikings as we could shoot from the shadows and were usually successful.

Sometime amongst these skirmishes I caught an arrow through my left side, just below my ribcage. At the time I was shooting at a charge of Vikings and although I felt the contact, I ignored it and kept at my shooting. I had to stop and deal with the arrow as it was a nuisance and was getting in the way of my shooting. The head of the arrow had nearly gone right through my body, so I was able, in great pain, to push it through the remaining skin, snap it off and pull the tail back out the entry hole. There was plenty of blood however I had no time to think of this now. Free from the arrow I was able to keep shooting at the shadows which attacked us.

The ebb and flow of battle continued like this up until daybreak. The day gave us a chance to inspect the damage and count our losses. It had been a costly night and we had lost just over five-hundred men defending

Torksey. In my mind Torksey was not worth the lives and I wanted to get out. The Vikings were nowhere to be seen but we knew that they would not be far away. They would know that they had us trapped. Someone would have been counting our losses and they would know that we were now hurting.

As the dead were given a decent burial the captains and I discussed our plans. I told them that I wanted to get to friendly territory. 'We are an army who is best in the open ground facing a foe we can see.' Last night had been awful and I didn't want a repeat tonight. Everyone agreed with these sentiments and we agreed that we needed a plan. 'We believe that the Viking army is the army which has returned from Northampton. This means that they now stand between Torksey and where we would have some degree of safety.' Riders were sent north and south to confirm what we were facing. This was critical information with regards to our next move.

Either way I would rather meet this army in the field then trapped in a walled city like sitting ducks. This was a sentiment unanimously agreed upon by our council.

John noticed I was still bleeding and asked how I was. He insisted on seeing the wound and said we needed to seal it to prevent infection. The wound was now painful, so I didn't want anyone to go near it. There was still blood coming from the entry and exit points so what John said made sense. I was given a rolled-up rag to bite down on as they heated up a length of hot iron. The feeling of fear I felt as that iron came toward me will stick in my memory for a long time. Pain so intense that I wished I was dead mixed with the smell of my burning flesh. I couldn't see for tears as I bit down harder than ever on the rolled rag. Once the iron was moved away it was all over. I removed the rag and closed my eyes, at the same time putting my head in my hands. Slowly my breathing and body came back to normal although the pain from the wound in my side would be with me for a while as it was still excruciating. I was sweating and felt like passing out.

By midday we had the information we needed although the detail of the information was not welcome. The riders confirmed that the Viking force were planted to the south of us in the valley between Torksey and Repton. It seemed that they were spread out and intended to prevent us getting back to safe territory. When asked about numbers we were told that there were at least ten thousand Vikings. A larger force than I had heard of and thus a number which struck fear into our hearts. What choice did we have but to fight? But my instincts told me to avoid this fight. This was a larger force than ours and we were without supplies and on foreign terrain. Everything was in the Vikings' favour and I hated our situation. Once again, a wrong decision could cost us everything.

Hereweald suggested that we ride north instead. He pointed out that the Vikings would not suspect that we would ride north further from our supplies. Hereweald said that Torksey was not secure against night attack. Heading north we had two choices with the first being to head north and then west into north Wales or secondly, we could take York which had an impressive stone castle. Taking York would be a strategic victory and do great damage to Halfdan and his hold on Viking power.

I liked having options and especially when they offered opportunity other than staying put or fighting a battle with bad odds. The command was given that we were marching north within the hour. I wanted to get to York before dark to surprise the Vikings and catch them with their gates open. They would not expect an attack just on dark and from deep within their land. If the gates were closed, I would strike for the west and make for home. There was a risk that we would be trapped in York but I was hoping for some decent supplies and I was looking forward to the security of castle walls.

Torksey was half in ruins when we marched north leaving it to the Viking force. The men were all armed ready and expecting attack as we knew the Vikings would be watching us. I expected that they would be wondering what we were doing, and I was hoping they would not have worked out what our target was. As a precaution I sent the entire cavalry to York to secure the gates and city against a warning from the Viking army. With the two-thousand cavalry gone our marching army was depleted to less than four thousand, leaving us vulnerable to attack. We needed to keep our pace up to stay ahead of the Viking army should they make the decision to follow us.

Overcast weather meant a mild day and a good day for marching. If the situation wasn't so serious than I could have enjoyed the scenery and company. My mind was racing, and I was concerned about being stuck in York. If I had a second army which could bring relief then I would have been much less concerned. I had only just taken charge of the Wessex/Mercian army and only the north army at that. King Alfred and the rest of Wessex may only just be being made aware of what happened at Worcester and could even be marching a second army on my homeland. They would not know what our plans were or even where we were. This unknown situation again made us vulnerable to Wessex who should be our friends. I needed to keep this army together and safe. Victory would confirm the righteousness of our cause and my leadership but a loss and disaster would have the opposite effect, even if I lived.

The sun had gone below the horizon by the time we reached York. I could see that the city had been secured as the gates were open and men from Worcester were stationed out the front of the entrance. It was getting darker and cooler rapidly now and everyone was keen to get inside and to safety. As I crossed the threshold, I once again felt a feeling of unease. It was a feeling that I was walking into a trap. I had already made up my mind to only stay in York for the one night and if possible, make for the west tomorrow. I had not conveyed this to anyone as I wanted to see what became of the night and whether the Vikings had followed us to York.

York was a big town about the same size as Worcester. The difference with York was that all the town was within the protection of its walls. I had heard stories of the north and how dangerous it could be with attacks from the Picts. The Picts lived in the northern reaches of our land and apparently even the Roman armies could not conquer them. I thought of how good it would be to have them on our side against the Vikings but I had heard stories that even the Picts are terrorised by the Vikings. What a land we lived in, full of war.

I gave the command for the men to leave the people of York alone. 'Anything we take we pay for and help them if they ask or need assistance. I want to sow the seeds that it would be better living under us then the Vikings.'

Hoping we would not be in York for long I studied the walls and defences with the plan forming in my head to return some time in the future. The town was now crowded with all our men inside the walls. Our time in York was not wasted as we restocked our supplies of arrows and food. The arrows were an inferior quality to what we normally used but they were better than nothing and would do the job, if we were attacked. I was still hoping to be home within two days even by going through Wales, so we did not take more food than we required.

The pain from the wound seemed to get worse over the day and by evening was giving me hell. I endured and ignored the pain as I did not want to show weakness.

I thought that sleep would come easily to us that night as we were all exhausted from the harrowing night in Torksey. The gates were manned, and a watch kept but those of us who could sleep did so soundly. I woke up with the sun the following day and felt a little renewed although still weak from my wound. It was a great feeling to emerge from bed knowing I had slept well and feeling slightly better but as I moved, I knew that something was wrong. The pain in my side was excruciating although once again I did my best to ignore it. Sleeping in a bed was unusual when on campaign as we normally slept clothed and ready for action. I couldn't imagine what state I would have been in should I have slept out on the hard, cold ground.

Runners were sent to determine the location of the Viking army. I wanted to know that we had room to strike west around them and over into the borders of Wales. At the same time, I told my command and the captains that we would be leaving within the hour so to make sure that everyone had eaten and was ready to move out.

John asked me if I was feeling all right as he said I looked pasty and seemed ill. 'Is your wound causing you problems?' John felt my head and said that I was burning up. I told him I was going to be all right and it was probably just a little infection.

The runners confirmed that the Vikings were still not sighted so I assumed that they may have spent the night at Torksey. Although a large army, they may not know the size of our force and could be acting with caution. Being in command was like playing a game of cat and mouse and I hoped that they had not anticipated my moves. Aethelweard and Deorwine were disappointed to be leaving as they liked having the castle for protection and thought that it gave us a great advantage. I agreed about the advantage but pointed out that we were a long way from support and eventually we would run out of supplies. We could hold the castle indefinitely if we had supplies to keep us going.

Led by Dunstan, the others agreed that it was best to keep moving and to get our men back to the safety of our lands. Thus, we left as planned and headed west over the rolling hills towards Wales and Powys. Before leaving I thanked the people of York and told them that one day, I would pay them for the weapons and supplies they had given us, which were still not paid for. We had travelled with some money but not all which was required for what was taken.

These lands were sparsely populated and consequently we only came across the odd traveller. We spoke to everyone whom we came across and each one said that they had not seen a Viking army. This news was welcome as I dearly wanted to get home without having to fight. My guess was that the Viking army was still stationed in Torksey or had marched south to Repton. There was a risk that they would see this as an opportunity to invade Worcester however this did not give me the unease that it would have in the past as we now had the castle for our loved ones to seek refuge. Northampton also had an impressive castle which I hoped had held out against an earlier attack.

There was so much which we did not know, and we continually made decisions on what we thought was happening. It is little wonder that our armies made blunder after blunder. I had heard of pigeons to send and receive messages and I thought that when I got the chance, I would try to get the pigeon messaging service working in Worcester. My current priority was to get these men home safely. The second priority would be to build the army so that we could counterattack. I was not so naive as to think it would be that easy as I knew we needed money and supplies for such armies. We needed to be prosperous if we were to afford a large army. There needed to be full granaries and stockpiles of weapons. It could take us years to get to the point where we would be able to march on York, London and Northumberland. At that point the Vikings would be pushed back into the sea and God willing our people would have peace and prosperity.

The travelling was painful for me and became even more difficult as the day wore on. My wound was bleeding and it was becoming obvious that it was starting to fester. Those around me could see that I was struggling but there was nothing they could do for me, especially out where we were.

We reached northern Powys nearing the end of that first day. The centre for trade in northern Powys was Whitchurch, a town surrounded by rich agriculture. As the men pulled up in the fields outside Whitchurch, I rode with a delegation into town to meet the local council and to let them know that we were no threat, that we came in peace and were just passing through.

A group of men met us as we were crossing a stone bridge on the outskirts of the town. The men were armed although they seemed at ease. We were deliberately not armed as our intentions were honest. I stepped forward and introduced myself as Godric of house Amity from Worchester. There was a noticeable easing of tension on this exchange and I took it that they had heard of me or Worchester. Bledri introduced himself as the council leader and Cadwal as the commander of the guard. In the exchange I asked for permission to camp outside of their town for the evening and said that we would move on at first light as we were making for home. We were granted permission and our delegation were invited to share a meal with their council in their town hall. They were hoping for news of the wars in the east and some hint of what was to come.

Falling off my horse confirmed to everyone what they thought. I was very ill and needed bedrest and medicine if there was a medicine man available. I was helped back onto my horse and led into the town right away.

As we had accepted the invitation from the Whitchurch council a message was sent back to the men to set up camp while the rest of us followed the council into their small but neat town. The buildings all seemed to be constructed of black stone which gave them a rustic charm. Whitchurch looked old, like it was built by the Romans, and indeed Cadwal confirmed that it was. Whitchurch looked to be a third of the size of Worchester and being only a day's march from York I was surprised they had not come under the control of the northern Vikings.

Cadwal took me to his house which was in the main street adjacent to the town hall. I was given some water and a light meal before being shown a room with what looked like a comfortable bed. As soon as my head hit the pillow it seemed that I was dead to the world.

The following morning, I was awoken and after a drink and being helped into a sitting position I was told how the evening had gone.

Bledri told them that their farmers in the east had been under persistent attack from both the Vikings and the Picts. Consequently, there were no farmers east of Red Brook. The Vikings just slaughtered the families while the Picts liked to take slaves to work their mines. King David had promised support but until now none had been forthcoming.

John and Leofric told me that I looked to be at death's door. They told me that Bledri had a medicine man who lived over toward Wrexham, a town further to the northwest. A runner had been sent for the medicine man, or healer as he was known. John then asked me what I wanted the army to do. They were silent as they gave me time to think.

We did not know where the large Viking army was and there was a possibility that they were destroying our homeland. The people should be safe in the castle but Worchester and all the farms would be burnt to the ground in this scenario. I hoped so much that it was not the case as I knew how much work went into building up Worchester and our homes. We also needed to get the Wessex men home as we did not want to antagonise King Alfred of Wessex. The men all had families and there would be work required as this was sowing season when all the fields needed preparing and crops planting. All this thinking was exhausting me, and I was gently shaken awake by John.

Apologising, I asked if John could lead the army back to Worchester. I told them that there was a possibility they might find the castle under siege. 'Do what is required to force the Vikings from our lands. If there are no Vikings and our homeland is safe have Hereweald take the Wessex army home and say that we will visit them by the end of summer. Have them begin to build for war building weapons to our new design. Let them take copies of our shield, sword and bow and arrow. These are the weapons which will free the Angles of the Viking.

'Have Hereweald increase the size of his army and send a delegation to King Alfred expressing our condolences for the loss of his son Ethelred. In a safe manner please convey that his death was honourable and by no means treachery. Worchester and our guard stand alongside Wessex in our battle to clear the Vikings from our land.'

Leofric then said that he would stay and keep a force of twenty guard for protection. I insisted he didn't need to stay however he told me I didn't have a choice. They said their farewells and left the room. I awoke later that evening when Bledri's wife Gwyneth woke me and said that I should have a little soup. I felt delirious and hot so knew that the fever had taken hold of me. The healer had better not be far away or there might not be much of me left. The soup smelt delicious but I declined it. Gwyneth would not hear about it and insisted I have a little and once I did, I certainly appreciated it. Gwyneth left me and I was once again fast asleep.

Trymman woke me the following morning. He was the medicine man from Wrexham for the region. Looking at my wound I could see that he was worried. In the room behind Trymman were Leofric and Andras who was second in command under Deorwine. Andras was only two years older than me and a brilliant archer, thus rising through the ranks quickly to become Deorwine's second.

Once Trymman had mixed a poultice together he rubbed it into the wound on both the entry and exit points on my side. I have always prided myself on being tough but I felt every bit of the pain as this practice was completed. Leofric and Andras assisted Trymman to roll me. A bandage was wrapped around my body to keep the poultice in place so that it could clear the wound. The poultice and dressing would need to be replaced every day until the infection was beaten. Trymman told us to expect a week when responding to the question of how long my recovery would be. He said that he would stay in Whitchurch to ensure that I recovered. I was also given sips of some medicine he had mixed.

I do not remember much of the coming week however Leofric told me that on those first two nights I was battling for my life. He had sat with Trymman and Gwyneth as they had nursed my body through a raging fever. They commented that God must have plans for me as he was not ready for me yet. I was so grateful to Bledri and Gwyneth for their hospitality and for keeping me alive. Without them and their connection to Trymman I would certainly be dead by now.

Trymman told me that my wound had now healed nicely and that my fever was gone. He told me to take it easy so that I could regain my strength. It was nice to be able to sit up and eat proper meals.

Chapter 9 — The Picts

That following morning Whitchurch was ambushed by a massive enemy force. This was my first encounter with the Picts, and I was at a severe disadvantage having just come back from death's door.

The Picts showed up at first light with an army of what looked like close to two-thousand men. They were much shorter than the Vikings and carried a range of weapons: such as steel balls on chains, pickaxes, hammers and the more typical swords and bows. Their clothing was mostly fabricated from animal skins but looked thick and warm. Highly appropriate clothing judging from where they were coming from. Resistance was futile although the guard did raise the alarm and try to hold them off. The attempt cost them their lives.

Leofric and Andras kept the Worchester guard together and close to me. We did not know what the Picts were planning and hoped it was not a mass grave. Trymman, Bledri and Gwyneth were also in our group along with Bledri and Gwyneth's daughters, Riannon and Seren. I was not even aware that Bledri and Gwyneth had children as I had been so sick and asleep for most of the last week. Riannon was sixteen while Seren is fourteen. Riannon is engaged to Cadwal's son Alun.

There were approximately five hundred of us who were forced into the town square. It was here that we met our new masters and the leader of this force. Gregor Scott introduced himself in a Celtic language and accent which I could just understand. He told us that we were now his prisoners and that most of us had work waiting for us if we did as we were told.

Gregor told us that some of us would be cleaners and house servants while others would work the pits for stone and iron. If we had skills with animals, we may get roles on the farms or with the royal horses. He told us that unrest would not be tolerated and anyone trying to escape would be killed on the spot. That was all that was said before Gregor Scott and his men ordered us to leave Whitchurch and commence our march north. As we crossed the bridge east of Whitchurch the Picts set fire to the town which just compounded the misery of the people we were walking with. In a way it was closure for the people as now they had nowhere to return to. I saw it as a cruel waste as I had a good idea of the effort which goes into building a town.

It was still early in the morning and the weather this far north was not warm although the walk was warming me up. I soon realised how weak I had become from my illness and week in bed. Gregor Scott was king of the Picts of Strathclyde and we were marching for their capital in Carlisle. I was told Carlisle would take us two days to reach given we were walking with women and children. From what I could see the Picts were treating us with decency and had allowed us to stop for regular ten-minute breaks to give the children and old people rest breaks. Judging by the language the Picts were relatives to the Welsh.

As we were walking along Leofric told me that Arthur and Bran, two members of the guard, had managed to slip out of Whitchurch. He did not know what had become of them however he hoped they had the sense to tell King David of Powys and the council back in Worchester. Without witnesses to our kidnapping our whereabouts could become a mystery.

At the end of the first day's walk, we were on open ground with the sea to our left and mountains to our right. It was getting bitterly cold again and fortunately the Picts allowed us to get fires going to give us some warmth. None of us had any food as we were all forced to leave instantly. The children were hungry and crying. The hunger was not going to get any better the further we walked unless the Picts came up with some food. Two of the Pict leaders came over to our group and started separating the older people from the group. This included Trymman who would have been close to fifty. This separated parents and grandparents from their families and community. It seemed that fifty was about the cut off age.

The separated group was marched away by two of the Pict commanders and some of their men. The commanders leading this group were Munro and Ramsay. Both men looked angry and mean as they had wild hair on their heads and faces. They looked to be handling the older group roughly although there was nothing we could do. I still did not have my full strength back and I was without my weapons which had been left back in Whitchurch.

Later when Munro and his men returned, they were without the elderly. I was about to step forward and enquire about the group when one of the ladies of the town yelled out the question. Munro Scott answered that they did not have the food to feed everyone so only the useful would be given food. 'The children will be accepted as they will become useful in the future.'

'What did you do to them?' a few of others cried with concern.

Annoyed by the harassment Ramsay cut in that they were killed and given a quick death. This brought an onrush of tears and despair from the group however I knew it to be true as Munro and Ramsay were both covered in blood and in any case, it was too late to change the past. Food was being prepared and started being brought around to the rest of us who were alive. I was still cold but warming by a fire and I was grateful for the warm stew which I was handed. The rest of the group sat in misery for the loss of their loved ones. Everyone would have known everyone in Whitchurch so such a massacre could not be easily forgotten.

We all slept close to each other to draw from each other's warmth. At some point during the night the fires had burnt down and gone out. With the fires out the real cold set in. As I woke with the first light, I could see we were surrounded by a thick frost. The wind was gone but it was bitterly cold. I got up and went to speak to the Pict guards who were watching over us. As I approached, they stood straighter and squared up to me, asking me what I wanted. I asked if I could get the fires going. They said there was no point as we would be heading off again within the hour. They asked me what I did as I was built like a house. I told them I was a blacksmith and used to working the forge. Useful, they said as they nodded. This sparked a conversation between us as I started to learn more about the Picts and their kingdom. We started talking about the Vikings and they said there were constant skirmishes along the boundary with Northumberland. The Vikings raided them, and they raided the Vikings back. There was no love lost between either of the parties. Although there were some struggles understanding each other we developed a good repour.

'Life is hard in the north,' the guard said, 'and it is important that we store enough food to get through the winter. Gregor Scott is a strong leader but considered to be fair. His son who is also one of the commanders is Munro. Munro Scott is a strong but harsh leader. On his own he is brutal and ambitious. This raid for slaves is the furthest from home we have ever been.' The raid was inspired by Munro and only accepted by his father after his father lost a horse racing bet. 'Munro talks about forcing the Vikings out of the land and taking lands all the way to London. He sees glory for the Picts and has studied all the stories he can find on Rome and their conquests.' These guards were really taking a risk by opening up in such a way. I thanked them for helping me to understand their mission.

Munro Scott sounded interesting to me and to some extent we had a lot in common. I hoped to achieve something like his goals however without the bloodshed and brutality to the people. It sounded like we were lucky Gregor travelled with their raiding party.

True to their word we headed off within the hour and to be honest I think everyone was grateful to be moving as this will help us warm up our limbs. We also wanted to get away from the memories of where close to a hundred of our elderly were just killed. We were given frequent ten-minute rest breaks and water to share around. It was nearing sunset when we came across Carlisle on the southern bank of the River Eden. The town had an impressive castle overlooking it which looked to be like our castle at Worchester. With regards to size, Carlisle township appeared to be like Worchester and was surrounded by farms just like home.

We were taken directly to the castle where we were given shelter in some vacant barns. The barn was cramped with little room. This did not bother me, as we were now slaves, and shelter was a welcome reprive after spending the night before out in the elements. Food was brought around, and we were told that we would be given our work the following morning. One of the commanders, Tadg, told us that every attempt would be made to keep the families together although this was not always possible, and we must be prepared to be separated. I suspected this would be the reality however it would still cause separation pain with many of the families.

That evening Leofric, Andras, Alun, Cadwal and I sat as a family with Bledri and Gwyneth and their girls. We thought we would probably be separated the following day so we vowed to look out for each other. The walk had restored much of my strength and spirit. The land we had travelled over was spectacular and I took the opportunity to learn everything I could from the guards on the way. With any luck I would be back this way some time in the future and God had delivered me this opportunity for a reason. I liked Bledri and his family and wanted to do what I could for them.

I told him that I would escape and that I needed to return to Worchester. The Vikings were priority number one however I had every intent on stopping the raiding for slaves as well. 'Farmers and families must be safe to work the lands all the way up to the borders with the Picts. When I escape, I will need to travel with some speed to ensure I am not followed and rundown. If I have the opportunity to free you, I will take any and as many of you as I can.' I told them that there would be risks as getting caught could mean certain death.

Leofric and Andras were with me a hundred percent and they vouched that any of the remaining guard would also be in. Surprising me, Bledri and his entire family were also willing to take the chance. Smaller numbers would have been easier however it was nice that they were so willing to take such a great risk.

The planning commenced with the need to be careful and not overheard. I told Leofric to ensure that the guard could all get jobs together either as part of a building team or in one of the mines. 'Listen for a big project and then have them all step forward on that. Bledri, you and your family should try and get work on one of the wealthy estates. You are a bookkeeper and your wife and girls can work as maids and cleaners. I will try and get work either as a blacksmith or on a farm working with animals. Either way I should get more freedom and begin working on getting some horses together for the escape. Let's try to keep in touch and at least work out where each of us is taken to.'

I told them to give me a month to put the plan together and gather the resources for execution.

The following morning, we were all taken into the main courtyard of the castle. Gregor came down and addressed us. He thanked us for not attempting escape and for generally being well behaved prisoners. Gregor told us that we were here for a reason and that we would need to assist the Picts to ensure they continued to prosper and defend their realm against the Viking attacks.

Tadg stepped forward and started to split up the people from Whitchurch. There were a hundred men required for a new iron mine in the eastern hills. This was a perfect opportunity to keep the men together. Unfortunately, this also pulled in Bledri who was separated from his family. The girls were all allocated to the same estate, a wealthy landowner by the name of Steward in the south east. I got my wish and was going to be sent to the royal estate in the south to work on the forge and with the horses. I thought this was perfect as this would give me the opportunity to scope the resources we would require if we were going to escape.

Seven women and girls accompanied me as we were led away by Ramsay and a guard of a dozen men. The women and I had been appointed to the royal estate which was five miles out of Carlisle. There were four older women and three girls about the same age as Wassa. They had all been given household duties at the estate and with it being the royal estate they were told they should consider themselves lucky.

On arrival we were given refreshments and separated to our different areas. I was shown to my quarters and introduced to the blacksmith and his apprentice. Ailpen was the blacksmith and looked to be a similar age to what my father would have been. He was broad shouldered with forearms like thighs. This was a problem most blacksmiths seemed to have. He looked to be a serious man as he didn't afford me any warmth, telling me he would not accept any trouble. Ailpen was one of the only bald men I had seen since my arrival as all the Picts seemed to be very hairy. The apprentice's name was Shug and he seemed to be maybe a year younger than me.

Shug was the opposite of Ailpen and I immediately took a liking to him. Shug had a big smile when he welcomed me to the estate. He promised to show me the forge and around the estate which he did after these initial introductions. For accommodation I was given a small space which was maybe ten square feet and was decent considering I was a slave. I was unlike most slaves as I was skilled and thus was probably being treated better than all the others. The estate was a large area with a dozen barns which were used mostly for the animals in winter although there were two large barns for horses. The tour was a quick one as Ailpen wanted us back at the forge so that he could gauge my competency.

There was obviously no fear that I was going to try and escape as the guard who had escorted us to the estate seemed to have disappeared.

Back at the forge Ailpen asked me if I was an apprentice or full blacksmith. I told him a bit about myself and how I had been apprenticed to my father. I told them that my father was killed when I was thirteen and since then I had continued with the trade and was considered a competent blacksmith. The similarities between Shug and I obviously had a softening effect on Ailpen as he seemed to weaken his attitude toward me although this could have been because I had lost my father at such a young age. I welcomed the empathy as it had been a tough couple of weeks, and I did not want to always be fighting everyone and everything. Ailpen and Shug were every bit a victim of their circumstances just as I was and likewise, I developed empathy for them.

I decided not to share my weapons advancements with Ailpen however I did show that I could produce any item which they were currently required to produce. Some of my techniques were more advanced than what he had been using which I was happy to show them. Over the coming week I worked closely with Ailpen and Shug and we soon developed a close bond. I could see that they both worked hard and tried their best to keep Tadg happy.

Tadg was one of the army commanders but when on the Royal Estate he was also in charge of the weapons and archers and thus the forges. They told me that Tadg was a reasonable man and they did not want to disappoint him. If we did not deliver what Tadg required, it would make him look bad to their King Gregor. If Tadg looked bad Gregor might replace Tadg with someone who was completely unpleasant. This reasoning made sense to me and I agreed with them that it sounded wise.

Although the days were getting longer and should have been getting warmer it was still chilly due to being in the hills and the north. For this very reason I thought I had been fortunate to be allocated to the forge. I wondered how the others were fairing although, from experience, it would come down to the individual who oversaw them.

Shortly after a week we had a visit from King Gregor and Munro Scott along with some young women who looked a similar age to me. One of the women had the family look so I guessed she might be Gregor's daughter. There was a close resemblance with Munro and even King Gregor. They initially spoke to Ailpen and were engrossed in their conversation. While watching this I noticed the girl, who I was yet to meet, looking over at me. Our eyes met and she did not look away but smiled. It was unusual for a girl to hold a look with a stranger, so this had me intrigued yet not surprised as the Picts were proving to be very open and trusting

Ailpen brought the party over to where I was working and introduced me, Kenner among them. I wanted to take Kenner's hand and tell her what a pleasure it was to meet her although I did not dare as I was a slave. Kenner was indeed the daughter of the king and Munro's younger sister.

King Gregor was pleased that I was a skilful blacksmith and offered that if I could complete a year of service, he would make me a free man. He did hope that I would stay on and continue in his employ. Gregor said that he wanted to build another larger forge as he was aware that he required more and better weapons. He told us that the reason for the new iron mine was to increase our resources so that they could take the war up to the Vikings. 'Every year we lose men, women and children to the Vikings and it had to be stopped.' I told Gregor that I was from the south and that we had the same problem with the Vikings. I said that we had the same plan to force the Vikings from the land.

Gregor invited me up to their estate for a meal so as to continue the conversation. I was honoured with the invitation and saw this as a great opportunity to continue my education about the north. Before dinner, I had time to go back to my project which was a set of cast iron gates. Ailpen and Shug were invited for the meal with me and this certainly pleased Ailpen as he had very rarely been up to the main estate. Shug seemed to be able to take it or leave it, such was his disposition.

We all finished up our projects approximately an hour before dark. Ailpen and Shug found some fresh clothes but I went as I was as I only owned one set of clothing. However, I did brush myself off and comb my hair.

The main estate was approximately one mile from our forge which made for a pleasant walk. On arrival we could see that the candles had been lit where we waited for approval to enter. On entry we were all given mugs of mead and trays of miniature pastries and sausages to snack on.

King Gregor and his wife Lileas joined us and we all fell into deep conversation. I remember how I had struggled to understand King Gregor at first and now I understood them as if they were my own family. We sat on the porch drinking our mugs of mead, eating fillers while watching the sun set over the countryside. It was such a picture of perfect peace it was hard to imagine that in other parts of the world there was so much suffering and death. Gregor questioned me about my directness as he said that there were very few he had met, who would keep eye contact. He also noted that there were even less who would feel comfortable questioning him let alone engaging in dialogue.

Kenner came in and joined us as we got up for the meal. She gave apologies for Munro saying that he had some other pressing duties. I enquired if she had any other siblings which made poor Kenner look to the floor. Lileas rescued the situation by saying that Munro was their oldest child and that there had been three others between Munro and Kenner. The second child, Cate, had married young and died in childbirth while the other two children were boys, and both had been killed in battles with the Vikings. Gregor explained that this was one of the reasons why they hated the Vikings so much.

The meal was served and the conversation continued to flow. Kenner Scott recovered from my previous ill directed question to make lively conversation. I told Gregor about the southern kingdoms and the dream of King Alfred to force the Vikings from the island. Our fates had been similar, and we were similarly affected. I kept my importance a secret as I was still worried how this could be used against me and my friends. I did mention how I was with a battle force which was in Whitchurch when I became ill from where I had been hit by an arrow. The rest of the army had returned to Mercia while I recovered. I had just recovered when the Picts had ridden in and taken us as slaves. Gregor pointed out how this showed that the meeting was meant to be.

Trying to steer the conversation to where I might be granted freedom to return home was difficult. I suggested an alliance between King Alfred and King Gregor, and this made Gregor thoughtful. I suggested I could be the go between, and we could set up a meeting in a secure middle ground. Whitchurch would have been ideal however we could use Wrexham which was in the same region. Gregor told me that he did not yet have the resources. Most of his men were farmers and spread out over a large area. At best with all his banners called he thought he could only muster five thousand warriors. He had enormous pressure from the nobles and particularly his son to launch an all-out attack on Northumberland. 'We cannot attack south as we would leave our homeland vulnerable. We are protected in the north by our mountains, the weather and our vast land area.'

It was a pleasant evening but I could see that I was not going to get my freedom as I was too valuable a resource. By showing interest in leaving, I would only be drawing attention to myself and be making my eventual escape even more difficult. Gregor loved his land and people and I was a means to helping him fulfil these goals. Unfortunately, this was not my current goal however much I wanted to help him achieve his. I knew how important I was to the Worchester plan and now the greater Angles Land plan. A united Angles Land plan had been discussed between the councils in Worchester and Northampton. I wanted to meet with King Alfred and put the plan to him. A united people under one king and one government. It was all possible if we worked together.

After dessert we all rose to leave. Kenner had been a real delight and her beauty was matched by her intellect. I could have kept talking to her all night and I knew that she had aroused something in me which had been lost since the death of my Sunngifu. After saying our farewells to them and thanking them for the meal Ailpen, Shug and I started back to the forge and our accommodation. Ailpen commented on how the world was so large but at the same time so small. Shug punched me in the arm and said that it looked like Kenner and I had a thing going on. 'I reckon that she likes you as she could not take her eyes off you.' I blushed at this although I can't say that it wasn't music to my ears. I knew that I was attracted to Kenner and was wondering how to get an opportunity to meet her again.

Our banter went on like this until we said good night to each other and went our separate ways. I had really fallen on my feet and was already close with Ailpen and Shug and was getting in close with the king of Strathclyde and his family. That night my dreams were sweet, and I was at risk of forgetting the bigger picture.

A few days later I was introduced to Seoc who was the chief horse handler. We were making a new series of bridles and replacing the old horseshoes. Seoc looked to be in his fifties and was an animal lover in every sense of the word. Seoc showed me around the stables and I could see the genuine affection that he had for each of the animals.

Over the following two weeks I was able to work out the routines with the horses of which there were almost a hundred. This was a large stable and all these horses were the personal property of the king. There was a separate stable up in Carlisle for the army's horses. I would not be able to remove the horses I needed by myself, so I was going to have to bring the others here before we left.

Seoc had provided horses for the new iron mine which was ten miles to the east up in the hills. Without suspecting my intentions Seoc gave me exact details of how to access the mine and the roads to get there. I have a great memory for routes and quickly locked these details away. Next, I needed the directions to the Peterson estate and again Seoc helped me out. He travelled there once a week to check on their stable and offered to take me along to see some of their beauties. Seoc could see that I had an affinity with horses and that the horses seemed to trust me. Although slow at first Seoc and I soon developed a trusting relationship.

I was beginning to feel a little rotten as although I liked it where I was, I knew I had a duty to leave Strathclyde. All along while being friends with these men, I was planning on abandoning them. I could think of no other way as I knew if I confided in them then my cover would be blown, and I did not trust the connection that much.

There was so much I could offer them with my skills I had shown them but also my skills which they were unaware of such as making superior weapons and now my knowledge of waging war. Thinking back, I could see that Worchester had a lot of similarities until we started planning and building our wealth and prosperity. Carlisle already had a castle so other defensive walls could be built out on the dales which would make the Vikings think twice. I knew it is not my problem and I did not have time to see any projects through but I still felt guilty.

The road up to the Peterson estate was truly gorgeous as it was a clean, tree lined gravel track. Winding through the hills I was able to catch glimpses of the valleys through the breaks in the trees. Dermit Peterson was the lord of Peterson estate and cousin to King Gregor, thus well connected. Coming into view of the main building I could see that Strathclyde truly had some wealth and I thought I understood why the Vikings were targeting them, as difficult as they were finding it. We went straight to the stables where I was shown the beautiful range of horses.

Dermit came out to meet with Seoc and give us an update on any issues. Dermit said that they were all enjoying the milder weather and were being taken for longer rides every day. Seoc introduced me to Dermit and I complemented him on his fine selection of animals. I asked Dermit how Gwyneth, Riannon and Seren were going within his household as I told him that I had come up with them from down south. He told me that they had been very pleasant and compliant according to reports from Agnes who ran the household.

'Is there any chance I could see them and say hello given I am up this way and may not be again for some time?' This was bold however everything I was learning about these Picts indicated that there was little risk in being forward and just asking.

Following Dermit to the main house we entered the kitchen and immediately I saw Seren. A smile lit her face once she saw me and I greeted her carefully as Dermit was still by my side. I asked how she was and the whereabouts of her mother and sister. Together we followed Dermit through to the washroom where I was able to see Gwyneth and Riannon. Fortunately, Dermit left us to catch up which was polite as there was no suspicion that we were planning an escape.

Even though we had not been friends for a long period of time our experiences had made us close. I let them in on my plan and told them we would be coming past on the south road three hours before sunrise. They were to dress warmly and make sure they were well rested in the nights leading up to our flight. Seeing the Peterson horses had encouraged me to change my plan so we would not go back to the royal estate. Peterson had thirty good horses which would serve our purposes.

We needed twenty-five good horses so these stables would be fine. On the way back through from the mine we would slip into the estate and walk the horses away. 'There will be a need to expect trouble as I do not know the workings of this property, however I expect the trouble to be less fierce here than at the royal estate.'

Everyone agreed to the plan and to silence so we all hugged and said our farewells.

The following afternoon I was visited by Kenner down at the forge. Kenner was enquiring what I was up to and asked if I could take her to the stables to find a horse. Ailpen did not want to deny the king's daughter so he assented, and I left up the road with Kenner. She was just delightful with one of the nicest smiles I have ever seen. As we walked into the stables Seoc was stabling one of the grey beauties. He bowed to Kenner and asked if she wanted to go for a ride. Nodding Kenner replied to Seoc that the horse he was just putting away would be perfect for me. Seoc checked himself but then nodded and said, 'As you wish, my Princess.'

Free of the stables I followed Kenner off track and into the forests of the estate. Kenner was a good rider and it took some skill to keep up with her. Fortunately, I was an experienced rider and my horse, aptly named Fireball, had no problem following me or Kenner.

Kenner stopped and dismounted at a clearing with a brook running through it. At either end of the clearing were some beautiful old willows. I followed Kenner's lead and dismounted and tied Fireball up to the same tree. This was when Kenner grabbed my hand and asked me to follow her. Holding hands, we made our way to what looked like a secret grotto in under the cover of the willow trees. Kenner really was a stunning girl and I could not imagine what she was doing with me.

In the grotto Kenner turned and looked into my eyes. I was quite tall, so she had to look up however this did not stop us coming together and kissing passionately. From this point everything happened naturally and we seemed to follow our instincts. Slowly I removed Kenner's clothes to reveal a body which matched her smile for beauty. It was a magical moment and showed me that my mourning period for Sunngifu was over and I was ready to love again. After making love we lay together in that grotto until it was almost dark. Kenner suggested that we had better head back as her father or Seoc would probably be getting a search party ready. I told her I wanted to stay there forever and turned over and kissed her passionately again. As I said those words, I felt the falseness in them as I had planned to leave in five days' time. Kenner agreed and said that this was the best afternoon of her life before telling me that she loved me.

It was dark when we arrived back at the stables and we came up to King Gregor, Seoc, Ailpen and Shug all on horseback with torches. Kenner rode straight up to her father and apologised profusely and in the torchlight, I could see that he was cross. I stayed quiet as I knew that I was in big trouble. Silently I cursed myself as I had probably blown the trust which they had given me and lost a lot of my privileges. I was hoping that I did not put my escape in jeopardy.

The horses were put away and before heading back to the forge Gregor pulled me aside and asked if I had taken care of his daughter. He reminded me that she was unmarried, and he had plans to marry her to a wealthy lord from Pictland. Gregor told me that no formal arrangements had been made however he was considering the proposal as it might be what was best for his people. These Picts were amazing people and incredibly accepting. The king told me that I was not to put this possible arrangement in jeopardy. I could spend time with Kenner but was not to try anything on.

I was expecting grief from Ailpen however he just patted me on the back and told me how lucky he thought that I was. Shug was beside himself and he couldn't stop his smile which crossed his face ear to ear. I knew I was lucky as Kenner was stunning and that was an afternoon I would never forget. Lucky for me the following four days were spent in a similar fashion and I thought that I might also be in love. What was I thinking? I was most certainly in love and in a real conundrum. I had an entire nation depending on me and here I had a girl as amazing as I thought it might be possible. The risk of being found out contributed to the excitement of our courtship.

Telling Kenner was a thought which I played with on and off and in the end, I thought that it was impossible to take the risk. There was a chance that she would follow me. However, as loving as Kenner was, she was still fiercely independent and strong-willed. Kenner was also super protective of her family and father, probably as a result of her deceased siblings. I just could not take the risk however much I wanted to. Our time together came to an end that last afternoon as this night was the night of our departure. It would have been two hours after dark when I left the estate without any plan of coming back unless by some change of fate or years into the future when Angles Land had been secured.

Leading my horse from the stable I hit the road and headed out to the mine. I had time up my sleeve as I was not sure how difficult it was going to be freeing the others from their captivity. We then needed to get back to the Peterson estate to get horses and grab the girls.

The workers at the mine were all kept in a barrack at the entrance road to the mine. I tied my horse up short of the quarry and walked the hundred yards attempting to make no noise. Looking from the cover of the trees I could see that there were two guards on the entrance to the barracks and quarry. This was when I wished I had my bow. Thinking what to do, I thought a less threatening approach on the access road might work best.

Approaching the two armed guards, I raised my hands and asked if they could help me. I told them that I was lost after being attacked out on the road to Carlisle. I told them I had been walking for hours. The guards told me to bugger off and both drew their swords. None of this bothered me as the ruse was enough to get me close enough to quickly disarm the guards. The last four weeks in the forge had helped me get back to full strength and a strength which could disarm most men, even the strongest, armed or not.

With the guards out of the way I went into the first wooden building and walked along looking for someone I knew. It wasn't long before I noticed Andras sound asleep. Stepping quietly, I had so far not woken any of the workers who were all exhausted from a hard, physical day in the quarry. I slipped in beside Andras and quietly prodded him awake. As soon as he saw me, he knew why I was there. He looked like a changed man with hardened chiselled features, the features of a man working stone day after day with barely enough food to keep him going.

Slipping out of bed Andras dressed and was able to identify all our men, at the same time waking them and telling them it was time. Seeing Leofric alive and well filled my heart with joy as we both embraced.

Outside we all gathered but did not hang around for long. We had to get to the Petersons' estate and to the horses before daybreak. Once news of our escape was received, I was sure there would be horses on the road instantly and they would know exactly where we were heading. I could have done things differently and even killed Gregor and or Dermit however I knew this would provoke them and would certainly work against me working with them ever again.

My luck held and as we reached the Petersons we came across Gwyneth and her daughters. They were all emotional as Bledri and his family were reunited. While they caught up the rest of us headed for the stables to liberate the horses. The stables did not have any guards as they had not expected anyone to attempt to steal their horses. One by one we led the twenty-five horses free from the stable and as quietly as we could we led them down the road to where Bledri and the others were.

I told them that we now had to ride as sun was not two hours away and we would have death on our tails. Up until this point we had not come across anyone else using that road and I hoped it would stay the same for at least another two hours.

Our speed was restricted due to the darkness although the horses with their better night vision were able to keep us moving forward. It was only a half moon and under the cover of the trees near impossible to see for any distance. I had a picture in my head of the roads we needed to take and slowly but surely, we wound our way out of the hills and back down to the main road south from Carlisle.

Light slowly began to filter through the trees as we rode south. I could suddenly see the road in front of us and with this our party sped up. The first light also gave me the chance to look at our group and especially all the men. We looked like a ragged bunch, but a bunch large enough that nobody other than an army would come near us. We were a wild looking group which I would want to avoid, if not part of it.

The men looked the worst as they had spent the month in hard labour mining stone and iron. I felt a little guilty as I knew that I have been well looked after and had far from suffered. There was no way I was going to tell them about Kenner as this made me extremely uncomfortable given their circumstances.

As we were stuck on the main road, I wanted speed and as much distance as we could create before the men from Carlisle were on our trail. We were very lightly armed with only a half dozen swords between us and some cutting knives. I did not mind being seen by passers-by as Gregor and the Picts would know exactly where we are headed. The road was still empty as it was another bitter morning. The horses we had stolen were exceptional and would be a big loss to Peterson. Peterson had not done anything to me, and I had some guilt about the theft although I suspected he benefited from his relationship with the king. By association he was at least partly guilty for our abduction.

By the time we saw the sun break the horizon we were nearing the border lands between Strathclyde and Northumberland. This section of road was lonely and remote. There was a reason why it is lonely and that was the ever-present threat of attack from bandits or Vikings. Consequently, the quality of the track was poor which again forced us to slow down. There was one section which we walked to give the horses a rest and to avoid breaking one of their legs.

Nearing the end of the day there were some grumblings to make camp for the night. I told those responsible that we were making for Chester. Bledri had told me that Chester was the northern most point in Powys and it would offer us some protection. Bledri knew the mayor of Chester and although they had had their differences, he expected he would be loyal to his own kind. I was a little less confident as a group of twenty-five riders in the middle of the night is never welcome. Trouble will usually be following, and most people would not want any part of it.

We were stopped at the gates of Chester a few hours after the setting sun. We had been forced to slow down to a walk once night fell as again it was overcast and a moonless night. Steadily we had followed the track and found our way to Chester. The guards raised the alarm on the sight of us as they could not be sure whether we were friend of foe. At the gates we found ourselves facing fifty armed men in different stages of dress. Another chilly evening and what looked like a cold welcome.

From what I could see the walls around Chester were not large however they would offer protection against raiding parties without the resources of war. Made from stone they would be the height of two or maybe three men. Stopping fifty yards from the gate Bledri stepped forward with his hands raised as a sign we came in peace. The rest of us stayed still as we did not want to give them an excuse to start shooting. We had all been on foot for the last half an hour as we knew we were close, and the horses were exhausted.

Bledri yelled out who he was in response to their demand. A man stepped forward and came right up to Bledri. As they embraced, I released a long breath which I had not realised I was holding. There was no guarantee here, however it looked like Bledri was true to his word and he did know people in Chester. I was called forward to meet the mayor of Chester, Caerwyn son of Gronw. Caerwyn eyed me and added that at last he had the chance to meet the fabled Godric of Worchester. 'A strange place and time to meet when war ravages our land.'

I added my pleasure on first meeting and then being welcomed by Caerwyn and indeed Chester. 'Are you able to offer us a bed for the night and maybe something for our stomachs?'

Caerwyn then welcomed us all into Chester and seeing that there were women he was quick to wake his household to assist him in finding us a place to sleep and some food. Carwyn's wife Heledd was extremely efficient and before long we had the horses stabled and we were all sitting around with a hot cup of soup. Caerwyn introduced us to his commander of the guard. Gerallt was a man of similar proportions to me so one you would avoid if you could. Although looking as tough as they come Gerallt still has a full mouth of teeth and a warm smile.

They told us that it was tough times and there was increased activity from bandits and particularly the Vikings. They believed that something big was brewing and the Vikings were preparing for their moment to strike. They did not know where the hammer was going to fall, however, they suspected it would be Worchester. Looking a little guilty Caerwyn added that he hoped it was Worchester and not Chester. They told us that east of Chester was dangerous land and it was no longer safe to hunt or farm in the lands from Chester to York. 'Walls and castles are being built wherever possible and people are living in fear.'

I told the group that we needed to get home to Worchester and a little about our adventure with the Picts. I did not speak poorly of them although I was careful not to speak glowingly either as Leofric, Andras and Bledri were sitting with me and they had been in the quarry.

They confirmed that Whitchurch had been burnt to the ground and looters had been over the place. We told them that we were going to pass through there on the way south to check it out. Caerwyn also told us that he had heard that Northampton had fallen to the Vikings after a long siege. This was a major blow as immediately I thought of Wassa and her safety. Although I could do nothing now, I struggled to regain control of my mind. I needed to get home and start building and protecting the people.

After supper we all turned in as we were exhausted from our long day. It had not been easy however we had made it to Chester all the way from Strathclyde. Our escape plan had worked, and we were only a day from home.

Chapter 10 — Building for War

We were up and away at first light although I know I wasn't the only one sporting aches and pains. We just had to get back home and especially now that we had heard that Northampton had fallen. The fall of Northampton would explain why the Viking army had not come after us back to York if that was at the same time. It might also indicate that there was a much bigger Viking army roaming around our land. I needed to be home and I needed time to continue the work we were doing building the guard.

Our first destination was Whitchurch where I was still hopeful that the guard and I could retrieve our weapons. These were high quality and would take time to replace and I did not want to be facing them in battle. Whitchurch was less than two hours by horseback, and we reached it mid-morning. The town had been burnt however the walls and some roofs remained.

Bledri and Gwyneth's roof had collapsed, and their house was a mess. Looking from the open doorway I thought I knew exactly where to look for my bow and swords. Digging through the mess I was able to locate my weapons although there was little of the bow or quivers of arrows. I collected as many tips as I could find and retrieved the swords. Not quite perfectly equipped for war however I now felt menacing again.

It is interesting how having your weapon in your hand makes you stand taller and think more recklessly. I almost welcomed the Picts or Vikings, thinking how I would love to cut some down. Most of the other weapons for our men were gone although we did retrieve some swords and supplies. It seemed that the looters did not hang around for long as there were many things of value which had not been claimed. Following this thought I suggested to Leofric that it was best we move on. A nod in my direction told me he was thinking the same thing.

We quickly found our horses and started for the south road. A shower of arrows came our way just as we had left Whitchurch. As soon as I heard the familiar sound of arrows in flight I screamed out to ride. I sensed that we had casualties as we took the horses to a gallop. Looking around, I saw two of our guard, fall to the ground, dead, and another two get hit with arrows. I stopped as the others rode by to see if the guards were all right and as I did, I noticed Seren had come off her horse and Bledri had stopped to help her. Seren's horse had been hit and it had bolted. I yelled for Bledri to ride while I rode back and with one hand reached down and pulled Seren onto Firebolt, sitting her in front of me. Bledri was a heavier man than me and his horse not as well built. Besides I suspected Bledri's best riding days were behind him.

As we again took off along the south road, I heard arrows in the distance. Judging by their sound I did not think they were going to make me, so I ignored them and pushed on by the south road. Looking back, I could no longer see any evidence of Whitchurch and it did not look as though we were being followed. It was funny to me how one minute I felt like I could take on the world and would have welcomed trouble and the next I was fleeing for my life. Fortunately, common sense was guiding me.

The others had slowed down and thus we were able to catch up to them. Firebolt was a good horse and again had served me well. The boys, Archer and Cynefrid, still had the arrows in them. They understood that it was not safe to stop and fortunately they were still able to ride. Archer had been hit in the right shoulder while Cynefrid had an arrow through this thigh. The bleeding looked to have stopped for both and although they both looked in pain it was a relief that there was a good chance they would recover once we got home.

From where we were, we took the direct route through Powys and back to Worchester. We passed more and more travellers as we made our way south although on sight of us all the travellers cleared the road and did their best to avoid us. It was now summer, and the weather had been improving ever since we had left Strathclyde. Our path was through a beautiful part of the country with spectacular mountains to our right and streams and rivers on our left. There was a late fog lifting from the tree covered mountains and a mist hanging over the water. Although passing travellers the fog gave me a sense of isolation and peace.

Coming over the Malvern Hills it was a sight to behold seeing our beloved valley again. We had a great view of the castle and Worcester. The roads around there were busy as there was a hive of activity around all the properties and down into town. The Worcester valley and regions had been expanding for at least a decade and this had also triggered wealth for all the new settlers to the area.

This was home for all of us but it was all new for Bledri and his family. I was conscious of the newness for them and told them that they were welcome to come and stay at my property until they could set themselves up. This earnt a hug from Gwyneth who I could see was also teary eyed. As we were passing our farm first, we stopped when Hilda came running out followed by Tata. Leofric was with her in an instant and they embraced with so much passion that most of us had to look away. I told my sister that we would be back however asked if she could make Gwyneth and her girls at home as they would be staying with us for some time. Ruffling Tata's and Osgar's hair I told them I was looking forward to spending some time with them and telling them of our adventures. I scanned around hoping to seeing my Edgar again as he must be around somewhere. He was a fine boy who looked to be taking after his father, at least physically. However, I could not see him and we did not have the time to hang around.

Leaving the farm Bledri thanked me again and commented on how beautiful and tranquil the area was. Approaching the river, to my surprise I could see a welcoming party coming to meet us with John at the front. It was great to be back around so many familiar faces and John's was the most familiar of them all. We were taken into town where those of the guard who were injured could be cared for and the others could be reunited with their families. It had been a significant adventure which had started with the confrontation with Ethelred a month or so back.

John filled us in on events in the south and said that Hereweald had taken the Wessex army back to Winchester to fill King Alfred in on the situation. Refugees had been flooding in from Northampton and its region as the Vikings had breached the walls. Word had come through that they thought that Halfdan was involved in the attack and that he had made prisoners of the castle leaders to use in negotiations. This was all John could tell me of Wassa or Ethan and Evan.

I ate and drank and enjoyed the feeling of being home but I could not relax as I knew there was significant work to be done. I was given an account of the sword, archery and cavalry units in the guard and with the refugees they had been able to expand the ranks to two thousand. The forges were running all day every day to provide the weapons we needed for the new recruits. Buildings were springing up everywhere as Worchester continued to expand. Deorwine told me that work on the cathedral was progressing at pace and we had a continuous guard posted on the roads into and out of town from the east, west and south.

It would not be wise for me to make any decisions while being as tired as I felt. I left the meeting and with Bledri headed back out to the farm. Bledri asked me about my sister and Northampton as I guess he could see this news was sitting heavy on me. I told him that my current thoughts were to ride off and attempt to help them escape or at least confirm where they were, although I needed to sleep on the decision.

'I am aware of my importance to our town and its people and I am conscious not to risk it all to rescue one family member. However, Wassa is my younger sister and I have looked after her since the death of our parents. I feel responsible and so much want to make everything all right for her.' I also wanted to get Northampton back as this was a strategic castle which protected the underbelly of Mercia and Wessex. I had already lost one sister in horrible circumstances and did not fancy losing another.

There was plenty of room for Bledri and his family and it was nice having the additional noise in the house. It must have been exciting for Tata and the children to have some other young people around. Tata and Seren were of similar age and already seemed to be getting on. I was told that Tata had been doing some exceptional work as a blacksmith which made me proud of my little brother. I also found my little Edgar as he terrorised the household. He was now in his terrible twos and full of energy. I did not have the energy for him this night and I had plenty on my mind. The night was young when I left the company of family and went to bed. I needed sleep and needed time to consider the next move.

The projects in Worchester were in place and on schedule. It was now time to continue building our army to take on the Vikings. Part of me wanted to strike back hard on Halfdan and to take Northampton back. I was uncomfortable with the Vikings having a stronghold so close to our community. The Vikings could easily raid Worchester and its farming communities and get back to the safety of their castle by night fall. How had the Vikings penetrated the walls and conquered such an imposing castle? John had mentioned lots of refugees and I wondered if any of them may have come from the castle. As I lay in bed, I slowly began to concoct a plan of revenge although I needed some more pieces to this puzzle.

The following day I felt renewed, so I grabbed one of my bows and headed to the practice grounds. I saw that Leofric and Tata were also up and already at it in the forge. Greeting them and our apprentices I told them that I was planning something so needed to hit the practice grounds. It felt odd having a bow in my hands however by my third shot it felt like a natural part of me again. The bow was a weapon I had used most days of my life and in a way, it was like having the use of another arm. It was automatic to pick up the bow, string an arrow, line up the target, pull and release. There was no real thinking involved unless it was an unusual shot which was required. The practice did me good and I was able to see a clear path forward.

Back in the forge I told Leofric that he would be needed for a special council meeting which I was going to call. Bledri and his family were welcome on the farm or in Worchester, wherever they chose to venture and settle. I kissed Hilda goodbye and went to grab my horse. She tugged on my arm and looking back I could see she had tears in her eyes. 'You will bring her home, won't you?' This made me turn and embrace my older sister. I also now had tears in my eyes as I told her that with every breath I take, I would not stop until Wassa is safe. Leofric and I rode away from the farm, with Hilda balling her eyes out, being comforted by Gwyneth and the girls. The truth was I felt the same way but did not dare show the emotion in the way my older sister had.

I was back and had my favourite war horse, Mountain Force or Mountain, as I affectionately knew him, beneath me. I say favourite although this is a little unfair to my first horse, Bolter. Bolter was killed in the raid a couple of years back and since then I have been riding Mountain Force. Bolter was a fierce war horse and had been my saviour on many occasions, not least the first battle for Repton. John Archer would be dead if it was not for Bolter. Fully armed, I had my bow with quivers full of two hundred of the best arrows. Along with my swords and knives I was once again ready for war.

Once in town I went straight to John and asked him if he could organise a council meeting for the full council including the captains. Leofflaed asked me if I was all right and welcomed me home. She gave me condolences for Wassa however I stopped her and told her that all was not lost, and I would be getting her back.

Leofric and I split up and spent the next hour riding around to the refugees and asking them what they knew of the fall of the Northampton castle. It turned out that most of them were in the castle when it fell. They said that the Vikings took charge of the castle and town but within a week they had opened the gates and relaxed their control. People could return to the town. The castle itself was still heavily guarded although the Vikings were generally not harassing the businesses in town. However, given this freedom many of the residents had fled to Worchester and some further south.

The messages which Leofric and I gathered were similar. It seemed that the castle walls were tunnelled under and once breached the castle garrison had fought bravely but were eventually overpowered by the Vikings. I could see many opportunities with these accounts which I used to make additions to my earlier plan.

It was a full town hall which I addressed as I explained the danger of the Vikings establishing a stronghold so close to Worchester. 'I do not want our homes burnt in the night and our farmers and their families raped and slaughtered. Northampton must be taken back, and we are the ones to do it. We cannot wait for support from the south or Wessex as this will give the Vikings time to reinforce what is already a difficult situation. They will not suspect a counterattack as they will know that the Wessex force have gone home to Winchester. There may never be a better time to strike then now.'

This statement caused a commotion and I could see as I spoke that there was widespread agreement around the room. It could never be said that the people and council of Worchester were cowards. In my short life we had dealt with many hardships, setbacks and battles. Most of them were older than me and like me knew that there were no safe havens unless we were the ones to create them.

I went on to give them the information which Leofric and I had been able to glean from the refugees. 'There may be tunnels which the Vikings had dug through from the banks of the river Nene. The Vikings have let people return to the town and only killed those directly related to the army. There is trade going on into and out of Northampton, so the gates are open at various times during the day.'

From there I laid out the plan of how I saw us taking back Northampton. There were many clarifying questions and a couple of position suggestions, but the plan was generally accepted in whole.

'The sword unit will slip out of town tomorrow morning and head north. They will ride toward Repton and rest just south of it. On dark they will make their way down to the River Nene and along it to Northampton. I expect the tunnels to be heavily guarded although we may get lucky. Approaching from the north I am hoping the Vikings have less eyes on the road. If there is a guard the guard is to be taken out as quietly as possible. There is a chance that the tunnels have been filled in. The sword unit is to wait for the cavalry to attack. Either way, the sword will then make their way through the tunnels or join the attack on the gates.

'We will take the full cavalry which is currently a thousand strong. We will leave around midnight on the following night and wait out of sight for the castle to open its gates. This mission will be full of stealth and could be costly. Our goal is to get inside the gates and secure them open. We do not know of the numbers inside however I do not believe that they will be keeping their full army there as they have had the castle for over two weeks and the weather is perfect for raiding.'

Everyone agreed that there was great risk however our security relied on us taking Northampton back. John questioned whether an attack would put any hostages in the castle at risk and I agreed that it would although I saw no other choice as there was nothing we could use to negotiate with for their release. It was sad for me to admit this however I knew it to be the truth.

Messages were sent out and preparations were made. The following morning the swordsman of the guard left for Repton while I worked with the other councillors to communicate what we were doing with the rest of the community. The swordsmen were being led by captain Aethelweard, as reliable a man as you could find.

The rest of the council went around calling for volunteers for the guard as I had the idea of building a home guard of one thousand warriors to help defend our community while the main guard was away. They would all learn archery and sword and be supplied with the latest weapons.

The response we got was overwhelming. It appeared everyone wanted to be involved in what we were building, and food and security were at the top of everyone's minds. That afternoon Deorwine, Dunstan and I stood with over two thousand prospective guard members. The offer was not only open to men but also to women, women who had the right physical qualities. I could immediately see that we were going to need another forge and some more apprentices to keep up with the demand for weapons.

Using the existing guard and the weapons we had we began showing the recruits the correct techniques for archery and sword. Practice went on until an hour before sunset and I could see many of them were getting sore fingers, hands and arms from their archery work. Some had blood from blisters while all looked exhausted from the training.

Bringing everyone together, I thanked them for joining the guard and told them that some did not make the cut and had been given other duties. I reminded them that the guard had a part to play which was as important as the farmer who provided our food, the blacksmith our weapons, the mother of the next generation and the stonemason responsible for our buildings. 'The point I am making is that we are all part of a successful community which supports each other whenever and wherever we can. There is no part which is better than the other and even though you are now welcomed to the guard it is still your responsibility to work hard on your other occupations and help your neighbours and friends. You are also to give two hours of every day to Wulfstan, our amazing stonemason. Wulfstan built our imposing castle and is now working on our inspiring cathedral where we will be able to come together to worship

Jesus in style. Wulfstan will establish a roster which fits with your other requirements and please let me remind you one of the key purposes of this project is to bond the guard and to build on your inherent strength by working with stone.'

It was midnight when the cavalry led by Dunstan rode out of Worchester and off to retake Northampton. This was going to be our first real resistance to the Viking expansion. The raids of Repton, Torksey and York were simply raiding, and we were not in position to hold these lands, but Northampton was different. The Vikings were holding the East Angles, London, through to Repton, York and Northumberland. If I'd had a map, it would have felt like they would probably have more of our Angles Land, than we had. It was time to push back and tomorrow was going to be the day of the Angles. During the day I had heard us being referred to as the English and to us being England. It was a slang that had sprung up to describe our people and region. We were not Mercia any more since the fall of Æthelstan to Wessex and we had never been Wessex or part of Powys. Angles were who we were but I did like the sound of England and English when describing ourselves. It would be interesting to see if it stuck and for how long.

Once dark, I had left with Leofric as we were going to make our own way direct to Northampton to scope the castle and ensure that our plan was set for the morning. Two riders would be no threat to anyone, and we did not want to be raising any suspicion. We were still heavily armed as we were only two and we were at risk of attack from bandits or other bands of Vikings on the roads. It was a dark windy night which was ideal for covering our sounds and later the sounds of our cavalry. The flip side was that it also meant we would not be able to hear any would-be attackers or defenders.

From the protection of the trees, we could see that Northampton was shut up. The castle gates were closed, and the town looked dead to the world. I had the urge to try to get in and down to the dungeons. The risk of this move was that if we were seen or caught, we would raise the alert level in the castle which could ruin the entire plan.

Instead, we confirmed the existence of the tunnels and could see that there were guards at the entrance with horns to blow should they be attacked. We watched these men for some time and at last we saw a handover for the nightshift. I knew we could have taken them down with little effort although again we risked alerting the castle before our cavalry could hit their open gate. It became a long night as we waited for the battle to begin.

I sensed Aethelweard and the sword before I heard and finally saw them. Leofric and I joined them as we waited for the first sign of light. At this first sign I carefully scaled the riverbank and found a spot under the cover of trees where I could view the castle gates. It was still windy and overcast which continued to work in our favour. I did not have to wait long for the gates of the castle to open for the servants and the early morning trade. Foot traffic increased by the minute as the town and castle woke to the new day. It was time for the sword to secure the tunnels and start making their way through, with the plan that the cavalry should be ready to strike very soon, and the battle would be at full pitch instantly once they are through the gates. Should the gates get closed on them then they would have to wait and hope that the sword division got into the castle and could open them from the inside.

Dropping back to the sword unit of our guard, Leofric and I quickly shot the two Viking guards. Immediately we headed for the tunnels followed by a thousand of our highly trained swordsmen. There were four tunnels, so we split the group amongst the four openings. The Vikings had built the tunnels well and to a size to fit their bigger bodies. This suited us well as there were only a few sections where we needed to duck or squeeze through.

On entering the tunnel, I was hit by the damp soil smell and the temperature seemed to drop considerably. Expecting guards at the other end we proceeded with caution. The tunnel began to climb, and we were met by a ladder. The top of the ladder looked like it was in a room of some kind. Expecting trouble Leofric grabbed my arm and said he would go first. He told me that I was too important to lose, and it was not worth the risk. I was angry at first as I wanted to get to the top of the ladder and into the fighting; however, I realised the wisdom in his suggestion even though I also thought Leofric too valuable. Aethelweard and his men climbed up the ladder and secured the room above, where three of the tunnels come out. The fourth must be in one of the adjoining rooms. There had been guards in the room but they had been killed before they had had the chance to raise the alarm. We had lost two members of the guard while securing the room. They had heard us on the ladder but had not suspected an attack. They may have been thinking we were their friends from the tunnel entrance. Fortune continued to follow us around, a good sign for what was to come.

As quietly as we could the swordsmen continued to fill the room. The room was only big enough for about a hundred of us, so the others had to wait in the tunnel. The plan was to now wait for the sound of the cavalry. I opened the door a crack to get a better view and this was when I first heard the horn and knew the fighting had commenced. Pushing open the door I could see the battle as there were groups of people and Vikings engaged everywhere. Immediately we were set upon as we worked to get out of the storeroom and increase our area of control. We needed to secure the room and the surroundings to give all our swordsmen a chance to clear the tunnels. This was a problem with our plan as we really needed to be getting over to support the cavalry and the gate.

The numbers through the tunnels grew rapidly and I signalled to Leofric that I was heading for the walls. Leofric and a dozen of the men came with me. With the men protecting our path I was able to use my bow to great effect. Once at the walls we were straight up the stairs to the parapet where I got my first chance to scan the battle scene. It seemed that half of the cavalry had made it through the gates but the gates had now been closed. They were now fighting for their lives to reopen the gates. All the cavalry were both archers and swordsmen and now most of them had their swords in their hands. We cleared the parapet of Vikings and from this elevated position I began taking down the Viking archers who were also on the wall on the other side of the gate.

With the swordsmen free from the tunnel our men were able to secure the gate and open it to the remainder of the cavalry. Vikings continued to pour into the central square below but they were now outnumbered and easily taken out by our forces.

From my position on the wall, I saw Aethelweard and his men head for the open doorways to begin clearing the castle of further threats. I remembered my sister and headed off the wall and to the location where I knew the dungeons to be. Luckily, I had spent some time in the castle when I was in Northampton for Wassa's wedding. On the path to the dungeons, I came across small resistance which was no match for my skill and desire to find my sister alive. Killing the last of the Vikings guarding the dungeon, I was able to find the keys and open the doors leading to the dungeon itself. While I had swordsmen guard the entrance I stepped into a world of horror. There was a cacophony of sound as the prisoners jammed into the closer cells saw me and started yelling for help. The numbers in the cells were too much and their living conditions horrific. It smelled more like a sewer then a dungeon which only raised my concern for my younger sister.

There were many chambers down a central hallway. I was screaming out for Wassa with all hope that she was in one of the rooms. I cannot explain how but I heard a reply from the end of the hallway and took off down the hall at full speed. At the end of the hallway there was a central chamber where Wassa was chained to the wall by the wrists and ankles. She looked terrible but at least she was alive. The room was full of prisoners in a similar restraint such as Ethan and Evan and their steward. At least there was room to move in this cell unlike the other cells I had seen up the corridor. I undid their chains as quickly as I could. Once Wassa was free she fell into my arms in tears before helping me with the others. The prisoners were in all different levels of hurt although Evan and Ethan both looked to be well, albeit filthy and beaten.

The reunion was brief as there was still a battle to be won in securing the castle. I gave Alric, the steward, the keys and he said he would sort the remaining prisoners. Some may have been genuine prisoners who would be dangerous to release although most seemed to have been members of Evan's household or in the guard. The rest of us left the dungeon and ran up to where the action was.

Once out in the square I was met by Aethelweard who confirmed that the castle had been secured. All Vikings have been killed and there was no sign of Halfdan. The castle commander was Ivan and he fought until the end.

At once I ordered that the tunnels be filled. I sent runners to the township and to Worcester to tell them of our great victory. Now I really hugged my little sister as my eyes filled with tears to match hers.

We spent the rest of the day assisting Evan in getting his castle and town back to some level of normality. There appeared to have been limited looting and damage caused as Halfdan had the intention of making Northampton a permanent Viking kingdom. Halfdan had left Northampton close to a week earlier to support London against an attack from Wessex. This had conveniently worked with our timing.

There was a need for us to return to Worchester but we agreed to leave Aethelweard and the sword division with Evan as we had no doubt that the Vikings would return. The tunnels had been filled in but the Vikings have proven themselves to be cunning and we had no doubt Halfdan would throw everything at getting Northampton back. We told the men that it was not permanent and there would be some form of rotation system set up. In the meantime, Northampton would be working hard to rebuild their own guard. Aethelweard and his men were also given the task of training these new guard.

It was sad to once again be saying farewells to Wassa and her new family. Evan and his family could not thank us enough for coming to their aid. He told us he could not have hoped for better friends and allies. With a cheeky smile Evan told us that Northampton would always be a part of England. I smiled back and said, 'One land, England!' We finished our farewells and we were off back to Worchester.

Riding back into town we were once again greeted as heroes. We had had our losses but these were relatively small compared to what they could have been. The attack was audacious and only with luck on our side were we able to achieve what we did. We had roughly two hundred dead of the fifteen hundred which set out. Even though elated with the victory there was still great sadness for those two hundred families who lost someone. We carried these bodies with us on carts which we pulled into the town square. From here people were able to find and retrieve their deceased loved ones.

Graves were excavated in a field on the outskirts of Worchester. Father Frank held a service and I spoke to the gathered crowd. 'These men are the first to die in what will be the reclamation of our island. Their sacrifice will bring their families and our community security and freedom. We thank them for their sacrifice. Their foundation will be honoured, and we will free our land. The English are innovative, persistent, strong and loyal and will not be held down for long.' Although there was still great sadness with this speech ending there was a great cheer and the mead was cracked open to celebrate the lives of the men we had lost. Worcester was a close community, and everyone would help each other to cover our losses. There were no families who were not accustomed to facing the death of someone close to them.

That afternoon and evening was the first time I had had to really relax and celebrate my return from the Picts. It was wonderful catching up with Leofflaed and John and even Hilda and Tata whom I hadn't spent any time with for over a month. Bledri and his family were settling in and Alun, who was engaged to Riannon, had joined the guard. Seeing that we had a great need of blacksmiths I thought Alun would be a good addition to our forge. This was a good opportunity to press him with an offer and gratefully he accepted. We had the two forges side by side and with the high demand both needed to be operated every day. Alun was old for an apprentice however his size and strength would be an advantage where age was a disadvantage.

Given all the work to do we continued to push on with expanding the guard and construction of the cathedral. With all the work in the region we were continuing to attract new settlers to the area. Word had spread about our innovations. The sales of different weapons and farm equipment was supplying much needed wealth to support all our projects. Several mills had sprung up along the river which had various uses including grinding wheat for flour mixing, barley for the mead and even for pumping water for irrigation and farming. The fertility of the region and these innovations meant that crop yields were high creating a need for additional granaries to store the food. Food also meant security and the region of Worcester had this in abundance.

New settlers were coming from Powys and the other Welsh states as much as from the south. In the past it had only been refugees from the north and east escaping the Vikings. Worcester was like a beacon in what had otherwise been a dark period for our land.

I kept feeling a tug to take a delegation to Winchester to introduce myself to King Alfred. Concern was being raised in the council that we could be perceived as a threat to Wessex. The last thing the council wanted was an attack from people who we saw as our own, an attack from Wessex. I agreed, however, I wanted to stay and focus on building our guard and consolidating Northampton and its surrounding region. We also set up patrols with the cavalry covering the area to Repton in the north and to Huntingdon in the East. The Repton and Huntingdon towns were not engaged as we knew we did not have the strength to hold them. However, all the countryside in between was kept free of Vikings for as long as we could.

Thus, the council kept agreeing with me and my priorities. The hard work and dedication of our people kept going right through winter and before long another year was behind us. With the great progress which was being achieved in Worchester and as spring rolled around, I was itching to hear and see how Hereweald was going with building Alfred's army. I know that we had been buying thousands of the new design of sword and longbow for Wessex and hoped his training had been every bit as successful as ours had been.

Alun and Riannon were married in what was another enjoyable celebration for our families. We had helped Alun build a house on some of our land so that he could easily access the forge and Riannon was not on her own out on a distant property. It turned out that Riannon was already pregnant so we would have another baby before the end of the year as we were already expecting another from Hilda and Leofric.

Chapter 11 — Wessex

As summer rolled around, I felt that I could not put off my visit to Wessex any longer. John and I would go to Winchester as representatives of Worcester and England. Our cathedral was more than fifty percent complete and our guard had grown to four thousand. Northampton was secured and Halfdan had not returned to attempt its capture. There felt like something was afoot as the Vikings had been relatively quiet. Raiding was down for this time of year. Winter was normally a quiet time but as the season changed so did the Viking activity. Some in the council suggested that maybe Halfdan had gone back to Scandinavia to visit their king or family. Whatever the cause the reprieve had been welcomed as it meant an even better season for the farmers and an opportunity to continue building our defence and attacking capabilities.

With all going so well at home now was the perfect opportunity to make the journey. We took an escort of twenty archers from the guard, enough to discourage any bandits that might see opportunity. Winchester could be reached with a full day's ride, but we would be pushing the horses hard, so a decision was made to split the journey over two days. We made our way to Marlborough where we would find accommodation if it was available. Unfortunately for us the only inn in town was almost full so although John and I could get accommodation the rest of the guard would have to make camp on the outskirts of town. In the interests of fairness John and I stayed out of town with the guard. It was also safer having the extra men about.

We were now well and truly inside Wessex. It should have been friendly territory although I was not sure how welcome I would be. I had killed the king's son and two of his senior captains. The king had every reason to doubt me and even want my head. I was relying on his knowledge of his own son and on the accurate accounts of those who were on the field when he sent the Worchester guard to their deaths in the first battle for Repton. I also hoped that he understood the circumstances of Ethelred's death and that we had had a fair duel. Even though he had champions to assist him I gathered it was fair as the numbers were heavily in his favour and I had a natural fighting ability which I understood.

There was a lot of traffic on the roads which was a good sign for me. Traffic meant people feel safe to travel and the traffic on the roads meant commerce and wealth.

Marlborough was like any small town back in England. England was what I had started calling Worchester and our surrounding valleys. It was Angles Land for a long time as we were descendants of the Anglo Saxons. Angles Land soon became England when warriors and townspeople started using it while drinking and celebrating. England was neat and the one single word was easy to say and easy to remember.

We had our own food so did not require any supplies in Marlborough. The people of Marlborough, and those we met on the roads, all showed us respect and some seemed interested enough to spark up conversations. They wanted to know about Worchester and the Vikings. Once they knew who we were they wanted to know if some of the stories they were hearing about us were true. I was intrigued about the stories however they seemed to be stories about the battles we have had over the last decade and they seemed to be a true enough account. That night John and I discussed it over some mead. I was telling John that these battles and skirmishes had not seemed heroic at the time. We were generally fighting for our lives and fortune had followed us on these occasions.

John agreed however he did note that although one event of fortune was luck and would not warrant a story, everything I had touched I had come out on top and that was a story worth telling. John went on to say that people followed people like me. They wanted to be with someone they believed in and could trust. 'All the stories have you as the trustworthy righteous victor,' he said. He pointed out that we all might need that reputation before too long. I caught his drift as we were going to be meeting the king on the following day, or so we hoped.

The approach to Winchester had us pressing for space on the road. I thought that Worchester was busy but Winchester was double what we saw at home. The roads were packed with traffic in both directions. It was high summer and the day happened to be a scorching one with next to no wind and a sun blaring down on us. We were lightly dressed although fully armed. As Winchester came into view, I could see a palisade wall around the township, and in the distance, I could also see a massive castle under construction. The castle looked as though it was being invaded by ants but I knew this was the workers pushing hard to complete their tasks. It made sense that the king of Wessex would want a castle but still it gave me some pleasure knowing that we already had a fine castle well ahead of Wessex.

We were stopped at the entrance of the outer palisade wall. Although there were merchants and travellers passing all around us, we stood out as all twenty-two of us were on horseback and not just any horses. Our horses were larger than the average horse one would see working the fields. Our horses were bred to be large and strong so that they could carry armed men and their supplies. Together we would have made quite a sight and drawn a lot of attention.

It made sense for the guard to stop and question us as we were also well armed, and I would be doing the same if in their situation. John and I got down from our horses and answered the questions from the guard. They were happy with our responses and gave us entry to the outer limits of the town. This was where the greater Winchester was and where we started looking for an inn to accommodate us and our animals.

Eventually we found The Retreat which sounded too good to be true. The Retreat promising a comfortable stay with well-priced mead. We could all do with a drink so when they said they had rooms to house us all and stables for twenty-two horses we were not going to knock it back. John and I decided that it was too late to be making ourselves known to King Alfred, so we decided to get our group food and drink and eventually have an early night.

The Retreat had a rowdy and rough front bar. We did not know this at the time but were soon to be initiated. We had eaten in the late afternoon and were on our fourth mug when trouble started. One of the boys in the guard was pushed off his chair by some burly man and his friends. They had obviously had too much to drink and were looking for trouble. I did not see this happen however was told about it later as being the first engagement in what became a messy business. At the time I was still relaxing with my drink listening to the sounds of a new town.

The guard by the name of Warwick did not respond to the provocation but did try to get back onto his chair. This prompted the men looking for trouble to pull the chair away and call poor Warwick a weakling and sissy. By this stage a crowd had gathered, and I guess they knew what was coming.

Still, Warwick was disciplined as he and a couple of our guard who he was with came over and joined us on the other side of the room. The front bar was quite a large smoke-filled room with a low ceiling only just above our heads. Warwick sat down and told us there were patrons who were looking for a fight. I told Warwick and the others how impressed I was that they had not been provoked. 'It is not worth the trouble as our mission is to meet with the king and then be off home.'

As I was saying this, I noticed some men starting to build around the outside of our little circle. When one lives and dies on their instincts these instincts are something which one comes to rely upon. They were really picking on Warwick and he had done such a great job of avoiding the conflict. I did not think that anything I said would avoid a conflict but it was worth a try. Warwick is a great guy and one to one he could have handled any of these bullies.

Standing up, I turned to address the antagonists. Before I could even say a word, I sensed a threat coming toward my head and on reflex was able to parry the first strike away. There was now no way of avoiding the fight which these men wanted although within a small period I had already dropped five of them with punches to the head and superior strength. The men did not fall far when hit as there was such a press of men surrounding us. This press of humanity kept them on their feet, and they were able to stay a threat time and time again.

The rest of us all ended up engaged in this brawl and before long the entire bar was into it. There was a dozen of the guard with John and I which was enough to ensure that none of us were permanently or badly hurt. Although these men were heavy set and tough, we were seasoned warriors, well trained and at the peak of our game. Everyone in the guard was assigned time on construction projects as well as practice so we all had innate strength. For close in fighting this innate strength becomes another weapon.

Sometime later I could hear screams as it seemed that a consequence of the brawl had led to somebody falling into the fire. Now alight, this man had rolled around and then got up to try and get his burning clothing off. We were in a very cramped and potentially combustible space. There were a dozen people with fire on their clothing by the time I had heard the screams. Looking around I could also see there was furniture and wallpaper alight all around the far end of the bar. This was a catastrophe unfolding before us so I forgot about fighting and caught the attention of John and some of the guard and told them to get out as soon as they could.

I went to make for the entrance however there was no way of even making it there as people were jammed into it trying to force their way out. At the same time the fire was spreading quickly from person to person as the whole place looked like it was about to go up.

Instead of joining the press for the entrance I indicated we look for the rear exit, so we all jumped the bar, which was on fire at the other end, and headed out into the inn. The fighting back in the bar had ended as everyone was now fighting for their lives. Running down the hall we were able to find the exit. As we went, we banged on doors to alert everyone that there was a fire. After finding the exit I sent some of the guard over to alert the rest of our group who were in our rooms. The others went to the stables to ensure that our horses were safe. From there I stood with John and Warwick and watched as the fire took hold. There was little which could be done as there was not enough accessible water and the fire was now too substantial.

All the men were safe, and our horses had been removed from the stable and tied up in a secure location. Six of the guard were staying with them to make sure that they were not stolen or even overly frightened. Our horses were so critical to us in everything we did, but especially for our archers and cavalry. We could build more forges and make additional weapons but increasing our stock of good war horses took years of breeding and patience. Every horse was like gold to us and we could not risk losing any of them.

It looked like we would be spending the night outside which was not all that uncommon for us. We were lucky to have retrieved all our weapons and supplies.

We could see that the city guard had arrived and was helping people out of the inn. There was a large crowd gathered around standing well back from the blazing inferno. I could see some people pointing in our direction and many of the guard heading our way. I thought that this might be an interesting encounter.

Introducing himself as the captain of the Winchester guard, Wulfsige suggested that we had best come with him and not to cause any trouble. I enquired if he wanted all of us to go with him or just a few of us. He suggested that we were all under arrest and accused of starting the fire at the inn. I replied that it would be incorrect to think that we were the party responsible as we were just there for a meal and a quiet drink. 'You can tell by looking at us that we are sober. We are here on business to see King Alfred.'

The man beside Wulfsige said that we would see King Alfred from a dungeon cell.

To avoid further trouble, I suggested to Wulfsige that John, Warwick and I go with them. 'Our men will not go far as we will be in your charge. This way we can leave our weapons and come with you without any trouble.'

The man beside Wulfsige began to laugh at this and said there will be no trouble for you will all be dead, and with this he moved his sword in front of his body as though ready to strike.

Wulfsige was looking directly at me during this exchange.

'You do not even know who we are, yet you stand here and threaten us as though we are your common thugs. I am Godric of house Amity, commander of the forces of Worchester and England and beside me is John of house Archer, head of the Worchester council.' I could see that this had an impact on Wulfsige if not on the men beside him. 'If you want trouble, we can give it to you however it is not our intention to cause you any. We are heavily armed and as you would have heard, we know our way around a fight.'

With this Wulfsige changed tack and instead stuck out his hand to welcome us to Winchester. He told us we were all welcome and should follow him as he would find us different accommodation which should prove to be more peaceful. Trusting Wulfsige and this change I relaxed and began following him. We came to a second palisade wall and gate which was opened for us. Walking into a large open space this looked to be where all the civil buildings were such as the town hall, sheriff's building, barrack, stables and castle which was under construction.

Wulfsige led us to some stables for us to leave our horses. Next, we crossed to an armoury where we were told we could leave our weapons and they would be secure. From the armoury we were taken to the king's existing palace. John, Arture, Warwick and I were told we could come through and wait for the king. Wulfsige had one of his men take the rest of our guard to our accommodation.

Inside the central walls there was much less traffic and movement. It appeared there were no civilians present within the walls although we did see the odd servant scurrying around. A large number of guards and soldiers were evident which made me wonder what they were defending themselves against.

Thinking about Worchester, we only had a rostered system for the guards in the lookout towers on the roads into town from the east and north. There were no guarding duties apart from the twenty who had ridden with us on this mission. Our guard were spending their time with their families on their own business, practising weapons and on the town construction project. Worchester was still a town but was fast becoming a city. We were in the city of Winchester which was already much larger than Worchester. The cathedral is in the area of the city between the two palisade walls which is also the area where most of the people live.

Inside the palace we were told we would need to wait for the king in one of the adjoining rooms. There was something wrong as the number of men with Wulfsige had tripled and they were all heavily armed. Stopping before entering the hallway I questioned Wulfsige about his intent. Turning he told me there was no point resisting and that my men had already been arrested and were being taken to the dungeons.

Looking directly into Wulfsige's eyes I asked him if it was true, that he was arresting the designated leaders of England. I reminded him that this would be a big mistake as our lands were allies and the Vikings were our true enemies. 'We have come here in peace and of our own free will to strengthen an alliance which I believe already exists.'

He told us that there was little point resisting as we were without weapons and outnumbered. What Wulfsige said was true but he did not know our strength. I could easily disarm one of the guards and be armed within seconds. However, there were only four of us and the others might not fare as well as I would, and I did not want any on our mission to be harmed.

Nodding to John, I told Wulfsige we would do what he had requested. John must have been thinking the same as me as he knew my abilities and John was also a tough old character who would be difficult to bring down. Accepting our fate, we followed the guard to our cells.

In the prison cells we waited patiently for someone to come and sort out our meeting with the king. Initially we thought the meeting would be the following morning however this became very wishful thinking. We had been in the cells for over a week and only been fed one poor quality meal per day. My frustration and anger were great by day two so by day ten I was ready to tear down the walls. The lack of food was also feeding my temper and slowly weakening me.

I had got to know one of the servants who had been coming and dropping off the food. Although I could not see her, she always asked if we were well and told us our meals were coming through the hole at the bottom of the door. Deciding on another option I asked her if she ever saw Aethelswith around the palace and she told me she did as she sometimes waited on her. I asked her to give Aethelswith a message to tell her, 'Godric of Worcester is in the palace dungeons. You don't need to say anything else and try not to let anyone else know I gave you this message.'

It felt as though we were rotting in this damned dungeon. All four of us shared a small cell with only two palette mattresses on the ground. We had been alternating who got one of the mattresses as I insisted that John be given the other one. John was like a father to me and was the oldest in our group. Warwick and Arture were not much older than me and with our youth we were more likely to get sleep on the cold stone floor. Our cell was not much more than ten by ten feet and there was very little light. At the top right-hand corner there was a small hole about the size of a fist which allowed in the light of the day. At night there was some candlelight which sneaked under the door but unless there was a full moon at night it was usually totally dark. We had a lock up in Worchester but it was less like a dungeon as there were open areas closed in by cast iron bars which I had hand made myself. The prisoners were given dignity and if found guilty of their crimes their punishments were carried out without degradation. I much preferred how we treated prisoners than to what we were now experiencing.

A day after speaking to the servant I heard her voice at the door to our cell. 'Godric, is that you in there?' Telling Aethelswith that it was and that we were being held unfairly I asked if she could organise a meeting with her father.

She told me that we were getting tried for arson and for destroying The Retreat inn. Aethelswith told us that the captain said that we would hang for this crime. 'I will go to my father now that I know it is you. He must see you and pardon you this crime.'

I thanked her and told her there was nothing to pardon as we were not responsible for the destruction of the inn. We were attacked by the local thugs who would just not leave us alone.

Early on the following day our servant did not arrive with our meals. I asked the new servant where Ebba was, and she told us that she had disappeared. She told me that she dared not talk to me as she may face the same fate. I wanted to know more about the word disappeared but the new servant did not say another word.

Two hours later the door to our cell was opened and I was ordered from the cell and given an escort by six guards. Although I had been locked up for close to two weeks, I had kept up my exercises in the confined space and had plenty of physical memory to draw on. Although weakened I was ready to attempt overpowering my escort but I was curious as to whether Aethelswith had been able to get me an audience with her father.

I was taken into a throne room full of people including many guards, retainers and servants. In the middle of the room was an impressive throne and two minor chairs or thrones. One of these was empty while Aethelswith was sitting on the left side of the man who must be King

Alfred. Behind King Alfred stood a man who I gathered was the bishop of Winchester.

In King Alfred's presence I was told to kneel and with this I was whacked by a spear across the back of my legs. The whack forced me to drop to my knees. I pushed my hands down to force myself back up when I felt a whack across my back. Seeing Aethelswith jump to her feet and to my defence the guard backed down and enabled me to stand. I must have been a horrible sight having been imprisoned in a cell for two weeks without a wash. The smell must also have been testing for those present but judging by the way we had been treated they may have been used to the smell and worse.

The king put up his hand and all in the room became silent. I was surprised by how elderly the king looked as to my eyes he must have been in his seventies at least.

'You dare to seek an audience with your king after killing his son. You dare to come into our city fully armed with the intent to cause a civil disruption. Destroying one of our much-loved inns. Your presence in our city does not bode well and our council cannot understand why you would lead a delegation to parley with Wessex when it is your head we are after.'

Looking around the room I could see Hereweald near the front of the room and was wondering if it was my turn to speak. 'Is it my time to speak, King Alfred?' I could sense another wack was coming before the king quickly put up his hand. Alfred told me I may speak however warned me that a poison tongue would not be tolerated.

'Worchester or England, as our region is now being known, is and has always been at war with the Vikings. We have ridden to war with Mercia and Wessex on more than one occasion. We have won battles alongside the fine warriors of Wessex. The common foe of both Wessex and England is the Vikings and our delegation comes to strengthen this alliance with the aim of forcing them from our island forever. We are a farming people who would be without war. We seek a life with peace, prosperity and security. This is what we seek for all the peoples of our island. Is this something which we can discuss and plan for?'

The king then spoke again. 'Mercia is no more, and Worchester was a region of Mercia. England is now owned and ruled by Wessex and thus you have no say in the affairs of Wessex. You are a citizen of Wessex and will therefore be judged under our laws. For the death of my son, I have many witnesses who tell me you are guilty. The burning of The Retreat inn again has many witnesses. Confession will get you a merciful death however denial and you will be tortured until we get a confession. How do you plead to these crimes?'

I really felt like laughing at my situation. I was so naïve in this mission although at some point I had to try. Looking around I could see Hereweald was distraught and Aethelswith had tears in her eyes. What I said now had to really count. I was nervous but probably not as nervous as I should have been. This was life or death and I really was at their mercy.

'My lord, you are right with what you say about Mercia and Wessex. Worchester stopped being a part of Mercia the day that Æthelstan betrayed us on the battlefield. His death was welcomed by Worchester and the surrounding regions. Worchester then followed your son, Ethelred into battle and again we were betrayed. Our forces were engaged only for the Wessex forces to be pulled from the battlefield by your son.'

There were gasps from those gathered in the throne room and some shouts to kill him, to kill his lies. One guard even yelled 'blasphemy, Ethelred was a hero'.

I went on as it seemed like it may be my last chance to tell my story. 'Some years later Ethelred came to Worchester to force us to ride with his army into battle. I told him that we would not follow him into battle after the previous treachery. After he called me a coward, I challenged Ethelred to a duel and allowed him to choose his five best heroes to fight with him. I fought Ethelred and his five heroes and was able to win a fight, a fight which I considered to be fair. After Ethelred's death the army of Wessex, under Hereweald, vowed to fight alongside the guard of Worchester with me as their battle commander. We fought and won battles at Repton, Torksey and York. This campaign cemented the relationship between Winchester and Worchester. I come here as part of a peaceful delegation expecting to discuss the building of our joint forces to take the war up to our foe the Vikings.' As I spoke, I realised I had to speed up as the commotion in the room continued to grow as I told the story of Ethelred. I hoped enough in the room had heard the words I was saying.

Guards came forwards and began smashing me over the head with the flats of their swords and others with spears. Turning I was able to grab a spear and disarm the guard with his spear. I thrusted it through the arm of another guard where I then disarmed him and took his sword and shield. A dozen guards descended on me but I was able to keep them back from me and unfortunately, I had to cut a few of them down. I knew I was in the zone of passion and when in this space I was a formidable enemy. I was still trapped like a dog in a cage but had stopped worrying about my situation.

The commotion, screams and accusations being hurled toward me went on for some time before the king stood and took a couple of steps forward. He raised his hand and the room fell silent. There were guards all around me in a circle making sure I could not get to the king or get out. I believed I could get out now, however, the rest of my delegation would be doomed.

The king looked directly at Hereweald, the king's reliable old captain. 'Is what this man says true?'

Hereweald stepped forward and confirmed that everything which I had said was as he himself knew it to be. There were gasps from around the room and at that moment I felt great affection for the man who had risked his life by confirming what I said to be true. On the day of the duel Hereweald had shown himself to be true and today he confirmed his integrity and honour.

Alfred was now staring at me as though he was staring into my soul. Alfred then turned to Wulfsige and commanded him to free me and my men who were being held.

Wulfsige questioned, 'What about my men he killed?'

The king responded by telling Wulfsige that they should have done more practice.

The king then commanded that the throne room be cleared with only Wulfsige and Hereweald to remain along with the bishop, Aethelswith and his clerk. My fortunes had suddenly changed as I was now able to move freely around the room and even approach King Alfred. Alfred stepped down from the raised section which had the thrones and we crossed to a large wooden table at the back of the throne room. This area of the room was hidden behind the raised throne and must be where negotiations took place if things progress from the formal meeting.

Coming around to the table I was at last face to face with King Alfred. Although Alfred was much shorter than me and was very grey looking with white wispy hair. He was older than I had thought he would be, and must have had his children later in life. Alfred and I came together and shook hands and I apologised for having to kill his son adding that I did not think he was a good man. Alfred nodded and said that he had had his own concerns. He added that Hereweald had conveyed the events of Worchester with him although in his mind he did not wish to believe them. That Hereweald would confirm these events so publicly with an enemy of the public confirmed that what I had said was true. 'Hereweald is as good a friend of Wessex as a king could hope for and, Godric, you have now shown that you also are a friend of Wessex.

Aethelswith looked as stunning as she always had, and she now came up and embraced me with tears in her eyes. I knew she was on my side all through the hearing as she had shown her emotions through the ordeal.

I asked the king if I could have John Archer brought to us as he was the head of the Worchester council. Alfred signalled to his steward who set off to bring John to the meeting. When John arrived, I got a good look at the damage two weeks in the dungeon had done him. He looked ragged but still very stoic. Fortunately, we were invited to share some food and drink before continuing on. Following this Alfred asked me a lot of questions about the Vikings and our interactions with them. I spent the following hours with the king and his key men.

Hereweald confirmed that since the offensive on London, which was unsuccessful, they had seen very little Viking activity along the frontier. This matched with our experience and confirmed, at least in my mind, that they were building for something. The Vikings would be using the time to gather resources and armies to target either England or Wessex. An organised and thoughtful Viking army scared me, although there was little we could do about it other than prepare.

'If we pre-empt and attack them, we will deplete our forces and leave ourselves exposed to a sizeable counterattack. This might be what they want us to do as going on the offensive will slow the building of our own forces and strain our resources.' The room agreed with me, so I suggested we use the time to build our own forces. I told the king that we had developed new superior weapons which we would show his blacksmiths how to make. Hereweald confirmed that they were indeed superior, and I could see that this pleased the king and his commanders.

A plan was agreed to use the coming year to continue building our forces and supplies and we would reassess in a year where we were at and whether it was time for an offensive. Any attack between now and then would be communicated to each party so that we were all aware of the Viking activity. An agreement between England and Wessex was made with these details, with Hereweald as King Alfred's witness and John as mine.

We spent the following week in Winchester which gave us a chance to reconcile with the Winchester guard and their nobles. In their eyes we had been the enemy as we were part of Mercia and were responsible for the death of Ethelred. The real story was now out and the stories about Worchester and England were now freely being spoken about. The Worchester guard was now this mythical army which had pushed back the Vikings and was unbeatable in battle. Myths or symbolism serve a purpose and I could see this one serving ours as people would want to follow and join such as army.

It was great having the opportunity to inspect Winchester's new castle, their supplies and population. I could see that much of their wealth was going into the construction of the castle. Winchester was also full of refugees and overpopulation tends to lead to poverty, such as had happened in Worchester. Winchester was less than a day's ride from London so always under the threat of a major Viking attack. For me London needed to be in our hands and the following year we might make it so. With the Vikings pushed back these refugees could settle on their own land and contribute more to Winchester and Wessex. There was great risk settling any land between Winchester and London and thus a large area of fertile lands was being underutilised.

Most of my time was spent with the blacksmiths discussing weapons, styles and material. I was able to show them how to make a lighter yet stronger iron. The iron could be used for many purposes but particularly for light armour and swords. The most important weapon for us was the longbow and I was able to demonstrate its power once we were reunited with our weapons. I did this with a demonstration for the king and his men in the main parade square. On seeing its benefits, the king ordered, that thousands of them be made.

While practising my archery one morning I felt her presence. It was the feeling that you know you are being watched and turning I saw Aethelswith leaning on a veranda rail watching me. I was out there with half a dozen of the guards' archers shooting arrows but on seeing her I stopped and walked over to take the chance to thank her for getting us out of the dungeons.

Aethelswith smiled as I approached and wow, what a lovely smile it was. I thanked her but she turned it back on me and thanked me for opening her father's eyes. She told me he had been dying for years from a loss of hope. She said that her father knew deep down what his son had become but for the sake of the realm he had not known what to do. Events had unfolded as they had and hearing our plan had given the king his hope back. He had dreamed of a united land where we did not war with each other but lived in peace and security. The Vikings had always been the problem and clearing them from our land would be the solution. This is what her father thought, and it was the same as our thinking. Naïve or not, at least it gave us a starting point.

We talked for some time before Aethelswith invited me to breakfast with her. It was exhilarating to be conversing with someone who was so well educated in matters of state and worldly affairs. King Alfred had established the scriptorium and had monks translating the old Latin scripts into the language of the people. Aethelswith had been assisting the monks and through this process had had the privilege of reading and learning some of this knowledge. She was at her father's side as often as can be so understood the political motivations of the regional leaders and the power struggle between the commanders and the church. She told me that her father was in such a state of confusion that he had effectively been immobilised as all decisions were going to ostracise one group or another.

I told Aethelswith about how I had been able to read John's book of war and how it had helped me to explore battlefield strategies. John had taught me to read Latin however a translation of the text into the local tongue would make the work accessible to more people. However, we will still require time and techniques for teaching the people to read. This was a long-term plan which Aethelswith and I both had. It seemed we both understood that learning would lead to knowledge which in turn would drive innovation and prosperity. I had seen the benefits of innovation with our weapons and being in her position as king's daughter, Aethelswith had seen the benefits the Scriptorium had brought.

Reluctantly, I left Aethelswith as I was required at the armoury. Fortunately, I got time later that day and on a couple of further occasions we were able to share company.

Aethelswith gave me a tour of the scriptorium where I got to see some of the works which were being translated. Besides books from all around the world there was a book on the different battles from Roman Britain through to the current day which I now longed to read. A quiet conversation with the monks and the book was in my hand on loan. There was a copy of the history book John owns which covered wars and battles of the ancient world. Being in the scriptorium was a special experience and if nothing else this was an extraordinary creation by King Alfred and an amazing legacy to leave. Books are extremely rare and enormously expensive, both points only adding to the wonder of this place.

I knew that I was getting distracted and was spending much more time in Winchester than we had ever planned. John finally reminded me that the season was getting close to changing and we needed to get home to continue our work. Aethelswith had also shown John the scriptorium and like me John was in seventh heaven when within its walls. Together we spent many hours sifting through the books which had been completed. The monks were very accommodating and showed us the piles of scrolls of literature which still required copying and translating. John knew I was enjoying the opportunity to learn, and I guess he saw that I was distracted by Aethelswith as well. John was also looking much recovered after the damage from his time in the dungeons.

Leaving was difficult and it was like my heart was being stretched into two. However, it was on a fine early autumn's day that we finally rode out of Winchester. We said our farewells to King Alfred, Aethelswith, Hereweald and his other commanders before turning and leaving. The plan was to return for council in twelve months to discuss the coming offensive together. In the meantime, we were to build supplies and recruit for our armies while consolidating our defensive positions. It was agreed that the Vikings were planning something as nobody could remember there ever being this low level of raiding and activity.

Arriving back in Worchester was an amazing feeling as the difference between home and Winchester is stark. Worchester had wide roads which had been enhanced from the Roman days. The buildings were clean and well-spaced with the cathedral close to being completed. There were low levels of poverty as building had been a priority for years and we always did our best to provide shelter and opportunity for any new arrivals. Towering above Worchester and the landscape was our mighty castle which was new and always impressive to look upon. Then most importantly were the people of Worchester who looked happy and secure compared with the common people of Winchester who were cautious and insecure. It had not always been this way with Worchester but the castle and our guard had had a big impact on the lives of the English, as we were now known. Heartache was still fresh for everyone but even this was relative and at that exact moment Worchester was full of hope and the promise of peace.

There was no greeting party as our arrival time was unknown and we were not returning from a battle. I expect there were a few worried discussions at the council meetings and around the family meals. As there were no organised engagements, I suggested to John that we hold off on a council meeting until the following day and all go home to catch up with our families.

Taking this advice, I went straight out to the farm where I found a life of peace and bliss. Bledri, Gwyneth and their daughters had settled into our family and Alun was progressing quickly with his apprenticeship. Gwyneth was helping Hilda with the children while Seren was assisting Bledri and Riannon with fencing of their new farm. Leofric and Tata continued to be flat out keeping both forges running along with maintaining the three apprentices.

My role on the property was mostly as a blacksmith but like the rest of them I had a responsibility to the animals and the farm. With my role as commander of the guard and position on the town council I was also extremely busy. None of us begrudged our duties as we knew no other way. When we celebrated, we tended to make up for the hard work we had put in by going a little over the top. My arrival home did not warrant a celebration however everyone did finish up early this day and we finished off a half barrel of mead.

That night I did most of the talking conveying details on our entire trip from the fire, dungeon to the courtroom where Hereweald stood true and backed my story about the king's son. These stories were a night's entertainment and broke the monotony of life on a farm. I wished everyone good night and told them that I would tell them the details of our plans the following night after I'd had a good sleep and had a chance to meet up with the council. Story telling was so integral to our life and thus most of us had a natural gift of telling a good yarn.

Everyone was tired, and although there were some grumbles, they accepted my word and went off to bed at pretty much the same time.

The following day at the council meeting we heard how all the planning had been progressing. There was a big push to finish the roof of the cathedral before winter. Once protected from the elements all the fine ornate work inside could commence. Many of the tapestries and decorations were already underway by separate groups of men and women in the community. The guard had continued to grow and there was a call for an additional rank to captain to assist with organising everything. A rank of general was then voted in as well as an additional captain responsible for organising training. The numbers were now at approximately five thousand with the additional numbers being used to build additional granaries, roads and bridges for crossing the river.

Reports from new settlers confirmed that the roads seemed quiet and both north and east Viking raids were at an all-time low. Although welcome news the sudden change was noted as being a worry to all on the council. The Vikings were definitely up to something.

Chapter 12 — Aethelswith

That night I filled everyone in on news from the council and the plans which were discussed with King Alfred. I told everyone of the wonderful scriptorium in Winchester and some of the books I have seen and had an opportunity to look over. I produced the copy of the Battles of Britain which I had been loaned by Aethelswith, and received oohs and ahs from the family. I promised to commence teaching them how to read, explaining how reading was a part of the future.

There were doubts as Leofric claimed there was no time for reading. 'Nothing will happen if everyone decided to read. I cannot see it taking off although I can see the need for academics and recorders of history.'

Hilda enquired about Aethelswith and my time with her. She asked me if I had any interest in marrying her. I love how my sister can be so forward and ask the questions everyone else is probably thinking. Everyone was silent waiting for a reply when Hilda asked the question again. I told them all that I did have feelings for Aethelswith and that she was an amazing woman with strength and integrity with a great breadth of knowledge. In short, I told them that I thought she would make a powerful ally and wife. I thought that my honesty would quiet everyone down however it just seemed to excite them, and they nagged me as to why I was back here while she was away in Winchester. I told them that if it was meant to be it would work out although I didn't think the women liked hearing this as I received a reproach from Hilda and Gwyneth.

Eventually the nagging subsided and life on the farm and Worchester continued into the harvest season and then into winter. Before winter word was sent over into Powys that we were considering an offensive against the Vikings over the following summer. Our training academy was open to recruits with the opportunity to be trained in the use of the latest weapons. An academy training centre was set up with full arsenal and barracks for accommodation. The barracks required expanding as the numbers joining up continued right the way through winter. Our wealth was sustaining us as there was considerable cost arming and feeding the growing army. Most of our guard were now settlers and citizens of our region known as England however with close to fifteen hundred in the barracks there were a lot of meals required.

Deep into winter we were a foot deep in snow and traffic on the roads was at a standstill. Last season was a bumper harvest so with full granaries we were mostly all comfortable to hunker down for the winter. During times like this we did not travel into the town unless travel was essential. The forges continued working through all weather conditions and the forge was ideal for the freezing winter days we were currently experiencing.

It was on one such day that we received three surprise visitors. Surprise because they were not expected and surprise due to the weather conditions at the time they arrived. Standing at the door was Hilda with a smile on her face. I was covered in grime and soot and was hammering away on another sword for our guard. The grime and soot mixed with my sweat which fell off me in droplets. Sensing and then seeing Hilda, I asked her what she wanted, maybe a bit curtly but not without love.

Hilda told me that we had visitors in the house who had come to see me. Looking beyond her to the outside I could see that it was still snowing albeit gently. Hilda told me to clean up as she turned, dropping in that Aethelswith was waiting. Ouch, Aethelswith here in these conditions and with me looking like I had done ten rounds with a fire and come off second best. I took my sister's advice and went around to the bath house where I cleaned myself off with ice cold water. It wasn't pleasant but it was better than looking like I didn't care.

Inside I found Aethelswith with Hereweald and his wife, Cynefri. Although standing beside the fire they still looked frozen. On seeing each other we all embraced like old friends. They already had some mead, so I grabbed some to join them, taking a seat facing the fire. There was all the customary small talk however I wanted to know the reason for their visit. True to form I asked them directly what had brought them on such a hazardous journey given the season and the weather conditions. I did add that they were always welcome and for as long as they liked or needed.

I could see this amused Hereweald as he said to me, 'Always direct is Godric the Great,' with a smile. I tried to explain myself when he held up his hand. 'I have just made a joke of you, my friend. If I was in your position, I too would want to know why we have arrived. Purely out of interest of course.'

Aethelswith sat down across from me and told us that she had to get away from her father. She told us that her father had arranged for her to marry Æthelstan's cousin Wulfstan. 'Wulfstan is twice my age and a brute at that. I have only met Wulfstan once which is enough for him and my father. My father wants the marriage to tighten our control over Mercia. I tried to explain that marrying Wulfstan would be like handing Wessex to Mercia. Wulfstan is tarred with the same brush as his cousin Æthelstan. They are both treacherous and power hungry although Wulfstan is the only one to worry about as he is still alive. Father is hell bent on the marriage and it is set for the first week after the ending of winter. I just could not hang around while these arrangements were going on around me. Worcester and the Amity house was the only place I could think to go. Here I am a good distance from everywhere and my father will struggle to find me. I had my good friends to travel with and ensure that I remained safe.'

I told them that they were a pleasant surprise and that they were welcome for as long as they needed or liked. We spent the rest of the afternoon eating and drinking and enjoying each other's fellowship. There were usually few travellers and visitors in winter so having the visitors was really welcomed by our entire household. I told them that being forced to marry someone you did not love was unacceptable. I also quietly worried about what would become of the alliance should Wulfstan become King of Wessex.

Later when it was just Hereweald, Aethelswith and I the conversation turned more serious. I wanted to know what was being said in Winchester and particularly at the court with Alfred's nobles. Hereweald said that they agreed with the king in public however they were sceptics in private. They did not believe that Worcester was as strong as was portrayed and they believed that London should be attacked at the first thaw without the English. 'They are worried about the power shift should the English be involved in any Wessex campaigns. The nobles just do not believe that Wessex needs anyone and slowly they are poisoning the king against the English.'

The marriage was to please the nobles as they saw an alliance with Mercia as blunting any ambitions Worcester might have. It was a shame to hear these things as I was ambitious but I had been telling myself that my ambitions were for my people and my murdered loved ones. Peace and security were all I had ever sought, and life had shown me that if a person really wants something, they had better get off their backside and make sure that it happens.

The intent was for them to spend the winter in Worcester until after the date of the wedding had passed. Aethelswith told me she would be useful and not get in the way. She said that she had brought a book and could start teaching people how to read. Her eyes were sparkling as she told me this and I found that I was smiling from ear to ear. This was perfect as there were few within Worcester who could read. Hereweald followed on that he could assist with the training of the guard and he said that Cynefri was very good at tapestry work. I chimed in that they did not need to earn their keep and again that they were a welcome sight, although if they can help in the ways suggested it would be very beneficial.

That night I had trouble sleeping as I thought of Aethelswith arriving in the deep of winter. I wondered what King Alfred would make of it and if he would bother to send out a search party for her. It would be a good guess that she had come here as our joint affection, I believed to be joint, would have been obvious to everyone at his court. Trying to put my active mind at rest I kept telling myself that I could only control what I could control. However, for anyone who has ever been in a situation like mine, they know that the more one worries about their overactive mind the worse it seems to become. However, as morning broke, I realised I must have fallen asleep at some point as the last few hours seemed to have disappeared.

Life in our household became even more frantic over the coming months. Under our roof we now had Bledri and his family, the Wessex party, Hilda and her growing family, Tata and I, and Alun with Riannon.

Their house was finished but they had come back to the main house ass Riannon was further on with the pregnancy and Alun was working in the forge. We were some of the lucky ones who had good stores of all the essentials however I still hoped for a short winter.

Egbert took to Aethelswith which was another good sign. He had never known his mother but had Hilda doing the best she could as a stand in mother. Aethelswith seemed to adore Egbert and started calling him, mini Godric. He was still young and cuddly with his presence only enhancing my feelings for Aethelswith, as I watched them play together.

Aethelswith began teaching our household to read as I didn't see any reason why we should not be the first to benefit from our guests, ahead of those in the town. I could read as John had shown me how to read years ago when discussing the history book of war. I really wanted everyone to experience the beauty of being able to read.

When the weather cleared up a little, I took our three guests into town to visit the new cathedral and to introduce them all to the council. Although most of the council had already met Aethelswith and Hereweald it was just as big a surprise to them that they had arrived over winter as it had been to us. They were honoured that Aethelswith had come to Worchester and even more thrilled when she told them that she would be spending all of winter here. Hereweald offered his services and so did Cynefri. They congratulated us on our spectacular cathedral and said that they hoped to be around for the first service once the inside was completed. Once again, we found a barrel of mead and celebrated the arrival of our visitors and drank to the success of Worchester.

This winter turned out to be a long cold and bitter one which may have suited Aethelswith as it certainly did me. We grew closer living under the same roof and I so very much wanted to get intimate with her. The feelings and urges which I now had were like those I felt when in love with Sunngifu. I did not know where I stood with Aethelswith as she was the daughter of the king and had obligations to follow the wishes of her family and father. She was royalty and I a farmer come warrior. At times this was awkward however I could tell that she had feelings for me. The problem that we faced was that our house was so full of people that there was never any privacy. I needed a solution and I thought I had come up with a great idea which excited me.

Folding a blanket and some snacks into a bag I asked Aethelswith if she wanted to see our family caves. I told her it was an adventure and she needed to come ready for a hike with some warm clothing. We were to leave after lunch which would give us privacy and enough time so that we could get back by dark. Having organised this in the morning I set about my tasks with a certain spring in my step, thinking of nothing else.

After finishing lunch, I told Hilda that Aethelswith and I were heading up to the caves so I could show her where we used to play as children. Hilda smiled her all knowing smile and wished me a pleasant hike. Just as we were leaving the house Hereweald and his wife appeared and said that they were ready to come with us. I looked at them in despair, showing my feelings all over my face. Aethelswith realising my dilemma said that she had invited Hereweald and Cynefri as they were also interested in seeing our caves. Regaining my composure, I accepted their interest and chimed in that it was the more the merrier.

Despite not being the afternoon which I was planning it was a delightful afternoon and once away from the farm Aethelswith became very playful. We walked hand in hand and at times we were arm in arm just as Hereweald was with his wife. It seemed like the entire afternoon would be like two married couples out on some exercise and an adventure. I found that I liked this arrangement as much as if it was just Aethelswith and I as it felt good to be showing my affection for her to others who I cared about.

While eating our snacks Hereweald asked me if he and his wife could walk back down the hill by themselves. He said that they were also looking for some time alone as the house was so busy, they had been missing their intimate time together. Aethelswith smiled at them both and told them she understood. I told them that they just needed to follow the track to the bottom of the valley, and they would see the smoke from the forges and farm. Saying farewell to Hereweald and Cynefri I was finally alone with Aethelswith.

We spent way too long on the blanket and in each other's arms. It was only the loss of light which alerted me to the fact that it was past time to head back. Snow was falling outside the cave entrance and the temperature was really starting to drop. We had made love many times that afternoon and I knew that I wanted to marry Aethelswith. So, before leaving I dropped down onto one knee and asked Aethelswith if she would become my wife. Aethelswith looked so pleased that she said she would be honoured. We hugged, embraced some more and kissed again before I remembered that it was only minutes away from total darkness. I was not worried as I knew these hills like the back of my hand and could traverse them blindfolded. We were both in another world as we finally arrived back at the farm.

Asking Aethelswith to marry me was difficult however it was probably the easy part when thinking about it. We now had the logistics of getting her father to agree as this was important in our culture. The wedding would have to wait until spring when we would need to travel to Winchester where I would ask for King Alfred's permission. The stress of this could wait for now as we announced to everyone in the house that we were engaged to marry. Everyone was so happy for both of us and it seemed that they all knew it was going to happen and were enjoying themselves watching us keep our affections for each other to ourselves.

The people of Worchester pushed on over the long winter and although we lost many days to the snow all projects progressed well. The construction of the cathedral was finished with only the finishing touches to the inside to complete. We had four completed mills and the embankment and waterfront docks had also been completed. The benefits of communal labour and physical work on the moral of the community were evident to all. The benefit to the strength of our warriors was also obvious to all who observed our guard.

As projects were completed, we were compelled to start other significant projects. This latest project was kicked off in June and was the task of constructing a wall around Worchester which would link up with the castle. The castle was large enough for our entire community and had stores to see us through for months if required. However, now that we were building some decent civic buildings such as the cathedral, school and town hall, we wanted to protect them also as under an attack our enemies would do their best to destroy these buildings. This wall would need to be five miles long and would require thousands of tonnes of stone. The foundations had been pegged and the quarries were back to being worked as hard as was possible. This wall would take years to construct but the benefits would be significant.

Spring came around, and before I knew it the day I was dreading was in front of me. Aethelswith and I knew we needed to confront her father and neither of us was sure of the outcome. I hoped that with my allegiance and reputation Alfred would accept my proposal but I knew too well not to rely on hope.

That winter we had worked hard but we had still had the time to get to know each other and consolidate our love. Aethelswith was an ambitious woman with a sharp grasp of politics. I was aware that she was with me partly because of who I was, a young powerful leader. I would never admit this to her although I expect she would simply accept it and ask me if I would change anything. Aethelswith would marry for the benefit of her kingdom and she saw me as the best bet for Wessex and her people. Mercia, had been corrupt and inept for years, and she could not see what her father saw in a marriage to the old Mercia. Alfred's age had stopped him travelling outside of Winchester for at least the last five years. If he had travelled, he would have seen how poorly Mercia had been getting managed. Worchester and the English had a plan and it was being pushed by a committed leadership group. I was sure she loved me as I loved her but I could see her strength and determination and the loyalty she had for her people. I was lucky that I fit her requirements and very grateful that I did.

On a mild almost summery day we left the farm for Winchester. Hereweald and Cynefri were still Aethelswith's chaperones so travelled with us while John, Dunstan, Leofric and a guard of twenty also came along as we needed to get intelligence and plan our summer attacks if any. It was nice to see the countryside again after all the snow we had experienced. There were many travellers out on the roads, so it looked like others were thinking the same. There had been no news of raids to the north or out to the east so still I was thinking that the Vikings were planning something big.

We stopped at Marlborough as on my previous trip. That night Aethelswith and I took a room while John and Leofric also got a room in the same inn. We ate together beside a comfortable fire. That night back in the room Aethelswith told me that she was expecting a child. To my ears this was wonderful news as I loved children and the thought of having one with this beautiful woman was very pleasing. Egbert needed a sibling and who better to have one with then the future queen of the kingdom. We were up later than I would have liked but we had to celebrate the great occasion.

The following morning, I told John and Leofric and they agreed that it was best to keep it quiet until we knew what Alfred's response was going to be. John said to me that from his experience kings liked getting their own way. Leofric suggested that maybe I needed to deliver the king a great victory. I told them that I had been thinking the same however I did not want to risk our long-term plans seeking a personal benefit.

Chapter 13 — Conquest, Treaties and Betrayals

Arriving in Winchester we could already see the benefits of confidence. Since our visit and the uniting of our peoples the stories of Worchester and the English were now freely told. Stories like those will boost the morale of the people. There were also the weapons innovations within the army and talk from the soldiers can also do a lot for boosting the people.

The castle and building programmes had progressed over winter much as our building campaign had in Worchester. Our arrival was different this time as we are returning people of note and I noticed people bow and curtsey as they scurried out of our way. Aethelswith took us directly to the king's palace and I took a deep breath and said a little prayer that it all went well.

The guards greeted us as we entered the building. I kept alert trying to notice if there was a hint of trouble. John and Leofric walked in with us which gave me some reassurance as they were like family to me. Hereweald escorted Aethelswith all the way back to her father. The chaperoning was a show but all important to the people inside and outside of the palace.

Inside the palace throne room King Alfred met with us. Aethelswith left us and went up to her father and gave him a warm embrace and kiss on the cheek. Holding his hands, she told him that she was well and that she had spent the winter in Worchester. She apologised for running away however she refused to marry Wulfstan of Mercia as she did not believe it was the most beneficial match for Wessex and their people.

The King waved away her talk of marriage and told her that he would discuss it with her later. He said that he was pleased that she was back and welcomed his friends from Worchester. We told him that we were interested to discuss the progress they had made over winter and to share intelligence on our common enemy. King Alfred waved us all away and said that treaties and war could wait until later. 'Make yourselves comfortable and wait until you are called for.'

I attempted to press the king however he was already up, and the bishop jumped in front of me and said that the king had spoken.

Feeling jaded I looked at Aethelswith and she looked perplexed. She put her arms out on either side of her body and made a sad face. This was a face which lightened my mood and almost made me smile. We said farewell to her and left the palace to find some accommodation. Dunstan had found us an upmarket inn inside the inner palisade wall. The class of people at The Castle was much higher than at The Retreat where we had stayed and nearly got killed last time. We headed to the bar as we were all in need of refreshments. John and Leofric also thought the king's actions were worrying as we were not just street merchants attempting to sell the king some wares. He was an old man and was probably just befuddled seeing his daughter again. 'I don't trust him as there is something I didn't like about the meeting. Keep your wits about you and get a message to the men to do the same.'

While in at our table discussing the day's events, I overheard some nobles on a table behind us discussing the Vikings. 'Aren't they giants and so ugly! I would not want to have to fight them. What do you suppose they are here for? Don't know, maybe some kind of truce.' As soon as we heard that they were talking about Vikings we had all stopped talking and were concentrating on listening. This did not bode well with our dismissal and now news that there had been or was a Viking delegation.

I got up from our table and stepped around to the table behind us. Introducing myself I asked them what they knew of the Viking delegation. They had heard of me and seemed eager to please. They told me that there were twelve of them who arrived in the last seven days. They believed the leader went by the name Halfdan. They were all large men like me, or so they said. This could have been a shot at flattery although I know I am a big man and I know just how fearsome the Vikings are. Thanking them I returned back to our table. The Vikings were now a major concern of ours.

'We could ask the king directly as he would have to bring us in on any discussions if he knew we knew,' said John.

I did not know as the way we were dismissed indicated that he was giving whatever was being discussed some serious consideration. Along with the message to be on our toes I thought it best that we stay armed and ready to flee at a moment's notice. We were all warriors, and did we fear war with Wessex, but if we had stopped and thought about it then we should have feared it. Most of Mercia was now friendly to Worcester and the English and I knew Powys had our back, but a combined Wessex and Viking enemy could be our end.

It was time to get outside even as it was just on dark. I needed some fresh air and to have a look around. The four of us left the inn and decided to wander the streets for a bit. We saw many faces who we had worked with on our last visit. It seemed that they were all aware of the Viking host who was staying inside the palace. Most of the people we spoke to were concerned about the Viking visit and what the outcome would be.

Wulfsige approached us and wanted to give us some intelligence. Wulfsige was the captain of the Winchester guard. After telling him our news from the north he told us about the Viking host staying in the palace. He also told us that Halfdan had five thousand men an hour's ride from Winchester. I asked Wulfsige how many men they had built up in their guard and he told me he had eight thousand who were training regularly and another two thousand he could call on. We thanked him and told him that the English were no friends of the Vikings and anyone who wanted to fight them would always be welcome.

We left Wulfsige and after some consideration, which always comes with a walk, I thought that it was best to warn Aethelswith. At the doors to the palace our entry was barred. I asked on whose orders and he told me the king's orders. 'Are you able to get a message to Aethelswith?' However, the guard declined. So, I sat outside the palace in the dark to consider my options. I really needed to talk to King Alfred and as importantly I wanted to be with Aethelswith. Waiting was not good for us and things were not looking favourable as I had lost any trust I had of King Alfred and our agreement.

On the other side of the square, I saw Ebba walking with a basket of material, linen or something. I hurried over to her and gave her a bit of a fright. I told her it was me, Godric, and not to be alarmed. I asked if she had seen Aethelswith and if she knew where she was. She nodded to both of my questions so I asked if she could get her a message. 'Please tell her to remember the caves and that I will be back, and she knows where to find me.' Ebba enquired if that was all so I nodded and gave her some coppers. Looking into her hand she thanked me and scurried on. An idea had formed in my head and we needed to act now.

Walking up to the others I told them of my plan. 'We are leaving now and going back to Worchester. Leofric, please go and get the guard out of the tavern and organise to have the horses ready. We will walk them out so as not to create a commotion. I will tell you more on the road, however, suffice to say I am not comfortable being here now and I long for the open road and fresh air.' They all agreed, and we split up to get our things and leave.

It was still the early evening when we walked our horses from the city of Winchester. Out on the road we took the horses up to a trot. I apologised to the guard for ruining their night but they understood. I told them that we may have been trapped if Wessex had turned on us. 'We have intelligence that a Viking delegation was staying in the palace. The actions of some of their guard and the thinking indicates the truth of the intelligence. It will be safer to see what pans out from this meeting from the safe distance of Worchester.' The guard agreed and seemed pleased to at least have had a meal and a drink.

That night we headed back to Marlborough. The inn keeper was surprised to see us again so soon but was happy for the customers and the money. It was now late, and they had been woken up to serve us. They managed to squeeze the rest of the guard into rooms and the common room downstairs. At least those in the common room had the remnants of a fire even if they did not have beds. They all looked grateful and bunked down as John, Leofric, Dunstan and I went upstairs to the room we would share.

In the privacy of the room, I told them that we would attack and take London. We needed to send a warning to King Alfred that he was better dealing with us than with the Vikings. 'I am thinking he is feeling safer dealing with Halfdan and even a little threatened with five thousand Vikings not far from his capital city. With Halfdan and his army away from London it should be vulnerable. John and I will take ten of the guard and ride for Northampton. There we will prepare Evan and have siege towers on the road to London. Leofric and Dunstan, you two take the rest of the guard and ride hard for home. Tell the council what you know from Winchester. Do not tell them anything which we do not know for sure. Only tell them that the Vikings are away from London and now is our opportunity to attack. Have the army on the road the day after tomorrow and we shall meet up in Northampton.'

We sat up discussing plans and I could see the excitement in their eyes. It had been a while since the last campaign of the previous summer when we took back Northampton from the Vikings. It was now time to take back London which would be a key strategic city in the battle against the Vikings.

The next couple of days moved along as planned. John and I were with the Northampton guard and had the siege engines on the road from Northampton to London. We had sent out riders to watch all the roads into London and had riders sent to watch London to see if my assumptions were true.

As we waited the English guard started arriving and wow, they looked great. Five thousand highly trained and skilled warriors. They were all hardened from committed physical work and heavily armed with what I believed to be the most advanced weapons. The horses were powerful and strong, well-bred and cared for. Greeting Leofric and the captains we filled them in on the intelligence which we had received. The castle at London was indeed vulnerable and more significantly most of the city was only surrounded by two large palisade walls. 'The city is ours if we want it. Once we have the city, we can set about bringing down the castle. There are a hundred Viking boats along the Themes River which will need to be destroyed as these are weapons of war which can be used against us.'

Leofric and the captains were thrilled with the intelligence and went back to share it with their men. I went back with them as I could see the fires were going and knew that the mead would soon be getting passed around. The mead was to be for nerves, and I trusted that the men would not go too hard on it as tomorrow we could have a battle. I was thirsty and ready for some friendly homely company.

The following day we marched on London. I was still in two minds as I was considering attacking Halfdan and his men. while they were in the field and away from home. With six thousand men we should outnumber them, and I was confident that all the training would see us come out as victors. We may not get a better chance at Halfdan and a victory against him would then give us extra time to take London. I did not know London or the other Viking settlements so I was unsure how many men he might have in reserve.

What was stopping me from an attack on Halfdan was the knowledge that the Vikings were in discussions with King Alfred of Wessex. I was not aware of these discussions and at what level they were. Should there be some agreement between Wessex and Vikings an attack on the Vikings could be an attack on Wessex. I thought this unlikely but I was not to know. I had to trust that Alfred would not do anything stupid and trust in the alliance which we discussed last year. It was this lack of trust on my side that put London in my sights instead of Halfdan. I had been betrayed twice before and one of those times was King Alfred's son. It was time to wait and see and to use the time to strike a blow into the heart of the Vikings.

Coming upon London we could see that this was a large settlement as the land was all cultivated and there were many travellers and merchants going about their business. We stuck to the roads and did not attempt to hide. The men had instructions to be courteous to all passers-by and to assist anyone who looked like they needed assistance. I reminded the men that the people here were mostly our people and would be again soon.

From the smiles and bobs and curtseys I expected that we were a welcome sight to these people. Either the people were placating us out of fear or they had heard stories of our exploits from travellers. London itself had an impressive palisade wall with sections constructed of stone. Most of these stone sections appeared to be much older and I suspected they were constructed by the Romans. To the north of the city there was an impressive castle which looked like it would be difficult to pry open. Our goal today was to take the city and look for a way to crack the egg, with the egg being the castle.

Our archers would be the key to breaching the walls as they would provide the essential cover so that our infantry could set about forcing a way through the walls. There were many options, two of the most likely being to either go through by battering ram or with ropes and horses tearing a section down. We also had many ladders so if those other two methods failed, we would use a full attack and as many ladders as we could get onto the walls.

The main attack will be in the morning. Until then we would set up defensive positions and lookouts. It was possible that word could have got through to Halfdan even though I thought that I had all roads from London blocked. The lookouts were a precaution as I was also unaware of any other armies in the area. It had taken years for us to build the fighting force which we had, and I was not going to throw it away lightly. I knew most of these men and their wellbeing was my responsibility as their commander. Every life was precious, so we had fostered an environment in our community where we looked out for each other. With these values we had never struggled getting people interested in joining our guard.

The garrison in London was not going to get off lightly as I had set teams of archers to watch the walls and to pick off as many men as they could. Our longbows were superior to the Viking bow and could hit targets at an additional seventy yards distance. This advantage would leave the garrison guards on the turrets and at the walls vulnerable to our arrows. We had brought plenty of supplies as I expected we would be in London for some time securing the region.

Firing the boats would be the other target of this evening's entertainment. I wanted all hope of escape taken from the garrison and I do not want these unguarded Viking boats to be used against us in the future. Dunstan took a group of men to accomplish this task. Seeing their boats on fire should put the fear into the Vikings inside London. I was hoping they struggled to sleep and would be sitting ducks come the morning.

Dawn was hitting us earlier and earlier due to the changing season. Like the well-trained warriors and farmers we were, we were up and ready for action prior to daybreak. I had a good feeling about the coming battle as it felt as though we had had a heap of time to plan the attack. There had been no warnings of a trap or another army coming our way, so I gave the instruction for the men to prepare to get through the walls protecting London. The walls would take some resources but I was pleased that they are the best palisade walls I had seen as I knew that I would need them for defence of the city at some point in the future.

The archers, who had taken shifts shooting down the city garrison, seemed to have done their job as there were no defenders to be seen on the turrets or walls. The boats were a pile of smouldering timber and had made a distant spectacle over the night as they had burnt and sunk.

First the walls were breached with ladders as Aethelweard recommended that the horses would struggle to dislodge these wooden walls as they were weaved together and buried deeply into the earth. Aethelweard and a guard took me to the foot of the walls to see what the issues would be. We were safe under the cover of our archers and none in the garrison were game to pop their heads over the walls. A full charge was ordered for the walls on both sides of the central turrets and main gate. Archers had control of the airspace, so the infantry was sent over the wall to establish a safe zone to get more warriors into the city. We could hear the fighting on the other side of the walls and in maybe six or seven minutes our men had managed to open the main gate. It was now our turn to charge the castle as I led thousands of men into London.

As expected, the leaders and important people of London had closed the gates to the castle and were now locked into their own prison. We had time to weasel a way in or to sit out their surrender. Winter was not that long back so I was sure they would be getting low on supplies. Unless they had prepared as we had, most cities and towns only had capacity to feed their people for one season. Two bad seasons in a row usually spelt disaster with starvation.

It took two hours to hunt down the rest of the Viking guard and kill those wishing to fight and make prisoners of the others. I estimated that they had close to fifteen hundred men inside London and once we were finished, we were left with close to two hundred prisoners. The city was also full of citizens who had not fled or were not allowed to flee. I wanted to treat these people well as I wanted them to see us as the better leaders when compared with the Vikings. As always there were administrative tasks which we were required to complete to ensure the defences of the city were maintained and that the resources of the city were not looted or wasted. We posted new lookouts on all the approach roads and opened our gates to the surrounding farmers and merchants. The prisoners were housed in a central gaol which looked fit for purpose with the correct capacity.

Once the defences were established, we allowed the rest of the men to stand down. Leofric brought two men over to where John, Deorwine and I were sitting. The two men could speak some English and introduced themselves as Aage and Amund. Aage was the chief steward of London and Amund his assistant. Although with strong foreign sounding accents both men claimed to have been born in East Anglia and to be natives of the land.

I could see this would be another problem as many of the people in the Viking lands would have been born in this land and it would feel wrong forcing them into the sea and off our island, their island. I told the men that we may have a problem and asked them if they could exist under an Anglo-Saxon ruler? Both men said that they could as they were administrators and only wanted security and prosperity. They noted that they were aware of how prosperous Worchester had become under the English. John asked them about their supply of food and mead and about the provisions up in the castle. Amund noted that there was a well-stocked cool room full of mead barrels. He told us that there were only minimal stores of food items in the castle and that there were no more than two hundred guards and thirty nobles inside the walls. He informed us that the lord of the castle was Bjorn, and he was in there with his wife, Brit and youngest son, Gunne. Their other two sons were in the army with Halfdan.

This intelligence was welcomed and both Aage and Amund were offered a place at our table as we celebrated the victory with some steak washed down with mead. Over the coming days both men would turn out to be true to their word and both offered us enormous value in information about Viking society, key barracks and towns.

Aage told us that King Knut was ruler of the Viking lands. Halfdan and Eric were his two main commanders with Eric being one of Knut's sons. Apart from London, Tretford and Colchester were the two key settlements in the south while Lincoln, York and Bamborough were the strongholds of the north. We told them we had been in York which was something they told us they knew. It seemed that they had some privileged information.

King Knut was based at Bamborough as he liked the ease with which he could come and go across the sea to their homeland. Bamborough also had a mighty castle and walls which made the castle easy to defend. Both agreed that taking London would be a big blow to Halfdan as he had been using it as his castle when not on campaign or back at Colchester. Eric was based in Lincoln with good rivers to the sea. Eric was over six foot and a ruthless fighter. He liked to give the Picts grief but had been known to fight in the south as he assisted in the taking of Repton and Torksey.

The following days were a waiting game as we were not sure what the counter move would be. We had left the gates open and welcomed travellers and merchants alike. I liked to use travellers as a way of gathering news of who else was on the roads. We had experienced minimal losses in the taking of London with just under three hundred dead. Although we mourned their loss the rest of us knew that it could have been much worse.

Discussing options with John, Leofric and Dunstan, it was agreed that we would rather meet Halfdan in the field, although leaving London meant we would have to split our force to ensure that it was defended and not easily lost. Given the superiority of our archers it was decided to leave half of our archers and half of the infantry behind. This would leave a garrison of two thousand men to defend London. We would have roughly one thousand archers, one thousand infantry and two thousand horsemen in our force. Cavalry fought with both the bow and the sword. Scouts were sent out with every effort made to locate Halfdan. Riders had also been sent to Northampton and Worcester to tell them of our victory and to warn them to be on the lookout for Halfdan and his five thousand men.

All the scouts returned without a positive sighting. Given that they were not in the immediate vicinity we decided it was best we rode to where we last knew them to be. It was a full day's march to the fields to the south east of Winchester. On arrival we could see that a large group had only recently left, and it looked as though they had headed east. I could see that we were at risk of being outflanked so gave the order to turn around and head back to London. London was a prize and I did not want to lose it so soon after its capture.

Our garrison of two-thousand men would be vulnerable, especially without the castle and as such, an enemy within its outer walls. We needed to get back to defend London. Taking the Vikings east appeared to be a strategy of Halfdan's; to lure us away from London. If we took the bait and went on a wild goose chase the Vikings would find taking London back much easier. Halfdan seemed to know us and knew that we would come for him to take him in the field. We already knew Halfdan to be cunning, yet it appeared we had fallen into his trap for a second time. Thus, we raced back to London to reinforce our garrison there.

Back in London we made defensive plans for an imminent attack. We also discussed options for the castle and whether it was worth losing men trying to capture it. The decision was made to forget the castle but to keep an exclusion zone around it so that we did not lose men to sniping. From there we waited for an attack. We had lookouts on all the access road to London and yet still we waited with no news. The time was used wisely as it gave us a chance to reinforce the walls and to build catapults and other weapons. The catapults were initially to be used as a defensive weapon however as time went on it looked as though they would be used as an attacking weapon on the castle.

Weeks passed and the season slipped over into summer. Still we waited, for want of another decision. It was then that we received intelligence from a traveller that Halfdan and his men had crossed the Thames River downstream at Gravesend. They had hundreds of boats there to ferry them across the river.

At least we knew what direction the attack was likely to come from. Colchester was Halfdan's capital and I was sure he would want London back as strategically it was a real prize. London had excellent sea access, was defendable and was a day's ride to most areas of Wessex. We needed to know what was discussed with Alfred and I really wanted to meet up with Aethelswith again as she was carrying our child and we were engaged to marry. It was time to talk to Alfred, so I set off with John and twenty guard for Winchester. It would take less than a day on horseback, so we could see the king when we arrived. However, I thought it best we freshen up for the evening and evaluate what kind of reception we were likely to receive.

We booked into The Castle Inn and managed to get ourselves a table to ourselves as we had the last time we were there. The meals were good then and just as good now. After the meal John and I decided to look around and see if we could see anyone whom we knew.

Fortune was following us as we saw Wulfsige walking in our direction with a couple of men. Yelling him our greeting he noticed us and came over to greet us. We exchanged pleasantries about day-to-day concerns before he told us to be careful as the king was furious with us. I guessed he could see that we were confused as to why the king would be furious with us for Wulfsige then offered us an explanation.

'The King has signed a peace pact with Halfdan. There will be no more wars and a hard boundary will be drawn up between Wessex and the Viking lands. The Vikings will be given the eastern region of Kent and be allowed to keep the land east of the line from London to Leicester and west across to Repton. In return the Vikings will no longer raid or plunder Wessex towns. The clincher is that Halfdan agreed to adopt Christianity if King Alfred agreed to the truce.'

Wulfsige said that the ink had just set on the agreement when word came through that the English had taken London. 'We were in the throne room and we could see how embarrassed the king was although Halfdan brushed it off and said that he would deal with the English.'

I needed to hear how Aethelswith was, so I asked Wulfsige if he had seen her and if she was well. He said that he had not seen her around so did not know of her wellbeing. Wulfsige also noted that half of the army which they were building had been discharged and sent back to their properties. I thanked Wulfsige for his chat and advised that he try to keep the discharged men ready for war. 'Tell them to keep up their practice and to keep ready. I believe this to be a trap as Halfdan is cunning and the meeting with King Alfred was Halfdan's idea.'

There was nothing much more we could do that night and John and I wondered if it was worth the risk of even speaking with the king. We agreed to sleep on it and make the decision in the morning.

I slept well that night which was testament to how comfortable the bed was. Over breakfast John and I discussed our options. I suggested that maybe he should wait at the inn with the guard and should I not appear at least he could tell the others what had happened and about the agreement with Halfdan. What could he have meant by saying he would deal with the English? And yet he had slipped past us and left us with London. I would go in with Archer and if we did not come back out by nightfall then they were to slip out of the city. 'It might be worth changing inns and moving to an inn outside the walls. The gates will still be open, and I will make my way to The Red Pheasant.' This was an inn we had both noted on the way in. This way we were less likely to all be trapped in Winchester.

John suggested we could just as easily all leave back to London; however, we both knew that this was not an option. If the king was furious now, he would want my head if he found out we were here but had fled back to our army. I also needed to see Aethelswith as I really missed her and again had that teenage feeling of love. I wanted the king's blessing to marry her which meant I needed to forge a relationship with the king, as old and grumpy as he was.

After breakfast we put the plan into place. John and the others moved inns while Archer and I went to get an audience with the king. The last time I tried to get into the palace my entry was blocked. This time we had more luck and were led into the throne room and asked to wait. We stood there for half an hour which was an average time to be made to wait. The wait ended when a dozen guards came out of the doors on each side of the room behind the throne. That was a dozen from each door so twenty-four guards in all. Following the guards were the King, Hereweald, Wulfsige and Bishop Giles. Hereweald and Wulfsige both seemed to give me a look to be cautious while the bishop looked completely smug. I could not understand his look but then again, I was probably going to find out.

Archer and I both bowed as the king stood in front of his throne. We stayed in a bowed position waiting for the king to release us. The wait was far too long but eventually he told us to rise. I waited for the king to address us as we were in his throne room. The king sat and sized us up for a while before mentioning that he had heard we had taken London. 'We did, my King, and a great victory it was.' I wanted to say more but was cut off by the king.

'You put me in an embarrassing position as I was securing the safety of our lands and people and here you were making war on them. Halfdan has signed a treaty and we have set borders and before the ink was dry my subjects were breaking that treaty.' The king's voice had risen as he had continued to speak, and he was a little red in the face. I could see the situation from his side and understood why he had been embarrassed and was now upset with us.

I was given the chance to respond or at least I thought that I had been given that opportunity. 'We saw an opportunity and we took it. The last time we spoke we both spoke about clearing our island of Vikings.'

'Silence,' the king boomed at me. 'I did not give you permission to speak.' He had an amazingly loud voice for someone who was so old. 'You are my subjects and yet you go to war without my permission. It is treason to lead my army into battle without the blessing or approval of its king.' His voice was raising again along with his temper. Looking around the room the king asked Bishop Giles if what I had done was treason?

With that same smug look on his face the bishop eagerly agreed that it was treason and subjects who acted against their king and kingdom needed to be weeded out. I did not know If I was going to get another chance to speak. I was also getting a little alarmed as my weapons were on a bench outside the palace as we were told no weapons in the throne room. No one had obviously told the guard that rule as they were all heavily armed.

The king did surprise me and offered for me to have my say. He asked me if I thought my act had been an act of treason. 'We took London in your honour, my king, as we thought it would please you. At the time we thought that the Vikings were your enemy just as they are ours. The guard of Worchester is independent of Wessex and has not taken orders from Wessex since it was betrayed by Ethelred. I am commander of the guard and the guard will answer to me or the head of the council. Worchester is loyal to the king of Wessex and it hurts me for you to suggest that we are not. I am also surprised that you have struck a deal with someone who is a warmonger who cannot be trusted. We bow to your superior judgement and will of course follow your wishes until such time as the Vikings break this treaty.' I felt like I had probably said too much as I glanced at Hereweald and he looked completely alarmed.

'How dare you insinuate that Wessex is or was without honour and to my face. You will be punished for treason and your men will be disbanded. Worcester does no longer need a guard and as a sign of good faith your men will walk away from London and leave it to the Vikings.' Alfred was sending Archer with a message to take to our people. Archer also looked shocked however he did not dare open his mouth to protest.

I considered trying my luck against the guards as although they are many, I knew with a little help from either Hereweald or Wulfsige I could best them. That would not end my problems as I thought I knew that I would not get far as I was in the heart of the wasp's nest and would not find a way out. It would also surely doom Archer.

Since my fate was already set, I was not going to sit quietly and take it. 'I came to you and offered you our services to assist you against the Vikings. This is a massive betrayal, the second by your family against the free peoples of this land.' Guards were coming for me as I continued to tell the king what I thought. 'Halfdan will betray you as he is as cunning as a fox.' The whacking of my back, legs and body with their spears had commenced. 'Halfdan wants the whole island and is building for an all-out attack. Everything has been quiet for more than a year which means he is up to something.' I could not go on with my outrage as I had been knocked to a near unconscious state. The king ordered Archer to take his message to London and he ordered me to the dungeons.

I was heaved to my feet and shoved along in front of the guards. Once again, I was off to the palace dungeons although this time in a more dire situation. I was sore and had a death sentence hanging over me. The guards added to my misery, kicking and punching me until I all but blacked out. Lying there in the foetal position I was not considering my death but rather the welfare of Aethelswith. I was wondering where she had been taken as I was sure she was no longer in Winchester.

I must have lain of the floor for close to a day before I felt able to get to my feet. Food was coming through the service door at the base of the cell door which would help me with my strength. I steeled myself to be ready for whatever opportunity came my way. I needed to get out of Winchester and continue our preparations for the Viking wars which were sure to come, whether Alfred believed it or not. He was an old man who was being fooled by a dream of peace. I needed to warn our allies that Wessex was no longer friendly to our cause or at least not for now.

It must have been two weeks since I was put into the dungeon cell. I thought that Alfred would be in a hurry to execute me although I was not complaining as the time in the cell gave me time to recover and plan. The door was opened on this night and before me stood Wulfsige. Wulfsige asked if I could walk and when he saw me stand, he urged me to follow him. I followed him out through a series of tunnels which seemed to stretch on for at least a mile. We surfaced into a locked room which I found out was outside the inner walls of the city. In this room were Hereweald and Leofric. Seeing them I was overcome with emotion so I embraced them both warmly. They told me that we needed to move quickly to get out of the city before my absence was discovered and before daybreak.

Following them out of the building they took us through a series of buildings which ended up outside the city. Once outside we travelled a short distance where there were horses tied up and waiting for us. With the horses was Dunstan and to my delight my weapons, swords and longbow. I felt like I was back and in control with my weapons and friends. I still had some weakness and aches from the two weeks in prison and the injuries while being put there however with weapons I always felt a foot taller and wider.

Thanking them, I told them what I was thinking and gave them some requests. I asked Wulfsige if he could go to London and make sure it was secure. Wulfsige said that most of the disbanded units were loyal to Hereweald and Worcester and would join us if we requested it. I agreed and said that once the men arrived at London the units from Northampton and Worcester could return home for a break. I tasked Wulfsige to continue building the army and continue building the defensive lines, particularly on the road from Colchester.

I then tasked Hereweald with what was the more important task in my eyes. 'Hereweald, can you please return to Winchester and do whatever it takes to find out where Aethelswith has been taken? It is a dangerous task as you will risk being discovered and then accused of treason by Alfred. If your loyalty is discovered do whatever you can to get word to us and we will do what we can to free you. Once you know where Aethelswith is please go there and rescue her and the child, if it has been born by then. You will be a loss to our guard and army but this mission is dear to my heart and the future of England.'

Hereweald did not hesitate in accepting my request and we embraced before he headed off back into Winchester. Hereweald made me a request also. He wished for us to take his wife, Cynefri, back to Worchester. I told him it would be an honour. His was a dangerous mission and I really hoped that I would see my old friend again.

We waited an hour before Cynefri arrived at our hideout. Leofric, Cynefri and I left Wulfsige and headed back to Worchester. I longed to be home with family and to see that all was well. I was grateful that Leofric had come to see me home safe and cherished his lifelong friendship. Leofric and I were close before but since the loss of Egbert we had grown closer every year. We now worked the same forge and were responsible for delivering the innovations and advanced weapons which are separating us from our enemies. Leofric and I were family and as close as friends could be. Riding home he told me how worried he and his father had been. Looking into his eyes I could see how genuine this concern had been.

Chapter 14 — Union

We arrived back in Worchester without trouble which was testament to the work the guard had done cleaning up the main roads. I knew the safe roads were being helped by the absence of the Vikings as would be expected. The absence of the Vikings was odd in my mind, even if Wessex could not see it. The sky rained on us most of the way home but the weather was mild. We knew the rain brought life and we were raised to always be thankful for the rain when it came. The rain mixed with the summer warmth would be helping our farmers toward another bumper season, or so I hoped.

In Worchester we were greeted by John and Leofflaed. It felt like a long time since I had seen her and realised that it had been months. I was greeted with great warmth and could see that there was relief I was home. We stayed around for the remainder of the afternoon and discussed tactics.

We would continue building the guard for the imminent war which I believed was coming. John and Leofric agreed with me that the Vikings could not be trusted and were planning something big. The suspense of waiting was extremely annoying however we were grateful for the opportunity to prepare. The projects would continue at full speed including the work on the exterior wall around Worchester and the stockpiles of our resources including stone and food. Leofric and I also needed to get back to the forges to deal with the demands our guard had for weapons. Everything would be helped once the guard were able to return from London.

Arriving out on the farm I was overjoyed to see that Hilda had given birth to their child whom they had called Godiva after our late mother. Leofric was thrilled to be a father again, as was evident by his love for his older children and his immediate demand to hold his new daughter.

She was a little beauty and at four weeks old we could already see the fire in her belly.

Then there was my little Egbert. He came running up to me shouting, 'Papa! Papa!' Wow, my son had grown and was looking alive and full of energy. I picked him up and threw him up into the sky, catching him under the arms. My Egbert chuckled with laughter as I repeated this several times. He was much heavier than the last time I did this, and I could see toss ups as a good exercise for building strength.

It was great seeing everyone else who now called the farm home. There was Hilda and Tata and then there was Bledri and his family who had similar values to ours and had fitted in as if they were of the same blood. Riannon looked like she would have her baby any day as she looked extremely uncomfortable and was carrying a massive belly. Alun was fussing over Riannon, which made sense given her state, however he was supposed to be learning the blacksmith trade which I was hoping would be keeping him busy. Tata did say that there had been some trouble as Alun had been neglecting some of his duties which had put pressure on the others at the forge. I made note to discuss this with Alun in the coming days.

While discussing general farm issues with Tata he told me that he was in love with Seren and that she was now carrying his child. He wanted my permission to marry her as I was the head of our household. I asked him if he had spoken to Bledri and if Bledri had given his blessing. Tata nodded and told me that Bledri was thrilled and said that should Godric agree then he would support the union. I smiled and pulled my little brother in close to me. He was so dear to me and had grown into a strong man only slightly smaller than me in stature. I had become a father like figure to him since the death of our father when he was only six. Hugging him I told him he was special and if this was what he wished for then I would give him my blessing. He cried on my shoulder and I could feel a lot of pent-up emotion. I did also tell him he was now a man so he did not need to ask my permission. It would be nice if he asked me if I supported Seren and he getting married which of course I did.

I dealt with Alun and his neglect as a blacksmith apprentice with some direct but understanding discussion. His baby was due but the women would look after Riannon and call him when needed. 'When

Leofric and I are away all hands are needed to do extra to cover.' I think he understood as he certainly told me he did and looked to be suitably chastised. I also suggested that it was time he joined the guard and commenced splitting the time between the forge, guard and family.

Alun and Riannon's boy came three days later. I thought Alun would find it much harder work looking after a newborn than when the baby was in the belly. He now had sleepless nights and entertaining the baby to balance along with a full-time workload. Hard work but very rewarding, as I have been told. Their baby was named Wynnstan. Wynnstan was overdue and looked healthy enough. Apparently, it was a tough birth and Riannon bled a lot during the birth and in the days afterwards. I knew Hilda and Gwyneth were both extremely worried and were spending day and night with her in turns. Hilda had taken to feeding Wynnstan as Riannon was too week. What started as a joyous occasion was now starting to scare everyone on the farm.

Feeling a little guilty for the hard time I had given Alun, I sent him away from the forge to care for his child and Riannon. With Leofric and I back we could power the forge and start knocking off some of the orders. Tata had been swamped with the workload but had been doing his best to prioritise and keep the list down.

Unfortunately, Riannon did not recover and died two days later, too weak to go on fighting the blood loss. Riannon was tough but kind and would have been a wonderful mother. This was devastating for us and our first loss for a few years. Riannon was buried on our family plot with a service presided over by Father Frank. Gwyneth would now take charge of looking after baby Wynnstan with Hilda helping with keeping him fed. Alun was given additional time to mourn but insisted on returning to work as it seemed he just wanted to keep himself busy.

A week later the guard returned from London to great celebration in the community. They were a returning victorious army and were rightly recognised for this achievement. Meeting them in Worchester we ordered the mead barrels to be opened and the meat to be spit roasted. We were into autumn and already the weather was changing to the cool side. Bonfires were started as the returned guard gathered around the square for a meal and celebratory drink. It was good to see some old friends again and I could see they were pleased to see that I was well. They would have heard of my arrest and escape but until you see someone is safe, there can be lingering doubt.

Aethelweard and Deorwine gave me an update from London and said that six thousand men from the Winchester forces had followed Wulfsige back to London in loyalty to the English. 'They remember the battles against the Vikings and Ethelred's betrayal. They say that they will honour their vow to fight for Godric, a leader they can be proud to follow and rely on.'

This news pleased me, and I could see the benefits of living with honour. Being true to ourselves would either reward or cost us at some point in our lives. By not allowing Ethelred to bully us Worchester had earnt the respect of that Wessex army. They now had London to defend and I was sure they would do a great job.

The new country of England was now roughly the size of the old Mercia and we had a formidable force. With the discharged men from Wessex, we could now put over ten-thousand men into the field. With the potential for enemies on both sides of us, this at least gave me some sense of security.

Tata and Seren had agreed to get married the day before Samhain day. We have sent an invite to King David of Powys and his family. I was looking forward to seeing him and his sons, Cadfael and Emrick, again as it had now been years since we had last seen them in Worchester. Samhain day was the day we remembered all of those who had died, and we celebrated the renewal of life. The church did not like its pagan origins and I tended to agree but I saw it as a special occasion to bring our community together. With the wedding the day before, those who travelled for the wedding could stay for the Samhain feast.

The day before the wedding a full entourage from Powys arrived at our farm. There was King David and wife Anwen along with his sons and their families. I could see that both Catrin and Hafina carried children and there were older children sitting quietly in the cart with them. They were all welcome and we fussed about making room for their stay. We were fortunate that the farmhouse was of a size that it could accommodate a reasonable number of guests. It had been rebuilt at twice the size since it had been burnt down years before and when Bledri and Gwyneth's family moved in we had expanded it further.

Over a meal we all caught up on what was happening in each other's countries. David had heard that I was arrested and even heard that I had been executed. He said that he didn't know what to believe although he said, 'Nothing stands still for long in the land of the Angles.' We all laughed at this as it was so true of my lifetime that there had been constant change through our land from who was leading to where the borders were. David told us that raids into Powys had stopped over the last year. Normally the Vikings were harassing their northern towns however this had all stopped. I told them about the treaty between King Alfred and the Vikings and David scoffed as like us he could not see the Vikings stopping their warring ways. David also said that raids along the coastline of the other Welsh states had all but stopped. This was welcomed by everyone, but it gave nobody peace of mind. We agreed that a big attack was coming but where would the hammer fall?

It was great catching up with old friends again and I could see that Bledri and Gwyneth were thrilled to have their old king and his family attend the wedding of their daughter. King David reiterated that Powys would assist Worchester if the hammer blow from the Vikings was to land on Worchester. 'We are mostly hunters and farmers but we could quickly have over two thousand men on your doorstep.' I told David that it was nice having friends in this unknown world and I reiterated the dream that there would be one land with no Vikings. We all drank to that and continued our merry evening.

The wedding day arrived and besides being the biggest day of Tata and Seren's life it was also the biggest day for our new cathedral which had been completed and was waiting to stage a significant event. Its opening was attended by most in the city and it seemed that everyone was proud of our new addition to Worchester. Father Frank was prouder than anyone that day and ended up drinking himself stupid. Today was different as this was an official wedding service and not an open day. The cathedral could hold five hundred at capacity and today there were people extending out of all the doorways trying to follow the service. Most people in our community knew Tata as this was his community and he was one of the town's blacksmiths. Beside this he was my brother and as commander of the guard and one of the council leaders I was well known throughout our community. Worchester was now being called the city of Worcester, one of the few cities in Britannia. Winchester and London were also cities although I could not think of any others except for maybe Exeter although I was not sure if it was. I had never been to Exeter however I had been told they had up to ten-thousand residents.

The wedding and after celebrations went as well as one could have dreamed. Mother and Father would have been proud as Tata has developed into a fine man and would soon have a lovely young family. Seren was adorable and doted on Tata which brought a smile to my face every time I saw her fussing over him. Father Frank stayed sober for the service but once again was inebriated when he got the chance.

It was a day to remember and one enjoyed by our family, friends and guests. King David and his family stayed a further two days to give us a chance for a hunting trip up into the Malvern Hills. We did not get any scares on this hunting trip and again only found deer, hare and fox. We enjoyed the time together relaxing and not thinking about matters of state.

Winter was soon on us although this did not stop our work. The region had had another excellent harvest which needed to be stored and protected. The defensive walls around our new city needed to continue which meant that the quarries were as busy as ever and the forges the same. Things slowed down over winter as there was much less daylight and when there was snow, we hunkered down and came to a standstill. There was usually snow on the ground sometime between Samhain day and the year end and this year was no different. We could work outside through a light snow but once it was a foot deep all work was best done inside.

As winter ended with some warm spring days, I looked upon our city with pride. Our community was amazing, and I loved everything we had been able to achieve from the castle to the docks to the mills and now the cathedral. Worcester felt like the centre of the world and most importantly home. We had been keeping in contact with Northampton and London and like us they had endured the winter in relative comfort. There had been none of the feared attacks from Vikings or Wessex. Scouts sent north said that the roads to Repton and Torksey had also been free of raids and farmers in between had been unmolested. It was too much to wish and dream that there really was peace and that the Vikings were content not to raid and plunder although it was starting to look like it.

The seasons came and went and before long we were coming up to another winter. We had new additions to our family from Tata and Seren and again from Leofric and Hilda. There were still no open hostilities from Wessex, or the Vikings, and our peace and prosperity were continuing unabated. Egbert had his sixth birthday and was being given easy chores around the farm. He was now responsible for collecting the eggs and ensuring the chickens and ducks were watered. In another two years Egbert could be added as an apprentice blacksmith.

It was a week after Samhain day in the year 866 when my world changed. I was in the middle of fabricating a frame for a door when I felt a pair of arms come around my body. Usually more aware of my surroundings I jumped and was about to hammer whoever it was behind me when a little voice in my head told me not to strike. Putting down the burning steel rod I turned in the arms which after initially being knocked away had returned to my waist.

There she was, looking into my eyes, the women I had spent countless hours worrying about and loving. Aethelswith, and how wonderful she looked. The radiant smile was looking up into my face. I was stunned to silence and inaction. However, she took care of this by grabbing the back of my head, and pulling me down to kiss. Oh, how I had longed for this moment. I now cried for the first time since I had lost my father at the age of thirteen. I cried for all the horror in the world including the loss of my sister and mother, Sunngifu, Riannon and my old best friend Egbert. Sobbing into Aethelswith's neck, I at last felt complete and at peace.

We stayed this way for some time as Aethelswith was now crying with me. I still had no idea what she had endured, and I was sure she was scared for the future. To give us the time we needed I released the energy from the forge by dampening the fire. Alun came in and saw me with Aethelswith and immediately understood the situation. Alun said to leave the forge to him as he would keep going with the door. Grateful, I gave him a smile and took Aethelswith by the hand and went across to the house. Inside there was a hive of activity as there was Hereweald back with Cynefri. There was also Owen and another man I had yet to meet filling the reception room. Looking around I could see Hilda holding a big fat baby who looked to be almost a year in age. I could see Hilda with one of her biggest smiles as I grabbed Hereweald's arm and pulled him in close. 'Thank you, my dear friend, I am forever in your debt and I can't wait to hear your tales of adventure.' With this closeness to Hereweald I once again had tears in my eyes, tears of joy.

Turning to Hilda I could see that Aethelswith had taken the baby from Hilda's arms and was coming over to me. Looking into the baby's eyes I could see the Amity family line. I instinctively knew that this was my son and for this, as much as seeing Aethelswith, I was thrilled.

'Godric, meet your father, the one I am always talking about.' With that I put my arms around them both and lifted Godric out of Aethelswith's arms. How small, light and beautiful all at once. Godric was thrilled to be flying, as I tossed him through the air and caught him. I had played the same way with baby Egbert and now had baby Godric and hopefully more time to be a father. It was so wonderful and miraculous how we can create life. Everyone seemed as thrilled as I was and Leofric cracked the mead and we celebrated the rest of that night in style with singing and dancing and of course lots of drinking.

Hereweald told us that Aethelswith had been sent to the convent at St David's Cathedral in Wales. He said that the only person who King Alfred had trusted with this information was Bishop Giles. There was danger going back to Winchester as the king was outraged that I had escaped and he had ordered an inquiry. Wulfsige was blamed for the escape and a reward was out for his capture and head. Avoiding suspicion had been Hereweald's first achievement but enquiring about Aethelswith had only given him dead ends. He said that one morning he had seen the servant Ebba at the well gathering some water and she was sobbing. He had stopped to comfort her, and she eventually told him how she was being held hostage and was being raped by Bishop Giles. Hearing this angered me for many reasons, not least because Ebba was a beautiful innocent girl being abused by a person in a position of power. Ebba was a genius though as she had the key to unlock the mystery of Aethelswith's disappearance.

Finding another servant to assist, Hereweald took Ebba somewhere quiet and gave her some breakfast and something to drink. He said that

Ebba was like a daughter to him and the thought of her being raped by that fat bishop was too much. 'She told me that Bishop Giles talks in his sleep and he keeps getting worked up about Aethelswith and some place called St David's. A light came on and I knew this must be it. I left that day with Ebba and a couple of loyal men. We travelled light so that we could travel quickly staying in inns along the way. Our story was that we were pilgrims on a pilgrimage to the holy cathedral of St David's. I had heard about St David's before and knew roughly where it was. Once we were in Wales all roads seemed to point to St David's cathedral.

'Reaching St David's was like stepping into another world. The cathedral, vestry and other church buildings stand proud over a town which looks like it was a secondary idea after the construction of the church. St David's is extremely busy with pilgrims in great numbers but also many people of the church around every corner. After booking a place in an inn we decided we needed to pray in the cathedral and keep an eye out for nuns and the convent. At the cathedral we caught sight of some nuns however we were unable to follow them as they used restricted accesses and were not in the open for long. After a week we finally caught sight of two nuns in the foyer of our inn. Ebba and I were eating breakfast and a couple were there handing their daughter over to the nuns. The daughter must have been no more than fourteen and looked defiant but also resigned to her fate. I have no doubt she had brought shame on the family and this was her punishment. A life as a nun could be better than many lives but I would not wish the solitude onto anyone.'

Hereweald told us that he followed the three of them making sure he kept a distance so that they were not aware they were being followed. The trail led out of town and through a small forest. 'Coming out into a clearing I saw the convent. It had a single-storey wall around the exterior kind of like a castle with a large flat single-storey building inside. I was struggling to think how to get inside as I could see that the entry was guarded, and the three we were following, needed admittance. We were still not certain that Aethelswith was inside although we felt good about the hunch.'

The following part of Aethelswith's rescue had great risk and it is remarkable how it worked out. Hereweald and one of his two men took down the guards just after shift change which was in the early hours of the night. The guards were dragged into the woods and Hereweald's men quickly donned their uniforms and went back to stand guard at the gates. This gave Hereweald the opportunity to get inside the convent however he knew that Ebba would need to help. Inside the convent they kept to the shadows of the covered walkways around the central courtyard garden. Finding a lone nun praying before a statue of Mary, Hereweald knocked her unconscious telling us he did his best to be gentle. I could see he looked a little guilty telling us this part. Hereweald was a strong man and even his gentle knock to the back of the head could have killed the lady, and maybe it did.

'Ebba was now wearing a habit and was disguised as a nun. I stuck to the shadows but followed her to make sure she was not discovered. Hiding in the shadows Ebba found a common area where the nuns were praying and eating in equal numbers. Ebba had grown up serving Aethelswith so knew her better than her own mother. Coming back to the shadows Ebba pointed out where Aethelswith sat eating flat bread and jam. She had a habit on and did not look too different from the other nuns. I was appreciative that I had Ebba as I would have struggled and probably never would have found Aethelswith without her. Ebba entered the room and moved to sit opposite Aethelswith. I was able to watch events inside through the open doorway. The room was lit by candles which made everything inside easy to see.'

Wow, this was an amazing story. There was silence in the room as we all sat around listening to how Aethelswith was rescued. Ebba was being hugged from behind by Aethelswith and I could see she was grateful for her heroine and her courage. Aethelswith told us that she recognised Ebba the second that she sat down.

'As soon as Ebba sat down, I rose and stepped around the table inviting Ebba to rise. We needed to get out of the common room as there were many superiors in the room and any one of them would notice Ebba was an intruder. I guided Ebba to the door and out into the garden. It was there that I saw Hereweald and I just wanted to hug him so hard, but I couldn't, we were not yet safe. I whispered that we needed to grab the baby and led them both over to a small dark room. There were maybe a dozen beds in this room with a sister sitting in watch at the door. I know all the sisters at the nursery as I spent every free minute in the room feeding our baby. I told Sister Anne that I wanted to say goodnight to Godric. She told me that it wasn't a good idea as he was sleeping, and it would only wake him up. Telling me to come back in the morning, she stood to block my access. Some of the sisters are like this and certainly most of the superiors. I was a new novice and one who came in shame, so I was very low in the scheme of things. I invited Sister Anne outside to tell her my reasons and Hereweald came out from behind a column and with a thump to the back of the head had her knocked out. I rushed in to grab Godric and together the four of us made our way to the exit. Godric was sleeping and thank God he is a good sleeper.' Hereweald once again looked sheepish as Leofric made a joke about Hereweald and how he seemed to relish thumping defenceless women.

Everything seemed to be on their side as Hereweald's men were still undetected at the gate. 'We made it across to the forest to where the horses were tied up.' Hereweald then told us they rode through the night and checked into an inn the following day. This was the night before they eventually made it back to Worcester and safety. At the inn they took two rooms disguised as husband and wife. Aethelswith and Ebba had changed in the forest and Ebba had brought a set of clothes for Aethelswith.

Walking over to Ebba I also gave her a massive embrace and told her that I could not thank her enough. I offered her a place in our home and family if she would accept it. Turning to Aethelswith I got down on a knee and reiterated my love for her and once again asked if she would have me as her husband. Pulling me to my feet with tears she said that she would be honoured and there was nothing which would make her happier. It was easy to see why that night was such a night of celebration. The story of their rescue was one that should be remembered for generations.

Although late in the season we now had a wedding to organise. We would not leave it too long as the snow would block the roads shortly. Riders were sent to Northampton, London and over to Powys and King David. I longed to see family again but more importantly to marry Aethelswith.

News of the wedding for the following Sunday spread throughout the community and slowly close family and friends began arriving from everywhere. John and Leofflaed put many up at their home in town including King David and his family. The Earl of Northampton and his family stayed with us out on the farm. His family included his son Ethan and my sister Wassa. I had not seen Wassa for over a year and she looked radiant as a mother of two beautiful children. Our home was full of noise and excitement as preparations took shape for the wedding.

The week flew by as every waking minute was taken up with organisation, social catch ups and greetings. By the time the moment came to be married all I or Aethelswith wanted to do was sleep. The children, including baby Godric, were all being entertained by the older children which at least gave Aethelswith some respite. My Egbert seemed enamoured by his new little brother and fearlessly protective of him around the other children.

Wulfsige arrived from London mid-week and told us that all was quiet on the eastern front. The news was good and boded well for another year. Maybe we were free from Viking attacks for now and into the future. A little voice in my head told me that this just couldn't be the case. We had built the army to such a strength that we could start to think about reclaiming some of our northern and eastern lands. This was a discussion for the coming council meeting.

Our wedding day arrived, and God favoured us as the rain from earlier in the week had cleared up. Once again, the cathedral was full of people crammed into the openings, all wishing to be a part of the service. My good friend Father Frank presided over our wedding. The service felt personal and was deeply moving to me and looking around I could see it had the same effect on others. I was nervous for the occasion which was momentous in the extreme. Telling God, my loved ones and the world that this was the only woman for me until death do us part was very special and powerful. For some reason I now felt more grown up and my second wedding felt more intense.

To the sound of babies crying in the background, Aethelswith became an Amity and joined my family. That day there were many tears of joy and at last something which had seemed so improbable came into existence. The reception was held in the town hall and town centre. Aethelswith and I stayed around until well after dark even though we just wanted to be alone to celebrate in our own way. Eventually, we said our goodbyes and using Egbert and baby Godric as an excuse we made our way back to the Farm. Ethan, Wassa and their children came with us along with Leofric, Hilda and their children. The celebrations had begun to get a bit wild and it was no place for young children.

Back on the farm Aethelswith fed baby Godric and put him to sleep. At last, I was alone with my wife. At one point it had looked like this day would never come. I was lucky to have friends such as Hereweald who were intelligent and resourceful. Being old enough to be my father, Hereweald was a survivor in a world where survival is difficult. Hereweald had thrown his lot behind me long ago when he saw his commander commit murder against his own people. The easy option would have been to ignore what he saw, and many men would have. Instead, he had made the hard decision and looked for an opportunity to prove his loyalty to me. Since that day his loyalty and friendship had not faulted.

A couple of days later Hereweald and his men left for Winchester. He was going so that he could bring his family back to Worchester. Cynefri was with him, however, both of his sons were still with the Winchester guard and both had their own families.

Ebba would stay with us and help on the farm as a free person. I noticed that Alun had taken an interest in her and thought that would be a good match. Ebba was still young and could have her own family but she was already comfortable looking after children and Wynnstan needed a mother. It would be interesting to see if anything developed there.

Hereweald would need to be careful as King Alfred may have heard of Aethelswith's escape. He would also be suspicious of Hereweald's disappearance as Hereweald was supposed to be commander of his army. Hereweald reassured me that he had many friends in Winchester and that I should not worry about him but every time someone told me not to worry, I worried.

The snows came with vengeance a week after Hereweald left and although he would have had time to reach Winchester, with the snow his return would be delayed. The snow slowed everything down including news. The blocked roads also meant that a sneak attack or Viking raid was less likely so although making things difficult it was a chance to relax a little and catch up on the sleep we missed during the year.

With full granaries and plenty of projects to keep us busy, Leofric, Alun, Tata and I spent most of the winter in the forges. We now had four apprentices which made our work much easier. Bevan and Bert were our original apprentices who had now opened their own forge in Worchester. The four new apprentices were the sons of Aethelweard and Deorwine. Both men were dear to me so training their sons as blacksmiths was an honour and responsibility for Leofric and I.

Aethelswith was soon pregnant and was busy helping around the house with Hilda, Seren and Gwyneth. Having such a full house gave Aethelswith and I little opportunity for quiet time. We made opportunities to be alone as we both loved walking the hills and exploring our caves. On one of these outings, we found some better caves even further into the woods and one day we vowed to show Egbert, baby Godric and their siblings so that they could make the caves something special for themselves.

This was a beautiful period of our lives as we were surrounded by so much family and so many friends. Our land felt at peace and with the thick snow it felt like we were the only people in the world.

Chapter 15 — The Fight for Survival

Spring was late this year but sure enough the season changed, and we expected Hereweald could now get through. We have all become worried as he should have been back months ago as there had been breaks in the weather when he could have travelled. We comforted Cynefri with reassuring words about how Hereweald was a survivor and would be back shortly.

Riders were sent to all corners of our area of control which the locals now called England. It was effectively Mercia although that name died with Æthelstan. We needed intelligence on how each area had fared through winter and if there was any Viking or Wessex activity. It had now been two years since we had taken London and Halfdan had signed the treaty with King Alfred. From what we knew the peace had held although none of us who felt we knew the Vikings could understand what they were playing at. Consequently, we were still welcoming, arming and training men for our guard and army. Northampton and London were asked to do the same. Their progress was a little slower as they were coming from a lower base of numbers and they received less refugees, being on the front line.

Most of all I wanted to hear from Winchester and how Hereweald was. Therefore, I was delighted when Hereweald and his family finally arrived at the farm mid-spring. The boys, Swidhun and Leofstan, and the families were squeezed into our already busy house. A new property was going to be needed if we were to be comfortable in the long-term. With regards to the boys, Leofstan was over six foot and of equal size to me. I had seen him fight and was glad that he was on our side. Swidhun had a shock of red hair and where Leofstan was large and solid Swidhun was the opposite, being short and slight of build. This did not make Swidhun a pushover as I had seen him with a bow and in close with his knives and thought that he was probably the more deadly of the two.

Embracing my old friend and his wife, I welcomed him back to our home. Cynefri was overjoyed to see Hereweald was truly safe. There was much to celebrate but first I needed Hereweald's intelligence.

Hereweald and I went for a walk out to the farm to look at the horses we had been breeding. They spent most of the winter in the barns, so it was great to see them out playing in the paddock. 'What took you so long, my friend? You had us completely worried.'

Hereweald told me that he had to do some smooth talking to keep his head however the king's health was starting to wane, and his trust of people was very low. 'The king has not heard of Aethelswith's disappearance although this makes sense as I cannot imagine the convent would want to be advertising this to the king.'

Back in the King's confidence it was difficult to leave as the inner and outer gates are now monitored day and night and the secret tunnels had been sealed. 'We were now like prisoners within the city. The king's paranoia grows almost daily so we were desperately looking for an opportunity to leave. The king executes people easily if there is a weak link or claim of treachery from someone. His health is poor, and he spends most days in bed.

'Finally, our opportunity came but it came with ill tidings.' I expected to hear that the king had died but what I heard was far worse. Hereweald asked me to get Leofric for what he had to tell us, so I took us to the forge where I knew Leofric to be working. It was going to be quieter out with the horses, so we asked Leofric and Tata to join us for the coming news.

'The Vikings are attacking in full force. There are two armies each with over ten thousand men. The first army arrived by boat and were not detected until the attack on Exeter commenced. The second army also came in by boat and has landed at Hasting where they have built a camp and defences as more and more boats arrive each day. Both armies are huge and well-armed. Exeter has fallen and this army now marches on Winchester. Once news of the attack on Exeter reached Winchester, we sent out riders to the corners of Wessex to make sure there were no surprise attacks and to get help if there was any out there. This is when we came across a second and just as big army. The treaty with the Vikings was a chance to build their forces for one big push to destroy the Angles and Celts forever.'

This was a massive threat to our existence, and I knew Leofric could see it as I could.

'The king then sent me to you. He is pleading that you forgive his actions and loss of honour. The king says that he can see you were right all along, and he even told me he would send riders to St David's to bring back his daughter. The king broke down as he sobbed about how he had ruined everything. A sense of doom was coming over him, so I sought to reassure him. I told him that his daughter had already been rescued and had married Godric at the cathedral in Worchester. I told him that their son Godric junior was strong and healthy and most importantly that his daughter is extremely happy.'

Hereweald went on although I was already planning what the next course of action was.

'I told the king that the English had not stopped preparing for war and if he asked, they would come to his aid. England is strong and ready to meet whatever the Vikings come with. The king cried some more at this news and then asked me to come to you. He asked me to plead for forgiveness and to ask you to come to the aid of Wessex. He said that the Vikings coming from Exeter are the immediate threat however both armies need to be dealt with. He loves his daughter and has spent every waking minute thinking of her and how he has betrayed her. The king also said that he welcomes you as a son in law and can see your vision of peace once the Vikings are forced from our island. The king was then exhausted and needed to sleep, sending me on this errand.'

Everything in our world had just been turned upside down, from peace to total war. I sent Tata into town to get John to call an emergency council meeting. We would need to put this to the council but I was certain of what the outcome will be. They all knew what we had been building for and for the last three years it felt like this was an inevitable event. My recommendation would be to go with full force and to take up the king's plea for support. I would propose that we take the entire Worchester guard to meet the army coming up from Exeter and send riders to Northampton and London to send what men they could to the Viking army at Hasting.

Before leaving I told Aethelswith and the others the message from King Alfred. Aethelswith cried in my embrace on hearing how frail he was and how he was now begging for forgiveness. I knew Aethelswith and knew that she had already forgiven her father and had probably never blamed him for his actions. Aethelswith did not hold grudges but had a heart full of love and Aethelswith also understood the demands on a leader. Aethelswith pleaded with us to protect her father and the people of Winchester. Looking her in the eye, I told her she could count on it.

The council meeting went as I had suspected that it would. England would ride to war with the Worchester guard of seven thousand fully trained warriors set to move out on the following day. We would move south toward Winchester to intercept Halfdan's force. We were told that Halfdan was leading this first assault while King Knut's son, Eric, was landing at Hastings. If King Knut was involved this meant that the entire Viking kingdom could be coming down on us. Several of the cavalry groups rode back to the farm with us and helped load the weapons onto carts. We had been preparing for this and had weapons and other supplies in abundance.

That night we all shared dinner and discussed the coming battle. The walls protecting Worchester had been completed and should be able to protect our city against all but the most determined of attacks. Should the walls be breached everyone was to get back to the castle and to not open the doors for anyone unless the safety of the people could be guaranteed.

Tata said that he wanted to come and fight in this war. I wished he wouldn't but he was now a man, a father and of a similar size to me so denying him this opportunity would not be fair or indeed possible. Tata was a bowman in the cavalry which meant he would be fighting within my group.

The following morning all the guard were preparing to leave for Winchester when some riders came into sight coming from the north road. They were coming at speed which made my heart sink as a messenger coming at speed is a bad omen. Being pointed in my direction, the riders adjusted their direction and made straight for us. I was there with John, Leofric, Tata and Hereweald.

Pulling up his horse and almost out of breath, the lead rider told me that a huge Viking army was on the road from Repton. 'They will be half a day away at best.'

'How many men and do they carry siege engines?'

The rider behind the lead rider said he thought maybe twelve thousand but certainly more than ten. 'Mostly infantry and no siege engines.' At least they didn't have siege engines which would give us time, time which we would need.

Before I dismissed the riders, they told us that King Knut was leading this Viking host. I did not know if this was good or bad but I suspected the king would have the best men with him and would only ride if certain of victory.

Feeling trapped, I had to make a critical decision. If we rode to the defence of Winchester, Worcester and all we loved would be left with very little defences. If we stayed to defend Worchester, then Winchester would most likely fall and with it all of Wessex. With Wessex in Viking hands all their attention would fall on Worchester and the English. The men around me remained silent as they knew I liked to think through the different scenarios.

Looking at the men around me, I made my decision. I asked Tata if he could take some men and ride directly to King David of Powys. 'Tell him our situation and ask him for every available man to defend Worchester and its walls. In the absence of the Worchester council and town guard, Tata, you are to take charge of the city defences. I am sorry as I know you had your heart on riding into battle with us. Your time will come as there will be many battles to come. Send the warning to the entire valley and send riders to Northampton and London so that they can prepare. Tell them that the plan has not changed and the guard rides to Winchester.'

Through King Alfred's blind desire for peace, he had put the entire future of Britain at risk of falling into Viking hands.

London and Northampton would also be vulnerable as their men were riding to Hastings to confront the second Viking army. The pieces had all fallen into place for them and each battle from here would be critical to a possible total victory. Both London and Northampton would be easier targets then Worchester and with twelve thousand men against their walls I did not think they will last for long. For this reason, I was hoping that they did come against Worchester. I had faith in Powys and with two or more thousand men on them, our walls of our castle would not be that easy to breach.

Turning to Leofric I told him, 'We leave for Winchester.'

Leofric passed the message along to the other commanders and we pointed our horses south and rode out of our beloved Worchester. Like the others who now rode with us, we are all leaving our loved ones behind with the largest known gathered force bearing down on them. News of the northern Viking army would have already spread amongst the men and given them cause to doubt our current plan. However, I knew that I had utmost loyalty and faith from them and I did not fear that they would not follow me.

We needed to protect Wessex otherwise the numbers against us would be too one sided. I was so proud of my brother as I knew he would be disappointed about missing going into battle alongside me. I would be disappointed if I was in his position. King David would know the seriousness of the request if it came from Tata, like no other messenger. The familiarity between our families went back more than a decade and both our families were now very close. I did not doubt that King David would ride to our aid. I only hoped that it would be enough to hold off King Knut.

I had the same hope with Wulfsige and Evan and the need for them to halt the Vikings at Hastings. We required King David to halt King Knut at Worchester to give us time to sort the south. Aligned with Wessex, we need to defeat Halfdan at Winchester and get along the coast to Hastings to support the second battle front. Years and years of planning were going to come down to the next week or two. We were well prepared but we had not expected to be fighting on three fronts. The Vikings were evidently also prepared and seem to have been planning this attack for years.

We stayed clear of all the settled areas and spent the night in a field beside the road. The following day we might need to fight so we ate and went to bed early. Although a little stiff I woke feeling refreshed. I had thought that sleep would be hard to find with my mind racing but fatigue had taken over and once asleep it was a long and deep sleep.

It looked as though our two armies were going to meet at Salisbury. Salisbury was a beautiful old town not far from Winchester which was said to have rich agricultural land around it. There were Roman ruins throughout the area so we knew that it must have been a significant region for them. Riding into sight of the town I could immediately see why. Thousands of hectares of fields had been sown with crops for the coming season. The soil looked to be a rich dark brown everywhere I turned.

Unfortunately for some of the farmers their fields would be destroyed in the coming battle. There were always losers in war, and it was not always the warring parties.

Waiting in the fields outside of Salisbury were Eadwulf and the Wessex army. The size of their army was like ours which I saw as a positive. That they could raise these numbers at short notice showed me they were throwing everything at this confrontation. Eadwulf was the commander of the Wessex army and rode out to meet us as we came to join their position. He looked pleased as he looked on at our men coming into the field and forming ranks.

'Well met, Godric,' said Eadwulf in greeting. 'The Vikings are stopped over the rise and we expect battle either later today or first thing in the morning.'

Accepting Eadwulf's greeting we exchanged what intelligence we had. Hereweald and Eadwulf embraced as old friends which indeed they were. Eadwulf replaced Hereweald as commander when Hereweald came into mild disgrace by backing me. Eadwulf was a senior captain under Hereweald and was at the battle for Repton when Ethelred betrayed Worcester. Eadwulf told us he had seven thousand men and he estimated Halfdan had twelve thousand. After telling Dunstan to ask the men to be at ease and have a meal we went with Eadwulf to study the terrain and discuss tactics for the coming battle.

Coming to the top of the ridge we could see the Viking horde in the adjoining valley. How intimidating they looked, especially in the numbers I could see now. I could see that we were better off set up where we were as the open fields would give us an advantage. The following valley looked mostly forested and would be a disadvantage to our cavalry and longbow.

Back at the command tent I asked Dunstan to split his cavalry between the northern and southern hill tops on either side of central location. Having the cavalry on these elevated hills would ensure that we did not get outflanked. The sun was setting so we ate a light meal and discussed the possibility of a surprise attack in the evening or early morning. It was the eve of a major battle and everything seemed so calm. There was a lack of tension which worried me. It felt surreal as though there was not going to be a battle. Our men were so confident, and I understood this as they were well trained, healthy and strong and had the most modern weapons. They deserved to be confident; however, those of us who were leaders cannot afford to be confident or we would fall into a trap and waste the valuable resource which was our people. Most of our warriors had not been in an organised battle before as they had joined us over the last three or four years. They all knew hardship and every family was touched by the Viking invasion. Everyone knew how important the coming battle was going to be for our long-term survival and future.

Talk was going on around me and I realised that I was silent. Something was not right but I was struggling to put my finger on it. Breaking my silence, I asked Eadwulf about the terrain between Salisbury and Shaftsbury. Time was on the Vikings' side as they had two other massive armies marching against small forces which required our reinforcement. I felt like we were in a trap. This army was too large to leave at our backs especially as it was being led by Halfdan, a legendary Viking leader. Without us, we were most likely doomed on the other fronts. It was like a sixth sense, an instinct that was directing me to keep thinking of options.

Eadwulf spoke to one of his captains and came back with a report on the terrain. 'It is mostly forested with a river valley to the north and another to the south. There is a ridge of hills which runs from north to south dropping away at both rivers. Either side of the hill ridge is forested however the ridge is free from trees as it is rocky.'

All of a sudden it came to me and I could see that we were in a trap being delivered by time. 'We need to flush the Vikings out.' I sent a rider to Dunstan to have him return. Thinking this through I sent the full cavalry to the ridge Eadwulf told us about. They were not to enter the ridge until the morning on the coming day. They must be cautious to ensure that there was not a Viking force to the west of the ridge.

'Aethelweard and Deorwine, you will lead the sword and archery units into the forest at the break of day. Stay tight in your formation even if under attack. Archers will not be much use in the forest however my unit of archers will accompany you on horseback and take down whatever threat we can. The advance will be slow to ensure we take time back as our ally. Eadwulf, split your infantry into two groups and take one to the southern shore of the River Nadder in the north and the other to the northern shore of the River Ebble which is the southern boundary of the battlefield. Keep your position and after midday commence your advance to the centre of the battle zone. We do not know which way our enemy will move but I suspect that they will be stalling so will do their best to lure us into the woods. Once they find their retreat is blocked, they may make a stand or attempt to break out either north, south or east. Keeping a tight formation is essential as either one of these groups could feel the full force of this Viking army. We will number our groups as one for east, two for north, three for south and four for west. There will be a horn signal for each group, one through four. The horn will be blown long and loud the number of times for the group number depending on the direction the Vikings move. Once we hear the horn the other groups will move in the direction of the horn with caution and keeping a tight formation. The army being attacked will defensively back out of the forest ensuring the formation is kept tight. Unless the direction is to the west and the direction of our cavalry. In this instance the cavalry will split and ride the route outside the forest to reinforce the unit which is being attacked.

'We want to force the battle and flush our enemy out and into our trap. Time is something we cannot afford so this fight needs to be dynamic and taken up to the Vikings.'

I repeated the instructions to ensure that everyone understood the plan. Everyone seemed to naturally be following me as commander which I did not think much about at the time. Leading was coming naturally and could be a result of my father dying when I was still young and added to me being left as the blacksmith at that same age. Either way the commanders and captains seemed to understand the instructions. I told them all to get a good night's sleep as I expected we would not be attacked in this battle until we made the first move. Halfdan would understand his advantage.

Sure enough, the night was over and the battle to end all battles was in front of us. Everyone took their positions and had done the expected preparations. We knew what to do and the importance of fulfilling our part in the battle plan. Moving forward with the infantry I had the archers on high alert to take down any threat which we had a high chance of hitting.

The battle did not take long to be engaged and Halfdan moved his forces back as expected. The archers and I managed to inflict many casualties on their front lines as Halfdan's men underestimated the accuracy and distance of our archer's arrows. Our advance was slow as planned, not wanting to take any risk with the men from my home. The battle ebbed and flowed like this all morning. At around midday the Viking force stopped its retreat which brought our guard within striking distance of the Vikings. From that point there were regular skirmishes and casualties. We knew what to expect as the ground was slowly rising to the ridge at the back of the Vikings. The Vikings would know that their retreat was blocked. They would be franticly revising their plans. We were sure they would attack but not sure of the direction. I wanted to keep advancing to put Halfdan under pressure and force them into error.

Halfdan and his army hit us with force, and it took every bit of training and skill to stop our slaughter. Our warriors fought with such courage and kept their formation tight even as it came under constant barrage from Halfdan. Our archers now had continuous targets as we fired arrow after arrow to try and thin the Viking onslaught. The horn had been signalled and now we needed to hold until the reinforcements arrived.

The fighting continued over the coming hours with puddles of blood starting to collect across the battle front. Both groups giving no quarter with the Vikings using their fearsome reputation to inspire them while the Worchester guard enjoyed the reputation for being the elite fighting force in the Anglo-Saxon world. Neither group was going to let go lightly of their reputation. At the time that our reinforcements arrived we had lost more than half of our infantry and a third of our archers. I could see that exhaustion was taking hold of our men who had been fighting against much greater numbers. The pride I felt at that moment and all morning was immense and was the inspiration for my energy and determination. The cavalry arrived first and although not as effective in the woods, their bows were welcome cover and enabled the archers to throw off their bows and take up their swords to support those who had already abandoned their bows and were already fighting with the sword.

Shortly after the cavalry arrived both Wessex infantry armies arrived which enabled us to now press the Vikings with the advantage. The carnage continued until an hour before dark when ninety percent of the light in the woods had vanished. This was when Halfdan was finally cut down. Standing at six and a half feet, Halfdan was a monster and one who inflicted enormous damage to our men. Finally, we came together, and I got a chance to deal out the revenge I had been dreaming about since I was a child where he had left me without my grandfather and then later my best friend. He was strong and experienced but I was in the prime of my life and enormously strong. The fight only lasted a minute, and, in the end, I took off Halfdan's head. The Vikings around us were already exhausted and seeing their mythical leader lose his head seemed to take the remaining spirit from them. One last push by our remaining men and we finished off the Viking army. We could have shown mercy but I was in a battle frenzy and in no mood for it.

We recovered our dead and injured by candlelight and finished off the injured Vikings at the same time. Back at the camp our surgeons worked hard to save the injured while the healthy commenced digging graves for our fallen. Food was prepared and given to the men along with plenty of mead to wash it down. The other leaders and I went from group to group communicating how great the victory was and how it would be sung about for centuries to come. We wanted to keep their spirits up as there was still a lot of fighting to do and besides, the victory was a great and memorable victory. In normal circumstances we would celebrate such a victory for days.

Time was still our enemy and we needed to get across to Hastings to support our army from Northampton and London. The battle was worthy of some celebration, so the men were allowed some mead and the bards played and sang for us.

The battle had been costly with regards to loss of life as we had lost a third of our entire guard, close to two and a half thousand men. I was still going over the battle in my head and could not see how the battle could have been fought differently. Wessex had also lost the same number of men making our total losses five thousand. Considering the Vikings lost a force of twelve thousand this was a significant victory.

The following day I left the field with our remaining four and a half thousand men and commenced the journey to Hastings.

While we were doing this, we received word that King Knut of the Vikings had laid siege to Worchester. King David had arrived with two thousand men and was assisting Tata and the locals to defend the walls to the city. At least King David had shown himself to always be true and had come to our aid. The odds were not great so we really needed to deal with the Hasting Vikings as quickly as we could. At the same time, we needed Worchester to fight like hell to keep the Vikings out of the castle. If they breach the walls all our loved ones will meet a gruesome death.

I left Eadwulf the task of completing the burial of our men. I gave him a second task which was for the forges of Winchester. 'We need the forges to complete as many arrows, to our new design, as they can in the following two days. We will be coming back through Winchester and we will need to rearm on our way through.' These instructions were conveyed to Winchester immediately and given the highest priority.

That day we made a steady pace as some of the men had some minor injuries and all of us were exhausted from the previous day's battle. My hands and right shoulder ached from all the arrows I had shot. Although uninjured I felt worn out. None of us complained as we knew we had more work to do. We were the lucky ones as we had survived to fight again.

The following day our force came closer to Catsfield, a town not far from Hastings. The fighting could be heard in the distance as Leofric and I rode to the front and out toward the direction of the fighting sounds. In the middle of a field was a large group surrounded by an attacking army of Vikings. The group being attacked was our army from Northampton and London. Their men had a shield wall up and were fighting for their lives repelling the attacking Vikings. I could see that we had the advantage of surprise and the cover of trees. Racing back to the captains

I told them the situation and told them to set up a defensive position while the archers and cavalry should come with me to engage the Vikings.

From the cover of the trees, we came within range of the Vikings and started taking them down. The field was already filled with bodies, so our surprise attack only added to the existing carnage. Eric, the Viking leader, soon realised the changed circumstances and quickly made the decision to retreat to the cover of the hills outside of Hastings. We followed them for as long as was safe and inflicted as much damage as was possible. The more we could kill on the retreat the lower the number we would have to face in the coming battle. Doubling back, I went back to see who had survived out of Northampton and London. Evan and Wulfsige were together when I rode up to them. They both commented on our timely arrival and that they thought their men were not far from exhaustion at the time. Looking at the survivors they estimated that they had lost half of their men. However, it was not all doom and gloom as we could also see thousands of Vikings either dead or dying.

I was happy to see that Ethan was alive and well as he came forward. Ethan was married to my sister and father to their two children. The last thing I wanted was to have to return and tell Wassa that her husband was dead. We had all experienced too much heartache and I longed for a period when it would all end. Embracing Evan, he told me we were a sight for sore eyes, and I knew the truth of it.

Along with our men we now had a force of just over seven thousand. Our numbers would be the same as Eric's at worst and possibly greater than his, given the losses I could see. We decided to make camp and rest the men for the remainder of that day. I did not waste the time, though, as I wanted to know more about who we faced. I had not fought Eric although I had heard stories about his brutality. It had started raining as Eric retreated and as I stood in the rain, I thought it seemed as though the rain had set in for the day.

Sneaking forward on one of these scouting missions I had to shoot two of the Viking guards who were on lookout for Eric. Coming over the hills above Hastings I could see that Eric and his men had retreated to the town. We could see hundreds of their ships moored in the port. The sight of them sent a chill up my spine as it had for the people of our island for years. The thought of taking down their ships occurred to me as it meant their return would be difficult and less likely. Returning to camp I spoke to Deorwine and Leofric. Leofric suggested we organise a group of archers to sneak along the coastal path west of Hastings, keeping out of sight of any lookouts to make an attack on the boats. It was extremely dark as the clouds had covered the moon and the rain was persisting. It was going to be dangerous, but the exact morale boost the warriors needed. Leofric offered to lead the sortie while I took the high ground on my own, and again I was forced to take down several Vikings who were posted on lookout. I then raced down to join Leofric and the others.

Coming onto the port, we made sure we were in range of the ships before lighting up some oil. Lighting the tips of our arrows, we commenced the barrage onto the waiting Viking vessels. The ships began coming to life as fire took hold of first one then many at a time. The rain was light and no match for the oiled arrows. The fire then spread from ship to ship and our job was done. We retreated as quickly as we could back along the coast.

Then, out of the night, a large force of Vikings came down on us. We were all armed with sword however the surprise had caught many of us off guard and still with bows in our hands. Our front ranks were taken down in the attack and this included my close friend, Leofric. Seeing Leofric take an axe to the neck I threw down my bow and went into a rage. The skirmish went on for maybe ten minutes and ended with us losing over two hundred of our archers. I knew all our archers as they were the discipline of the guard which I was responsible for. Leofric was married to my sister and father to four of my nephews and nieces. He was the older brother of my old best mate Egbert and son to the man who was like a father to me. My rage helped me to beat the Vikings as I took down dozens of them to help finish them off.

I carried Leofric back to our camp and laid him at the feet of John Archer. I was crying although in the rain my tears would not be noticeable. Crying with John, I said that I should have known or expected an attack. 'It was a bold attack of ours and one which has done great damage to the Vikings. However, my boldness has led to the death of my close friend and another member of my family. It feels as though we are cursed although I know this trail of death has touched every family in England. This knowledge does not make me feel any better.'

That night the other members of the council and captains sat with John and I in the command tent. We did our best to remember Leofric and drowned our sorrow at the great loss of life. We discussed Eric and what he was now likely to do. I suggested he would be enraged as a Viking without a ship is no longer a Viking. It was a romantic notion but one I had heard many times and looking at the reaction from the men in the port I suspected it to be at least partly true.

'Eric will attack with every available man. I expect him to engage us while the weather is still poor. The weather will hinder our cavalry and archers which he will feel will give him an advantage. After all, the Vikings are used to the poor weather conditions of their homeland. I have been told it is cold and miserable in the lands of Valhalla.'

We knew the battle was coming as we saw the sky filled with smoke. It seemed that the Vikings were getting pay back by destroying Hastings. Judging by the smoke it seemed like the entire town had been razed to the ground. The fate of the people was anybody's guess.

As we had thought, the English and Viking armies met in the fields outside Hastings. It was another costly battle although we had the advantage due to our superior weapons. Surrounding the battlefield with archers. we fought in organised lines with the infantry protecting our archers for as long as we could maintain them. The archers would only put down their bows if they had used all their arrows or if the Vikings reached their location. All archers could fight with the sword and always carried their swords with them.

The Vikings attacked directly at the front lines which was mostly stopped with some strong work from our infantry. This shield wall was critical to maintaining the separation between our two armies. This separation enabled our archers to cause maximum casualties for the Vikings and then with superior numbers our infantry smashed their remaining men.

I was getting sick of all the bloodshed and collapsed in exhaustion as the battle was won. With tears in my eyes, I rose to my feet, pushing myself through the exhaustion to congratulate the brave men who had won this day. After collecting our dead and counting our remaining men I realised we had lost more than half of our original numbers. Northampton and London had ridden into battle with five thousand and we had left Worchester with seven thousand. Of the twelve thousand we now had between five and six thousand men. Resting the remainder, of the day I walked around and reminded the captains and warriors that we had one more critical battle. 'Our homeland is under attack and we need to get back there to defend it and defeat King Knut.' So much bloodshed and loss, was tough to accept, however we had little choice.

The following morning, we left Hastings and rode for Winchester. This was no race as we needed to ensure we had energy for the battle once we arrived. There should be fresh weapons waiting for us at Winchester and even some fresh men. I had been told that King Knut's army was twelve thousand strong, so I wanted to meet him in the field with at least equal numbers. Fighting for our homeland I expected that we would have the advantage. King Knut would not expect us as he was the instigator of the plan and would expect us to be caught up in Salisbury with Halfdan while his son, Eric, brought up the army from the east. The element of surprise is a key advantage in any battle, and I was planning on using this to my advantage.

Chapter 16 — Bad News for King Knut

King Knut had managed to breach the walls of the city and was currently battling at the walls of the castle. It had only been a week since he had engaged the English and he was now at the gates. Knut so desired to destroy the English and Worchester as they had been the thorn in his side for many years. He had not expected the Welsh to have come to their aid but simply saw this as an inconvenience which would soon be dealt with.

It became a major surprise to see an army, of similar size to his own, coming over the hills from the south of Worchester. The army was flying the flag of the English which meant one thing and that was that Godric and the guard had returned. Although annoying, this meant that the alternative plan he had agreed with Halfdan and Eric would come into play. Delays and concern for his home must have forced Godric's hand to return home. Winchester and Wessex would now fall and before long most of Britannia would be his. He now had a dislike of the Welsh so would then make it his life's mission to destroy them and the Picts who had been raiding his lands with annoying frequency.

Knut's plan was now to retreat and wait for Wessex to fall. His problem was that his retreat was blocked. The retreat was blocked by Godric who, it seemed, wanted a fight and not just to scare the Vikings off. The English had spread to cover the northern and southern exits from Worchester and Knut's men were in Worchester attacking the castle. With a series of horn blows, King Knut's men were turned around. He did not want to fight in the city, so they formed ranks on its outskirts. It did not seem as though the English were in any hurry as they gave Knut time to prepare. He could have fled west but had no knowledge of the terrain or threats of the Welsh countries.

Once out of Worchester Knut looked up to see a delegation from the English waiting between the two forces. The flag of the English was being flown and it looked like Godric wanted a negotiation. King Knut thought there was no way he would settle with the English. He knew he had the advantage of a well thought out and executed plan. Intrigued, he wanted to meet this Godric who was spoken about with such reverence. Some of his men feared Godric which is a shameful trait for a Viking. Godric was responsible for the fortifications at Worchester and its many construction projects. Worchester was the most impressive city he had seen since his invasion and sacking of Paris some years ago. He could see the work which had gone into Worchester and now thought that this would make a good capital for him. Knut took his two senior commanders and went to see what the English had to say.

Knut could see that Godric was an impressive man as they approached the parley. Heavily armed and at ease, Godric looked like a man in control. Godric also had two men with him who looked as menacing as the men Knut had with him. Although at ease, none of these men look pleased to be here. It was as though they would rather be fighting then negotiating. He was quietly wondering what they were going to offer him.

This meeting also gave Godric the chance to see the man who had been harassing and terrorising Britannia since as long as he could remember. 'Halfdan's and Eric's armies have been destroyed and both are being fed on by the carrion.' Godric opened the dialogue by telling them they came with every intent of destroying the Viking army. He told them he would take Knut's head and ensure the Vikings do not raid the lands of Britannia again. 'In God's way I have decided to give you one chance, a chance to save the lives of your men and that of your own. March out of here and leave Britannia forever and we will let you leave. Refuse to leave and the campaign of King Knut will be destroyed today.'

The loss of his son and Halfdan would have been a real shock and would be a complete disaster, if true. However, he could not trust what he was hearing as both Eric and Halfdan had led massive armies and were powerful commanders. Knut disbelieved the news and vowed to crush Godric for his lies, telling the delegation as much.

Chapter 17 — War to the End

It was quite a speech I delivered. I did not care either way as I wanted to save the lives of our men and I knew that a battle here would be costly given the size of Knut's force. I wanted to fight them to avenge the death of my dear friend Leofric. I knew I would have to tell my sister and their children, and I dreaded this more than the coming battle. Defeating Knut would leave the Viking lands exposed to repossession by the English. I could not imagine that the Vikings would have a sizeable fourth force in reserve.

Knut told us that he did not believe what we told him. He shook his head and told us it was fantasy as there was no way Halfdan's or Eric's forces could be defeated and so quickly at that. I reassured him that it was the case and that they had been costly battles for both the English and Wessex forces also. 'The war can end now with our choices. A great leader will protect their people by knowing when to walk away.'

Knut did not say another word but simply turned and headed back to his men. I did not know what action he would choose, and I did not have strong feelings either way.

The battle commenced shortly afterward and seemed to flow as we wished it to. Knut must have been angered by our parley as he sent his forces into the field without consideration for our archers who shot down hundreds of his men even before they struck a blow. Once engaged our archers continued to rain arrows into the Vikings. Our infantry had been commanded to be defensive and to form a wall to keep the Vikings from getting through the outer defences. I wanted to keep the Vikings separated for as long as possible to give our archers the best opportunity to reduce the Viking numbers and give us the advantage.

Our infantry did a wonderful job so that by the time our front ranks faltered we outnumbered the remaining Vikings two to one. With the archers now taking up swords everyone on the battlefield was engaged. I pushed my way through with every intent of getting to King Knut. The fighting was so fierce I did not get far before I was fighting for my life. I was starting to regret taunting Knut with the loss of Halfdan and Eric as he and his men were fighting with such ferocity. It might have made no difference but it seemed like they were men enraged. Our victory was assured regardless of their attempts as our numbers were too superior. Our men could also see their home and knew that it was our job to protect our loved ones. When fighting for our home we could easily find the extra energy required to finish an opposition or at least keep fighting beyond exhaustion.

At some point during the battle the Powys army joined us. Coming from behind the Viking defences, King David and his men had great success in cutting through the Vikings. I was later told that it was King David's son Cadfael who had cut down the Viking king. The bloodshed went on for most of the afternoon and in the end, it was a great victory for Worcester and the English. The battle between Cadfael and Knut is one that I wish I had seen.

Surveying the scene, I felt exhaustion take hold. Forcing it back I gave instructions for all our dead to be removed from the battlefield and to be buried on the slope overlooking our city. At that point King David came up to me and we came together as brothers. Our meeting years ago had been fortuitous and now we had fought together to destroy the Viking king. The king held me for what seemed like ages and tears came to me then. David told me that my father would have been proud of me. My friend had come to our aid as he had always promised. I told David how grateful I was for his friendship and for riding to the aid of Worcester but also noted that words could not do justice to how I feel.

The work clearing the battlefield would go on well into the night. The castle gates had been opened and the people who were not watching from the parapet began flooding back into the city and others out to the battlefield. I could see Leofflaed was in John's arms and thought that he must have already told her about her son. I scanned around and saw Aethelswith and Hilda making their way in my direction. Taking a swallow and holding back tears I greeted them with a long deep hug. As hard as I tried, I could not hold back and proceeded to break down.

Dropping to my knees and the ground my eyes were filled with tears. I told them that Leofric had been killed during a raid to destroy the Viking boats at Hastings. It was a risk too much and I should have done something else or at least have anticipated the ambush.

Hilda also collapsed and seemed distraught as would be expected. This left Aethelswith to comfort us, telling us that Leofric would have been proud of what had been achieved and that he lived a life full of love and would now be watching over his family from heaven. Death was nothing new for us however that did not make it any easier to accept. With Aethelswith's help we pulled ourselves together and went over and joined John and Leofflaed, to at least grieve together.

This war had been brutal and cost many lives. Of the original seven thousand men to have left Worchester only three thousand had returned. This would hurt our region and its families for generations but we would bounce back as we always had. The Vikings had thrown everything at us to wipe us out and we had not only repelled their attack but destroyed all three of their armies. I wondered if the sacrifice was worth it but for now, I wanted everyone to be proud of their fallen friends and family.

The losses for the Vikings were so significant this would hurt their homeland and overall survival. Unless their numbers were limitless, I hoped they would be unable to hurt us again.

Finding a raised section of ground, I addressed the gathered warriors and city folk. 'A great victory has been achieved against all odds. In little over a week our guard, along with our friends from Northampton, London, Wessex and Powys, has defeated the greatest of Viking armies. We have suffered deeply for this outcome as we have lost thousands of our loved ones. We are the ones who will benefit from their sacrifice and loss. Be proud of your family and friends and what they have achieved. Let us not waste their sacrifice but look after each other and build a safe and secure world for our children to inherit. Now is the time to press our advantage and take back the ancient lands of Britannia. We will bury our dead with honour and celebrate the great victory which we have all achieved.'

As I finished speaking a cheer went up from those gathered although it was muted due to the grief affecting almost every family. We did not celebrate the victory that night however late the following day the food and drink was prepared, and we had a subdued celebration of the lives of those who had died.

Reunited with my family all I wanted to do was get back to the farm and sleep. The night of the victory I made my way to the farm and it was not long before I was out to the world. Catching up on the hours of sleep I did not wake until midday the following day. Even then I ached so much that I just did not want to move. Aethelswith reminded me about the event that would be starting shortly in Worchester. Tempted to stay in bed I knew that I had to lead or at least participate in the event. I was too stiff and sore to stay in bed any longer anyway.

Hilda seemed much better than the day before and seemed to have come to terms with the loss of her husband. Most of the children were too young to understand the loss of their father but Osgar and even Godiva would grieve for him. I knew how they felt as I too was once in their position. They would come into town and celebrate their father's great victory. This and being around family would help them to move on through the grief.

Chapter 18 — Reunion

Over the following week we said our farewells to King David and his men, Eadwulf and the Wessex men. We kept the Northampton and London men together as we planned to set off to reclaim the areas of Britain which the Vikings had previously conquered and claimed.

Colchester would be the first target as this was the seat of Halfdan and a staging post for attacks on London. Making our way east would also give the men from Northampton and London a chance to see loved ones before the next campaign.

We reached Colchester a week after leaving Worcester and with close to five thousand men. The siege engines had been in London ready for use, so we took these with us not knowing what to expect. Colchester had city walls but these were only ten feet high so a straightforward attack with ladders was ordered. Our archers provided cover which enabled large numbers of men to clear the wall in the first stage of the battle.

It did not take long for the men who had cleared the wall to take control of the city as the gates were opened shortly after the battle began. Colchester had not been expecting us as they had also been assured that victory and all of Britannia would be theirs. On news of their defeat the city council were in awe of our guard and army. We told them that they were free to leave across the sea however they could remain if they renounced the Viking ways and joined England. The leaders of Colchester put this to the people and although a couple of hundred left on foot for the coast it seemed most of the town decided to remain. I had assured them that they would be treated fairly, and I hoped my reputation matched my words as I had always tried to follow my word and live with integrity.

From Colchester I sent out a raiding party of two thousand to secure the East Anglian territory of Tretford, a regional centre with wide canals directly to the coast. The rest of us began to make our way to Repton and Torksey. We did not expect either town to be difficult to repossess as we had won them in the past and most of their fighters would have died in the battle of Worcester. We would wait at Torksey for the men from East Anglia before moving north. Our target would be York and then Bamborough. A successful campaign taking these towns would have eliminated all the Viking strongholds in Britannia. With any luck this would ensure that they did not return, least not in my lifetime.

As expected, Repton and Torksey both fell to us without bloodshed. The residents did not see any point in losing their lives on a hopeless cause. Word had been spread about the great victory of the Worcester guard, the English. Word of the massive losses for the Vikings would be making its way through the Viking communities and they would all be wondering what was next for them. I hoped there would be stories about my leadership and how humane the English were, and I also hoped this would be enough to have them be willing to open their gates to us. In Repton and Torksey we found that close to half of the residents had taken to their boats and fled. Those that remained were the farmers and businessmen who saw the benefits of a secure and expanding community. If the war with the Vikings was finally over then maybe they could prosper as they had been watching Worcester doing for years.

While at Torksey a messenger arrived from Worcester. The ill tidings were that King Alfred had passed away in his sleep. He had been sick and erratic in his decision making for years. King Alfred was a great king and Wessex had come together and prospered under his rule. His death would bring in a changing era for Wessex after such a long rule. Fortunately, his death has come after the defeat of the Vikings which should give the new leadership a chance to establish their new rule. Aethelswith would need me now so I would have to make my way back to Worcester and Winchester. She was pregnant with our second child and although not sure how succession works, I expected that she would be made queen of Wessex.

I was grateful the king got to hear his dream became a reality with the death of King Knut of the Vikings. This might have been what he was hanging around for.

Dunstan was left in charge as commander of the guard with Wulfsige as second in command once he arrived with the men from Tretford. The plan would not change just because Hereweald and I had to attend King Alfred's funeral. York was the next target, followed by the rest of Northumbria.

Back in Worcester I went straight out to the farm. It was like stepping into another world seeing my wife, Egbert and all the young children. We prepared to leave the following day. John and Leofflaed, Tata, Bledri and Gwyneth joined us for the journey to Winchester. This was the first time that Tata, Bledri and Gwyneth would have seen Winchester and I could tell they were looking forward to the trip.

That night in bed Aethelswith asked me what I thought about being king. I told her I had not really thought about it but did not think that I would be king if she was queen. She laughed and gave me a kiss. 'You silly duffer, I can only be queen if I am not married but if married my husband will become king of the realm. Therefore, my choice of husband is so important. You will be crowned king of Wessex after my father's funeral.' This was unexpected and gave me pause for thought. Why be king of Wessex and keep the lands of Britannia fragmented? Lying next to my wife and queen the obvious thing to do was to merge Wessex into England. Our new country would be known as England and the people the English.

The following day we left for Winchester and the funeral of King Alfred. As we were leaving little Egbert came running over to the stables and begged to come along with us. I told him the answer had not changed as I thought he was too young. I watched as his shoulders slumped and the light in his face died. Looking up I saw Hilda looking at me with a questioning look. I knew I was beaten so jumped off my horse and picked up my little man. 'Will you do me the honour of riding with me to Winchester?' The light and life were back in Egbert's eyes as he wrapped his arms around my neck.

Although there was mourning a plenty there was also much joy at the sight of Aethelswith and me as we rode into the city. The crowds lined the road and cheered us through into the city and to the palace. Eadwulf and Bishop Giles were standing on the steps of the palace to greet us. 'Well met,' I told Eadwulf as we embraced. The greeting of the bishop was less warm but I had no time for hostilities or keeping old animosities alive. I did not like Bishop Giles and given what he had done to Ebba I really wanted to take his head. I calmed myself but made a note to make him pay for his crimes. We needed unity at this stage but the time of retribution was coming, and Bishop Giles would be made to pay.

I had not been back to Winchester since we had won the war which had freed England of the Vikings. I recognised many faces from the Winchester army whom I had fought alongside. Some came up and shook my hand in recognition of what we had achieved. Winchester was free because of the sacrifice of so many men and women. There would not be a family who was untouched by grief but we were a tough lot and a tight community so we would move on and support each other as needed. In a way I felt guilty as it seemed like I was getting all the credit for our great victory over the Vikings.

At the palace we were told that King Alfred was lying in state in the cathedral. Aethelswith requested that we be taken there immediately. I would have liked to freshen up and get something to eat but accepted my wife's wish and followed along quietly. It was King Alfred, and he was dead, no doubt, lying on the dais in the cathedral. Looking at the old man I felt honoured to be looking at someone who had achieved so much. Uniting Wessex and Mercia and the creation of the scriptorium would impact the lives of our people forever.

We were the last of the expected guests, so the funeral was scheduled for the following day at noon. From there we went back to the palace where we were able to eat, drink and freshen up. Hereweald was still with us and kept filling me in on protocol and what to expect. The announcement of the intent to crown a new king would happen seven days after the burial of the old king. 'The coronation of the new king will take place fourteen days after the death of the old king. The intent of the delay is to give anyone with objections the chance to make them and have them heard.' Looking between Aethelswith and Hereweald I asked them if they thought there could be objections. They both laughed and said this was their first coronation however they had heard that there were always objections. Alfred's younger brother had objected to Alfred being made king as his younger brother Albert was the stronger one and the better fighter. He claimed that the realm needed a strong warrior leader more than ever as the Vikings and Mercia were expanding into Wessex lands. The objection was taken seriously but eventually thrown out none the less.

That night we all stayed in the palace in fully serviced rooms. John and Leofflaed were told to be treated as very important people and Tata, being my brother, was also afforded special care. It was incredible the difference between life inside the palace and the life of the masses outside. Even the better inns were low quality compared to how we were treated inside the palace.

Aethelswith told me that this was normal for her and how she had been raised. I worried then about how we had been living out on the farm and how below this standard it must seem to her. Catching my eyes Aethelswith must have seen right through me to what I was thinking. She told me that she would live on the street if it meant that she could spend her life with me. 'The palace with all its luxury can be one of the loneliest places in the world.' She said that she could not imagine our farm as ever being lonely. Indeed, we had to go to the caves to get some time alone. This made us both laugh and come together again. I added that we might find more alone time in the palace which could be a hidden blessing. We laughed again and it felt joyous to do so after such a long campaign. Being pushed apart I then remembered that we had Egbert and Godric as Egbert told us not to forget him. Aethelswith and I both laughed again which made Egbert laugh which was a true delight for us all.

King Alfred was embalmed and buried in a crypt in the cathedral. He was the first burial in the cathedral and as the cathedral was King Alfred's dream, he was given a prominent crypt inside the entrance. Father Frank had travelled down for the funeral so assisted Bishop Giles with the service. I got the impression that neither man liked each other, however, they put these dislikes aside for propriety. During the proceedings both men kept looking across at each other, neither one sure who was going to do which part of the service. To me this was Giles's service as he had been bishop for the late king. Bishop Giles was made uncomfortable by Frank and I made note to question Frank when I got the chance.

Father Frank told me that he had confronted Bishop Giles about the story I had told him about Ebba and the bishop. 'I told Giles that he must come to the confessional box and confess his sins and beg for forgiveness from God. I then told him that if he failed to act then I would write to the pope and have him excommunicated.' Father Frank then said that Bishop Giles had threatened him and was also going to write to the pope. To which he had simply replied 'many know what you have done and should anything happen to me they would know where to look'. The looks throughout the service now made sense. I was so proud of Father Frank and the way he had handled the situation with Bishop Giles. I was thinking of having him bumped off however this would not have been a good start to my kingship.

As it turned out Wulfstan of old Mercia put in an objection to the announcement that I would be crowned King of Wessex. Wulfstan's objection was not the only objection I received although it was the only real challenge to my authority. Wulfstan was the cousin of the late King of Mercia, Æthelstan, and felt he was more entitled than me due to his royal blood line. Wulfstan was still an influential and powerful landowner so his claim was properly recognised. Aethelswith was due to marry Wulfstan at a command from her father. Aethelswith had fled Winchester in the deep of winter to avoid the fate. Coming to Worchester had sealed her future to mine. I was still so grateful that Aethelswith was so brave and headstrong as without these attributes we would never have ended up together. Wulfstan's objection was listened to but was eventually discarded by the panel which included, among others, Hereweald, John Archer and Father Frank.

The second serious objection was my own. I wanted to add to the title being offered or change it if possible. I wanted to be known as king of England but would settle for king of Wessex and England. I told the panel that I wanted to unite old Britannia under one title and flag.

The panel did not decide immediately, and it was only two days before the coronation that I was summoned back to the panel and told their verdict. Before the announcement I could see that they had agreed to my requests. The smiles on the committee faces told me as much. I was to be crowned the king of England. My dream was to become reality, one king for one land. Our land did not include the Welsh or the Picts but I would work on getting them to join. The big objection for change was that some felt that it would be being disrespectful to King Alfred who had spent his life building and protecting Wessex in its battle with Mercia and the Vikings. On a positive note, the panel could see that removing the names of Wessex and Mercia would reduce tensions and promote future harmony.

Details of my coronation were posted around the city, including news that the inner gates would be opened, and the common folk would be allowed into the usually exclusive inner-city precinct. They were encouraged to come in to meet and welcome their new king. I had insisted that the gates be opened as I disliked the privilege which so few of us seemed to enjoy. My first thought for when I was finally king was to explore the tax system. I had heard that Taxes in Worchester were lower than anywhere else. The low taxes encouraged entrepreneurs from all around to come to Worchester to take a chance and open a business. A low tax rate would have an immediate detrimental effect on the treasury although in the long-term the lower taxes would promote growth, lead to more jobs and prosperity. Worchester was an example of this and of how it all worked and this model could be shared throughout the realm.

Aethelswith and I left the palace with an armed guard and what looked like hundreds and possibly thousands of people lining the street to catch a glimpse of us. The palace stewards had tried to get me dressed up in some poncy king's clothing however I had refused to wear the garb. Instead, I was wearing my full battle gear including light armour. My horse had two full quivers of arrows on the saddle and I had my swords off my hips and my bow slung across my back. I wanted to make an impression and set myself as an individual. I was uniting the land, and this was done through sacrifice and bloodshed. There was almost no one alive who had been around when Alfred was crowned so there was nobody to object except for the palace stewards. Aethelswith looked pleased and that was enough for me.

If ever I had to do it again, I would reduce the length of the service. This was over the top and I was sure that it could be cut by half. Despite these thoughts Aethelswith and I endured the service, and we were crowned king and queen of England which included all of Wessex, Mercia, East Anglia, Kent and the lands through to Northumbria. At the end of the service there was an enthusiastic cheer from those inside the church and an even bigger one from outside the cathedral once they heard that it was done and complete.

John and Leofflaed hugged me after the service and told me that my mother and father would be as proud as they could be of what I had been able to achieve. 'Godric Amity, crowned king of England is surreal, but to those of us who know you it is plausible and deserved. You have worked harder than anyone we know to achieve prosperity for our people and the peace and security we all desire.'

I was humbled by the kind words and support everyone was giving me. The service ended and we joined the people outside the cathedral for a massive street party. I had instructed that food and mead be provided for the celebrations at no cost to the people. This was a surprise for those who had bothered to attend and was welcomed with appreciation.

The afternoon stretched on and morphed into the evening. I partied without a care in the world which was irresponsible when thinking about it the following day. I was sure to have enemies and I had just given them a perfect opportunity to take me out even before my kingship had begun. Fortunately, there was no attempt on my or Aethelswith's lives, and we bonded with our people and created a memory that all of those who were not too drunk could savour and fondly recall.

We rose late the following day as we had partied until at least midnight. I did not intend to stay in Winchester for long as I wanted to make sure the Vikings were cleared from the land. There were good people in charge of the army but there were still some formidable castles to get through and then there was the threat of the Picts. On news of the Vikings demise I was sure they would be ready to expand their lands into what I now saw as England. Thought of the Picts reminded me of Kenner Scott, the beautiful daughter of the Pict leader, Gregor Scott. I had abandoned her as I knew I had to get back to Worchester. I could not have risked telling her what I was doing as I knew she loved her father and was loyal to him and her family.

It would have been easy to fall under her spell and none of the following events would have occurred, or at least I thought they would not have. I would not have married Aethelswith and she may have ended up married to Wulfstan, cousin of Æthelstan. Our children and the future of England could well have never happened. The Vikings could well have destroyed England and Wessex while I was making happy families in Strathclyde. I had followed the little voice in my head which I liked to think was God talking to me and guiding my decisions. On this occasion and many others in my life this had paid off.